MURDER in BLUE

Also by Clifford Witting

MURDER
in BLUE

CLIFFORD WITTING

Galileo Publishers, Cambridge

Galileo Publishers
16 Woodlands Road Great Shelford Cambridge
CB22 5LW UK

www.galileopublishing.co.uk

Distributed in the USA by SCB Distributors
15608 S. New Century Drive Gardena, CA 90248-2129, USA

Australia: Peribo Pty Limited
58 Beaumont Road
Mount Kuring-Gai, NSW 2080
Australia

ISBN 978-1-912916-50-4

First published 1937
This edition © 2021

Cover painting by William Grant
by kind permission Hampshire Cultural Trust

Printed in the EU

A note from Clifford Witting's daughter,
Diana Cummings

Murder in Blue was my father's first book out of the 16 he went on to write. It was written while he was still commuting to London for his day job and he worked on it every evening. As if this wasn't enough to cope with, I was born in 1935 and during the early months of my life he could hear me screaming in the next room, distracting him from the very complicated business of writing a detective story! How thrilled he would have been to know that some 84 years later it would be reprinted amid a renewed interest in the Golden Age of Detection, introducing his name and distinct subtle humour to new readers. His style is still as fresh and easy to read as when he wrote it all those years ago.

He set a large number of his books in the small town of Paulsfield in the county of Downshire, behind the South Downs. This is based on Petersfield in Hampshire and he includes many references to the real town as it was in the mid-1930s: in the market place stands a statue of King William III mounted on a horse which in turn is mounted on a large stone plinth. My father demoted the King to a mere Lord but otherwise the statue is easily recognisable to this day although the surrounding iron railings have long gone. Local residents and visitors will also notice references to the pond as illustrated on the front cover of this book. Paulsfield again provided the location for a later book that he wrote entitled *Catt Out of the Bag*, also recently reissued.

I hope you enjoy *Murder in Blue* as much as I have enjoyed seeing it brought back to life.

CONTENTS

I.   I BECOME INVOLVED IN MURDER

I shielded the match from the rain with a hand that shook a little and looked down at the body of the policeman lying on the grass bank by the side of the lane, with the head, terribly battered, lolling grotesquely back over the edge of the ditch. Stretched on his back, slightly sideways across the bank, with his feet not quite touching the road and his arms flung wide under his shiny black cape, he seemed more like the carcase of some gigantic bat; and as the November rain mingled with the blood still seeping through his dark, curly hair and dripped, a dirty red, into the stagnant water of the ditch, I felt rather sick.

It was the bicycle that I had noticed first, as I walked along the lane. It was lying on the opposite side of the road to the body, with a handle-bar resting on the bank, just as it might have fallen from a man's relaxing grip. Then I had seen Johnson. I knew him well: a good-looking, smiling, friendly sort of chap. His teeth were clenched on his protruding tongue; and when I carefully felt his wrist, without disturbing his position, there seemed no flicker of life in the pulse.

Everything was deathly quiet. The hiss of the rain through the branches of the trees in Phantom Coppice and the dull beat of it on the bare cornfield to the other side of the lane, were the only sounds. The second match burnt down to my fingers, and I dropped it on the road. Suddenly, half a mile away, a train whistled as it entered Burgeston tunnel; and in the darkness I caught my breath.

"John Rutherford," I murmured, "pull yourself together."

I wondered what was the best thing to do. It was no good staying where I was, in the hope that someone came along that lonely lane. I might wait all night. Hazeloak village was the nearest place, but there was no doctor there. Paulsfield town lay two miles away. Would it not be best to get there as quickly as I could and tell the police? Speed was the first consideration, for, in spite of what I thought, Johnson might not yet be dead. Was I going to walk or was I going to take the bicycle? Its position might be valuable as evidence, but I decided to take the risk of moving it.

I lighted another match and picked up the machine. The lamp was out and a good deal of the oil had dripped on to the road, but the wick flared up when I put the match to it. I looked at the luminous watch on my wrist. Seven minutes past nine. As I swung the machine round, the light from the lamp picked out something lying in the road close to the bank on which Johnson lay. It was his cap—a dark blue forage-cap, with a waterproof cover. Police-constables in Downshire do not wear helmets. I picked it up and laid it on the grass by Johnson's side. Then I rode off.

The hands of the church clock were pointing to nine-seventeen, as I rode round the statue in Paulsfield Square and turned into the deserted High Street. I leant the bicycle against the railings outside the police station and ran up the steps. As I pushed open the door of the charge-room, Sergeant Martin looked up from his desk. He and I knew each other well.

"Hullo, Mr. Rutherford!" he greeted me. "What brings you 'ere?"

By this time I had got a grip on myself.

"Your man Johnson has been murdered," I said bluntly.

"Oh, has 'e?" chuckled Martin. "and who did it—the sparrow, with 'is bow and arrow?"

"I'm not joking, Martin," I protested. "This is dead serious. I've just found his body on the Hazeloak road, about a mile past Deeptree Corner. Head's battered in."

The smile disappeared from Martin's round red face.

"Good God!" he said.

"If he isn't dead, he's in a very bad way," I said, "and the sooner you get a doctor to him, the better. I've got his bicycle outside. It was lying in the road just by him; and I thought I had better use it to get here as speedily as possible."

Martin's finger eased the collar of his tunic.

"Johnson, eh? 'Ead smashed in. Murdered. Good God!"

He suddenly got up from his stool and went to the door behind his desk.

"Harwood come in yet?" he called.

"Yes, Sergeant?" I heard a voice answer.

"Got your motor-bike, Harwood? . . . Good. Bring it round to the front and get Chandler in the side-car. Sharp about it! Johnson's been found dead."

He closed the door and went to the telephone.

"Hullo! Get me 25. . . . Dr. Weston's house? . . . Police-sergeant Martin here. Doctor in? . . . Where? . . . Burgeston? . . . When's 'e due back? . . . Any moment? . . . Tell him to come round to the police station as soon as he gets in, will you? And if he's not back in ten minutes, please ring me. . . . Yes, it's urgent. . . . Right. Good-bye."

I heard a motor-cycle start up. The Sergeant's thumb made the 'phone-bell tinkle.

"Lulverton 2429. . . . That you, Weller? Martin here, Paulsfield. . . . Inspector Charlton in? . . . Gone home? What's his number? . . . Southmouth 8321? Thanks. Good-bye."

I heard the motor-cycle come along the side of the building. Martin asked for his number.

"Is that Inspector Charlton's house? . . . Is the Inspector in, miss? I want to speak to him urgently. Sergeant Martin of Paulsfield . . . Thank you, miss. . . . Hullo! Inspector Charlton? Sergeant Martin 'ere, sir. . . . I've just had word that Constable Johnson—one of my men—'as been found with his 'ead smashed in. . . . Yes, sir, I should think so, from what I hear. . . . On the Hazeloak road. . . . Yes, sir, 'e's with

11

me now. I'm sending a couple of men along at once. . . .
You'll come over, sir? . . . Take the London road, sir, until
it branches off to Burgeston, carry on through Burgeston,
until you get to Deeptree Corner. . . . You know it, sir? . . .
Turn sharp right at the Corner and you'll find 'im down
that lane—about a mile along. . . . Ask him to stay 'ere till
you come? Certainly, sir. . . . Good-bye, sir."

He hung up the receiver and went to the door leading
to the street, where Harwood and Chandler waited for
instructions, Harwood, a man of forty or so, with his rather
big nose now hidden by the collar of his cape, in the saddle
of the machine, and Chandler, a young chap of twenty-
three or four, in the side-car.

"He's about a mile past Deeptree Corner on the Hazeloak
road," Martin told them.

"On the left-hand side, about a hundred yards before you
get to the footpath that runs through Phantom Coppice," I
said over his shoulder.

"Get there as quick as you can," said Martin. "You stay
with the body, Chandler, until Inspector Charlton comes;
and you, 'Arwood, come straight back here, so you can take
over the station from me. If you're back in time, I'll go with
the ambulance, in case the Inspector doesn't show up."

"Right, Sergeant," said Harwood and his gloved hand
opened the throttle.

Martin closed the door and walked to his desk.

"Good man, Harwood," he said, as he again lifted the
telephone receiver. "That's his own motor-bike. . . . 'Ullo!
Ambulance, please, miss. Urgent call. . . . Uses it sometimes
for police work. . . . Lives at Burgeston. . . . Is that you,
Allnutt? Sergeant Martin this end. Can you bring the
ambulance round 'ere now? . . . . Yes, to the police station. .
. . At once. Urgent case. . . . Right."

He rang off and turned to me.

"Now, Mr. Rutherford," he said, "I'll trouble you to
answer a few questions. All a matter of form, you know.

Inspector Charlton'll want to ask you one or two things when 'e gets 'ere, but I'll just take down a few general particulars."

He dipped his pen in the ink. Then he paused, laid down his pen and pulled the telephone towards him.

"Just a moment, though," he said. "there's just one other little mat—Hullo! Get me the 'Porcupine' at Burgeston, please. . . . Don't I what? . . . The number? No, I don't. What d'you take me for—a bookworm? . . . Yes, the 'Porcupine.' . . . None of your lip, young woman! I never go into such places. . . . Hullo! Is that you, Mr. Rawlinson? Sergeant Martin speaking. . . . No, I haven't been round lately. May drop in for a quick one next Sunday. . . . Listen, Mr. Rawlinson, 'as my man Didcott turned up yet? . . . No, I don't want him, thanks. . . . Just rang to see if he'd arrived. . . . Thanks very much. Remember me to the missis. . . . I will. . . . Good-bye."

"Now, sir," he said to me, taking up his pen again. "First of all, Mr. Rutherford, what's your name?"

I smiled at this quaint question and answered:

"John Rutherford."

"John anything Rutherford?"

"No. Just John Rutherford."

"I know that as well as you do," he said apologetically, "but if I didn't ask you, the Chief Constable at Whitchester would 'ave a seizure. Address?"

"18, Thorpe Street, Paulsfield, Downshire."

"Householder?"

"No. The house belongs to Mrs. Hendon and I occupy the first floor."

"How is her ladyship?" Martin asked chattily, as he wrote down these details.

"She complains increasingly of 'them stairs'," I smiled.

"Occupation?" was his next question.

"Bookseller. I am the proprietor of a shop at 24, High Street, which goes under the name of 'Voslivres'."

"Thank you, Mr. Rutherford. That'll be all for the

moment. The Inspector will be along later and I'll leave the rest to him."

The street door was pushed open and a dapper, sharp-featured, pugnaciously moustached little man came in.

"Ah, good evening, Dr. Weston," Martin greeted him.

"Evening, Sergeant," The Doctor answered abruptly. "Well, what is it this time—another accident?"

"We don't know yet, Doctor," Martin replied cautiously, "but a man's been killed."

"Oh, indeed; and who is the unfortunate deceased?"

This with the shadow of a frosty smile.

"Police-constable Johnson."

"Ah-ha," murmured the Doctor significantly.

"Yes," said Martin. "Mr. Rutherford here . . ."

The Doctor nodded distantly to me.

". . .found his body on the Hazeloak road about half an hour ago. Just about a mile past Deeptree Corner. I've sent a couple of men off. . . ."

"Was he dead when you found him?" asked the Doctor, turning suddenly to me.

"I think so."

"What do you mean—you think so?" was his peremptory retort.

"Precisely what I say, Doctor," I said sharply, stirred by his bantam-cock arrogance. "I *think* he was dead. Unfortunately, I lack your expert judgment."

For one brilliant moment he smiled.

"I beg your pardon," he said quietly.

"Will you go and have a look at him, Doctor?" asked Martin. "You've got your car outside, I suppose? Inspector Charlton will probably be there by now."

"Damnably inconvenient!" said the Doctor, his acerbity breaking out again. "I'm expecting a maternity call any time now."

"Sorry, Doctor, but this is urgent."

"A dead man needs me less than a live baby," Dr. Weston answered tartly. "You should teach your constables, Sergeant, to look after themselves."

With this parting thrust, he left us.

"What a little spitfire!" I smiled.

"He's always like that with men," Martin replied. "With women 'e's a perfect angel—in a manner of speaking. Got the idea into his 'ead that men get all the 'a'pence, while women get all the kicks. He'll go a hundred miles to save a woman a bit of pain; but men, 'e says, don't deserve no help. I'll never forget the way 'e saw my wife through with young Ted; and dozens of other men I know willingly put up with 'is funny little ways."

"And how is that rascal son of yours?" I asked.

"Thriving, Mr. Rutherford, thriving. Wants to know when you're coming round to play Cowboys-and-Indians with him again."

"When I've got over the last time," I laughed. "I've the bruises from that tomahawk on me still!"

"'E's a spirited little devil," said Martin proudly. "Going to school next year."

He looked at the clock on the wall.

"'Bout time that ambulance was here," he said.

"Probably had to send out for a horse to pull it round." he lifted the receiver and again asked for "Ambulance."

"'Ullo! Allnutt started yet? . . . Not on the way? . . . Well, he darn well ought to be! . . . Tell 'im to put a jerk in it. What's 'e been doing—having a bit of supper?" he hung up before his sarcasm could be answered and turned to me.

"Harwood's taking his time, too. He should be back by—". He broke off and ran his hand through his thin sandy hair.

"Jumping Pete, Mr. Rutherford—I've forgot the photographer!"

He snatched off the receiver.

"Exchange! Hullo, Exchange! Come on, miss, who d'you think you are—the Sleeping Beauty? Put me through to Mr.

15

Hopkins, the photographer. His private address. Drat the number! Get 'im and get 'im quick!"

The Sergeant was getting excited.

"Is that you, Mr. 'Opkins?" he said after a pause. "This is Police-sergeant Martin here. Got an urgent job for you... Oh, they'll 'ave to play three-handed till you get back... Good. Bring a camera along to the station, will you, and your flash-light kit? And for Heaven's sake, hurry!"

He rang off.

"Phew, Mr. Rutherford! If I'd forgotten that, Inspector Charlton wouldn't 'alf have been polite!"

I was to have a fuller understanding of that remark, when I got to know Inspector Charlton better.

Martin roughed up the hair at his temples.

"Murder's an 'arrowing business, Mr. Rutherford," he said. "I've only just got over that 'orrible to-do we 'ad in the Square last summer. Where the devil's 'Arwood got to? I can't leave till 'e gets back. That sounds like him."

I heard a motor-cycle pull up outside. Martin went to the door.

"Where 'ave you been to, Harwood?" he called out. "On a holiday cruise?"

"Sorry, Sergeant," I heard Harwood say, "but I've been as quick as I could."

"All right. Take your bike round the back and come in 'ere ... Ah, 'ere comes Ambling Agnes! Now we shan't be long!"

I saw through the window the white shape of the ambulance, as it came to a stop. Martin took his cap and greatcoat off a hook.

"You'll stay 'ere, Mr. Rutherford, till we get back?" he asked at the door, and I nodded.

I followed him to the top of the steps and saw an ungainly figure hurrying along towards us from the direction of the Square. I took it to be the estimable Mr. Hopkins and as he drew nearer, I realized that the awkward protrusions from his person were occasioned by the photographic impedimenta protected from the rain by his voluminous mackintosh.

"Evening, Mr. 'Opkins," said the Sergeant. "Jump in."

Martin climbed up the steps at the back of the ambulance behind the frightened-looking little man, who had probably never snapped anything more alarming than the local football team, complete with ball, and the door was pulled shut. As the car started off through the still heavy rain, Harwood came through the door at the back of the charge-room.

"Well," I said, "Did you find him all right?"

"Yes," he said, with a wry grimace, "and a nasty state he's in. Looks like the work of a maniac."

"He *is* dead, I suppose?"

"Stone-dead. Reminds me of the sticky things we used to see in France. Were you in the War, Mr. Rutherford?"

"No," I said. "I was still on the sunny side of sixteen when the Armistice was signed."

"You were one of the lucky ones, sir."

"I didn't think so at the time!" I smiled.

"I went through four years of it," he said, "and tonight brings it all back again. The rain and darkness and death— and the mud."

"Did you come through the War all right?" I asked him.

"Yes, without a scratch; but when I think of the thousands who didn't—chaps who are still alive and suffering—it makes me go 'ot all over. Did you hear Lord Shawford on the wireless tonight?"

Lord Shawford was Paulsfield's local celebrity. I shook my head.

"'E was making the usual Sunday night Appeal."

"At eight-forty-five," I reminded him, "I was otherwise employed."

"Of course you were," he agreed. "I heard him at home— it was just before I came on duty. He was appealing on be'alf of all the poor fellows the War made wrecks of and what he said made me want to do my little bit to help. So the postal order I bought for some radio stuff that I was going to write off for went into the pillar-box tonight."

His earnest eyes gleamed. A good-hearted, sympathetic chap, I thought.

"Was Johnson in France?" I asked.

"No, he's only—*was* only about twenty-nine."

"One can hardly associate such a violent death with a country lane in peaceful England."

"I'd rather be killed like that than mown down by a machine-gun. It's more human. That's the dreadful thing about war—the impersonality of it. I can understand a man killing a fellow 'e hates, but to murder a chap who might, if you'd met him in peace-time, 'ave become your best friend, just because what your politicians think doesn't agree with what 'is politicians think—it's all wrong."

"Well," I said, "I concede you the humanness of killing a man you hate, but I question its justification."

"Oh, there's no justification," he said quickly. "Murder's a brutal thing. I can't get Johnson's face out of my mind."

"His dangling feet were more horrible than his face," I said.

He looked at me strangely.

"Did it get you like that, too?" he asked, and then changed the subject: "Are you waiting for the Sergeant to come back?"

I said I was.

"Perhaps you'd like to look at the paper?"

"Thanks very much," I said. "What did Southmouth do yesterday?"

"I think they won, but I'm not sure," he answered and left me alone with the paper and one of the most uncomfortable chairs it has ever been my misfortune to sit on.

After a while, my seat got too much for me and I was reading the police notices on the wall, when I heard the ambulance arrive. I opened the street door and saw Dr. Weston getting out of the closed car that he had brought to rest behind the ambulance. The door of the ambulance swung open and two men hauled a covered stretcher from the back, much to the excitement of the crowd of gaping townsfolk, who, having been noticeably absent when the empty ambulance stood earlier outside the police station, now miraculously appeared from nowhere and seemed fully compensated for the soaking they were getting by the thrill of the unusual occasion.

The stretcher disappeared down the side way and the Doctor followed it. I noticed now that another car had drawn up behind Dr. Weston's. From it emerged Sergeant Martin, Mr. Hopkins, who looked wet and unhappy, and a large man in a dark grey overcoat and a bowler hat. I heard Hopkins say something to the Sergeant that sounded like "first thing in the morning" and then he hurried off down the street, with his precious paraphernalia still bulging out his mackintosh. After brusquely ordering the crowd to disperse, which merely made them form a slightly larger semi-circle round the ambulance, Sergeant Martin followed the big man into the station.

"Sorry to keep you waiting, Mr. Rutherford," Martin said to me.

"Not at all," I assured him.

"This is Mr. Rutherford, sir," Martin addressed the big man, "who found the body. Mr. Rutherford—Detective-Inspector Charlton."

I shook hands with the man with whom I was to become so closely associated.

"Good evening, Mr. Rutherford," he said.

He was in the early fifties, broad-shouldered and, in height, a full inch taller than my own five-eleven. His thick greying hair, which I saw when he took off his hat, was brushed back from his forehead; and he was clean-shaven. His eyes were grey and they looked straight—and often quizzically—at you. His hands were large and strong, but well cared-for, and on the little finger of his left hand he wore a gold signet ring. His deep voice was gentle and cultured, and his lips seemed always ready to smile. He rather reminded me of one of those prosperous doctors, whose large practices make demands not so much upon their professional ability, as upon their social qualities. He had—how shall I say it,—a *comforting* air.

"It was good of you to stay," the Inspector went on, "until I came. If we can get your account of this affair while it is still fresh in your mind, it will help us considerably."

"By all means," I agreed. "I was walking along the Hazeloak road. . . ."

"Perhaps," the Inspector interrupted me, "it will be as well if you start at the beginning."

"I suppose the beginning was when I decided to go for a walk. I usually take a stroll after my evening meal and I didn't want to let the foul weather deprive me of it tonight."

"There is always a melancholy pleasure," smiled the Inspector, "In walking through the rain."

"I suppose there is," I said. "Anyway, I put on my raincoat and went out."

"What time was that?"

"About a quarter past eight. The clock in the Square said twenty past when I walked by it and I heard it strike the half-hour when I had gone some little distance along the road that leads to Burgeston and Hazeloak. About three-quarters of a mile from Paulsfield, when I was thinking how lonely the road was, I heard voices behind me; and a little while after, two policemen passed me on bicycles."

"Did you identify them?"

"No. As far as I was concerned then, they were just a couple of constables."

"Were they talking?"

"Not while they were passing me, but I heard them as they went on down the road."

"Did you recognize their voices?"

"No, I am afraid not."

"The only thing you are able to say with certainty, then, is that two persons, whom you took to be constables, rode past you on bicycles?"

"Yes."

"And after these two persons had ridden on?"

"I walked another quarter of a mile and reached Deeptree Corner, where, as you probably know, the road branches—one fork leading to Burgeston and the other to Hazeloak."

"And you took the Hazeloak fork?"

"No, I walked on towards Burgeston. About a mile along from the Corner is the entrance to a footpath that leads through Phantom Coppice to the Hazeloak road. Putting it geometrically, the footpath forms the base of an isosceles triangle, with Deeptree Corner as the apex. I paused at the end of this footpath and glanced at my watch. . . ."

"Which keeps good time?"

"It loses about fifteen seconds a week."

"And what was the time when you looked at it?"

"Just before five to nine—say 8.54. I took the risk of getting even wetter than I was already, and turned into the footpath, eventually emerging from the other end into the Hazeloak road, where I turned to the left to come back to Paulsfield. About a hundred yards down the road, on the right-hand side, I found P. C. Johnson's body."

"What time was that?"

"I referred to my watch before I left him and it was then seven minutes past nine. I hadn't been with him more than a couple of minutes, so I should say that I discovered him at five-past nine."

"Was he dead when you found him?"

"It is difficult to say definitely. I lighted several matches and had a good look at him. I decided in my own mind that he was dead, but I'm not prepared to swear it. I could not detect any sign of breathing and when I felt his pulse, without moving the position of his arm, there seemed no indication that his heart was still beating. His tongue was clenched between his teeth and his eyelids were half closed."

"Thank you, Mr. Rutherford," said the Inspector, "and what did you do then?"

"There was a bicycle lying against the bank on the other side of the road. It was, as a matter of fact, the bicycle that first drew my attention to the body. I nearly tripped over it. I stood for a few moments debating the advisability of moving it, and then decided that the most important thing was to inform Sergeant Martin at the earliest possible moment. So I picked it up, lighted the lamp and came here."

"In which direction was the machine pointing?"

"In the direction of Hazeloak, as if the rider had been cycling away from Deeptree corner."

"During your walk did you meet anybody besides the two cyclists?"

"I saw one or two people before I left Paulsfield behind, but after I got into the open country I met nobody."

"I am obliged to you Mr. Rutherford," smiled the Inspector." That I think is the end of my catechism." He turned to Sergeant Martin.

"You'll notify Mr. Trench, Martin?"

"Yes sir" said the Sergeant.

"Right I'll be in early to-morrow. What do you make the time?"

I looked at my wrist watch and Martin glanced around at the clock on the wall.

"Five and twenty to eleven" I said, and the station clock agreed with me.

"Thanks," said the Inspector. "Good night."

When he had picked up his hat and gone out to his car, I said to Martin: "That clock doesn't seem big enough Sergeant. The Inspector was facing it and he had had to ask what o'clock it was."

"He wasn't interested in the time," said Martin wisely.

"He wanted to make sure that your watch was right. If you'd had your glove off, he wouldn't have asked that question. He's deep, is the Inspector."

"Just before I gallop off to my stable, Martin, tell me one thing: who were the two constables who passed me?"

"Them, Mr. Rutherford? I should say they was Johnson and that other man I 'phoned up the 'Porcupine' about—Didcott. We've 'ad a special run of duty lately—policing Hazeloak and Burgeston at night. Sudden outbreak of robbery with violence. Every Sunday night, when the clock strikes half-past eight, Johnson and Didcott leave here together, cycle as far as Deeptree Corner and separate, Johnson to go to Hazeloak and Didcott to Burgeston. There's a couple of men go every night, of course, but Johnson and Didcott do Sundays. That's why I rang up the 'Porcupine'—to see if Didcott had arrived safely. They look after his bike while he's marching up and down on the watch for malefactors—not that he's ever laid hands on any!"

"Well," I said, "I don't think you want me any more tonight. I suppose I must say my piece at the inquest. When will that be?"

"Probably Tuesday or Wednesday. I'm just going to get through to Mr. Trench, the coroner."

"If you want me before then," I said, "You know where to find me. I shall be going on business to Southmouth to-morrow morning, but I hope to be back in the afternoon."

"That's all right, Mr. Rutherford," said Martin.

"Good night, sir."

Turning into the street I almost collided with Chandler. In the light from the lamp above, the young constable's usually ruddy complexion had now a pasty tinge.

"You don't look too good," I said sympathetically.

"No, Mr. Rutherford," he answered with a sickly smile. "It's turned me up a bit. Why couldn't the swine let 'im alone?" he went on with sudden heat. "Smashed 'is skull in—killed 'im like a bull! Dirty skunk!"

His open young Downshire face was twisted. He tried to control himself.

"Sorry, Mr. Rutherford," he said shamefacedly, "but Tom Johnson and me was chums. Saw 'im alive at 'alf-past eight. Pulled 'is leg about going out in the rain, I did. Told 'im not to get 'is feet wet. And now look at 'im!"

He didn't seem to trust himself to say more, but went into the station, while I turned into the High Street and walked back to Thorpe Street through the rain, which gave the impression that it had properly got into its stride, and hadn't the slightest intention of stopping before Christmas.

Mrs. Hendon, my landlady, of whom I shall have more to say later, was waiting up for me.

"Mercy, Master John!" she wailed. What in Heaven's name have you been up to?"

"Sorry I've been such a long time, Lizzie," I said,

"But I got held up."

"You ain't been doing nothing you shouldn't have?" she asked anxiously. "Why did Sergeant Martin and the big gentleman come round asking me where you were and what time you left the house?"

I comforted her by telling the whole story, and then went up to bed. As I got undressed, one remark I had heard that evening kept coming into my mind:

"He's deep, is the Inspector."

II WHICH HARKS BACK

When an author begins a book and creates, for the edification or amusement of his readers, a hero for his tale, he may, if he wishes, give a detailed and picturesque description of the man. He may say that he enjoys exceptional physical strength, or is the personification of frailty; that his features are chiselled on the purest Grecian lines, or rugged, with a firm chin and fine white teeth; that he is short and thickset or tall and lithe; that he has jet-black, exquisitely cared-for hair or a riot of unruly yellow waves.

But when a fellow tells his own tale, without any of the advantages of an historian and all the disadvantages of an autobiographer, he must do one of two things. Either he must give a fair and truthful description of himself, and if the picture he paints is a pleasant one, appear a thought conceited; or he must slur over—even entirely omit to mention—his physical endowments, and thus give rise to a misconception in the minds of his readers.

And I, who am, to all intents and purposes, the hero of this yarn—a hero, not in the sense of one who performs high deeds, but rather as one around whose doings the tale revolves—have found myself faced with these alternatives. After a deal of thought, I have decided that it would not be fair on you who are giving so much of your attention— especially if there is a good vaudeville programme on the Regional—to the story of an ordinary chap who became involved in a murder case, if I told you anything but the truth. Imagine, then, a man on the wrong side of thirty, but still on the right side of thirty-five; a trifle off six feet in height and fairly broad of shoulder, with features notable neither for beauty nor ugliness, eyes that are somewhere between grey and blue and that are beginning to need glasses more and more—principally during this hard work of making a book—hair parted on the left side and of a middling shade of brown, in which an anxious eye can sometimes detect strands of grey at the temples; and a small closely clipped moustache, which, in some lights, is terrifyingly ginger. Actually, I suppose, I am of the "Ex-officer" type, although my only point of contact with the War was when a bomb was dropped in 1917, three streets away from our house in Southmouth.

I know this reads more like a "missing-from-his-home" announcement from the BBC, but I can't avoid that; and if I add that an education at one of our lesser Public Schools could not cure me of a liking for Shakespeare and English Letters, or the just complaints of my friends separate me from the bubbly old briar that is for ever between my teeth—which, by the way, do not come out at night—the pen-portrait will, I hope, be complete.

Now that these irksome personal details have been dealt with, I am free to explain how I, John Rutherford, came to be living at Paulsfield. It has really very little to do with the story I have to tell of P. C. Johnson, but there will be so much talk, before this book is done, of that good-looking young constable and of his sudden demise, that I shall, perhaps, be forgiven for devoting a few pages to matters that have no direct bearing on Detective-inspector Charlton's investigation into the case.

My father finished his life in the mud of Passchendaele, leaving my mother with only one thing to live for—myself. We had never been poor and my mother was able to keep up our comfortable house in the seaside town of Southmouth, from which Paulsfield lies seven miles inland, behind the South Downs. It was lonely for her during term-time, but ours is a Downshire family and there was always some aunt or other of mine, or some cousin of my mother's or father's, to drop in to tea or spend the week-end with her. When

I left Mereworth, there arose the question of what I was to do with myself. Mother wanted me to go to a University and take a degree, but I managed to talk her out of that. I wanted to join the Navy, but Mother managed to talk *me* out of *that*. The end of it was that I didn't do anything—at least, not anything much. I bought myself a typewriter and dabbled in Literature. I wrote ghastly little poems and sent them to periodicals, whose editors were considerate enough to return my work to me, without taking the matter to court. I turned my hand to writing thrillers, which were ejaculation-marks and no plot. I sent humorous articles, running to about two thousand words, to *Punch* and was extremely surprised when I got them back. I spent pounds on stamps and used to hang over the gate, waiting for the postman to come. In fact, I went through what every other young writer goes through. And I thoroughly enjoyed myself.

Then my mother died.

That was five years before this story begins. When mother went, there didn't seem to be anything much left.

I stuck it for a while and then chucked everything up: sold Crawhurst for half its value, pensioned off the servants, warehoused the furniture and took my toothbrush to Germany. For a year I roamed about the world: France, Italy, Switzerland, Canada, the U.S.A. Then I came back to Southmouth, wrote a book about my journeyings—and burnt it.

In those far-off days before the War, Mrs. Hendon—then Miss Lizzie Jenkins—had been my mother's cook, but had left us to marry a Paulsfield plumber. While I was passing a thoroughly miserable existence in a Southmouth hotel, where the seven-course dinner left you feeling peckish and nothing so vulgar as a steak-and-kidney pudding ever figured on the menu—possibly because they didn't know the French for it, Mrs. Hendon wrote to me. She had always been attached to my mother and if numerous dainties passed through the kitchen-window were anything to go by, she was fond of me, too. she said she had heard with sorrow of my loss and that I had disposed of Crawhurst. Was I, she asked, wondering where to live, now that I had come back to England? Hendon, that doubtless worthy artisan, had wiped his last joint and gone where all good plumbers go, leaving Lizzie with a very small income and a very large house. Would I care to take the first floor, which I was to understand was comfortable and roomy, and let her "do for me"? Her apple dumplings, she added, were still as good as they had been at Crawhurst.

It was the dumplings that did it.

I selected a few pieces of furniture from the stuff at the warehouse and had them sent to 18, Thorpe Street. I paid for a small room on the floor that was to be mine to be converted into a bathroom, had the other rooms painted and the walls re-papered. In the decorator's good time, the place was ready for me and I shook the dust of the Hotel Frightful from my clothes, to take up residence in my new home.

In the peaceful atmosphere of the quiet little country town, I lived contentedly for several months. Mrs. Hendon fed me as if I was to be entered for the annual Stock Show on Meanhurst Heath, and the kindness and sympathy that she and her daughter, who was in daily domestic service, showered upon me made me feel, at times, decidedly uncomfortable. It is not until you have suffered a bereavement that you realize what a decent lot of people go to make up the human race. I spent my days in walking, with an occasional round of golf and visits, now and then, to London and Southmouth. In the evenings I used to read and, when the spirit moved me, write; or spend an hour or two at the 'Queen's Head,' where I could always find somebody to give me a game of snooker or billiards. It was, in fact, at the 'Queen's Head' that I first met Sergeant Martin, who, be it to his eternal credit, liked his pint of beer.

But as the days went by, a vague feeling of restlessness became gradually stronger inside me. It wasn't wander-mania—my travels had cured me of that. I think it must have been that my life was so entirely without motive: I had no goal, no distant lofty peak to reach. I even lacked such idiotic prepossession as absorbed the young gentleman who bore a banner with a strange device. What I needed, I decided on examining my symptoms, was action, either aggressive or defensive—it didn't matter which. I was in the position of a dog who always has his bones to himself and never feels the wild thrill of contesting their ownership with a rival—a dog, furthermore, who is quite happy with his modest little selection of bones and never casts envious eyes at the larger and more succulent dainties possessed by his canine contemporaries. Mr. Hornung's Raffles turned to Cracksmanship. I turned to Trade.

That is how 'Voslivres' came into being.

Paulsfield High Street is not a beautiful thoroughfare. Most of the old street, which must have been quite short, has been widened during the last seventy years and many of the original houses have disappeared, to make way for more serviceable, but far less captivating, buildings. Then, in 1923 or thereabouts, the Ministry of Transport decided that the increasingly heavy business and pleasure traffic between London and Southmouth-by-the-Sea (to give it its full name) was hazarding the lives of Mr. and Mrs. Paulsfield and, in particular, all the little Paulsfields. So where the old road from London turned sharply to the left and, ambling crookedly towards the High Street, joined it at another wicked corner, they now cut a new road through the fields. This joined up again with the old road a couple of hundred yards to the south-west of Burgeston village. It was along this old road that I had walked on the evening that I discovered Johnson's body.

The result of this "by-passing" was natural. No longer having the business advantage that being on the main road gave it, the tendency had been for the town to extend itself; and by the end of two years, the High Street had crept along the old road to meet the new road at the first-mentioned corner in my previous paragraph. New shops replaced the scattered cottages that had been before, and on the junction, there was now a large and ugly garage, with a cluster of petrol-pumps, disguised with so much care as lighthouses that they looked more like petrol-pumps than ever. Serried ranks of shops and houses now flanked each side of the new road; and by the time of which I write, the new road had become even more dangerous than the High Street had once been. The only solution open to the Ministry of Transport was, as far as I could see, to construct a by-pass to by-pass the by-pass.

Half-way down Paulsfield High Street, on its western side, is the market-square, around which a "one-way" traffic system prevails, except on market-days, when there is no system at all. In the middle of the Square is a statue of an illustrious forbear of Lord Shawford mounted on a horse. The only commendable feature of this monument is its surrounding iron railing, to which it is possible to tether fractious bulls on alternate Tuesdays.

I have said that, in my extremity, I turned to Trade. This is how it came about. Through all the changes that had taken place in Paulsfield, there had survived, on the south-eastern corner of the Square, a dear little shop, that dated back to somewhere in the sixteen-hundreds. For close on fifty years it had belonged to the Misses Rickthorpe, who had dispensed "Two separate pennyworths" of bullseyes and other delights to several generations of school-children. In due course, the dear old souls passed on—Emily, the elder, first and Maud scarcely two months later. Soon after, the property was put up for sale and, coinciding as it did with the unrest that I have mentioned, it gave me the idea of running a business. For a long time I had cherished a pet theory on the gentle art of persuading people that what you have to offer is the very thing that they themselves have long wanted—and never realized it. Now I saw the chance to put my theory into practice and at the same time relieve the monotony of a purposeless existence.

The Misses Rickthorpe left their small joint fortune to various charities, which were also to have the benefit of the proceeds of the sale of the shop. But a sentimental streak in the venerable ladies' dispositions made them decree that whoever bought the shop was to sign an undertaking not to effect any structural alterations to the premises until ten years after the demise of the Misses Rickthorpe. This, of course, must have discouraged many possible purchasers, so that when I visited the agents in whose hands the matter rested, I was offered the premises at a ridiculously low figure. After ascertaining that such work as would be necessary to convert the premises into a bookshop did not constitute structural alterations, I accepted.

The sisters had had the counter over which they had sold their lollipops placed right across the shop and parallel with the front door, on each side of which was a mullioned bay-window, where delicacies had been displayed. Behind this counter was a wooden partition, reaching to the low, raftered ceiling, so that the space behind could be used as a living-room.

When the purchase had been completed, I went into conference with the man who had decorated my flat. We decided that if we were to take away the counter and partition, we should have a room of quite reasonable size, occupying the whole of the ground floor, just as its original builder had intended it. An impression of informality was what I aimed at and I planned to scatter about this room a few comfortable chairs, so that my customers could examine books at their leisure or, if they cared to, pass half-an-hour with a magazine or in conversation with a friend.

While this work was being done, I had the distemper cleaned off the heavy oak beams of the ceiling and the ceiling itself re-whitewashed. The uneven stone floor I left as it was, and so with the great open fireplace. I would have mats on the floor and in the winter a log fire in the fireplace. All the available wall-space I had covered with bookshelves of seasoned oak, finished to match the old woodwork. The shelves to each side of the fireplace were only breast-high and above them were two little leaded-glass windows looking out into the tiny garden, which, in summer, was a mass of old-fashioned flowers: mignonette, hollyhock, love-in-a-mist, pansy and London pride. I think it was these flowers that really made me buy the place.

Upstairs, reached by a little steep stairway, were two more rooms and under the eaves, a loft. A little outhouse, on whose tiled roof grew moss and tiny cactuses, completed the establishment that was now mine.

I shall pass over my early months in business, when the little orange-coloured hanging-sign, with 'Voslivres' painted on it in black letters of the demurest proportions, saw few customers come beneath it. Suffice it to say that after a great deal of patience and hard work, I had built up, by the time P.C. Johnson came to his death, a flourishing little business. But no amount of labour would have had such satisfactory results without the assistance of two powerful allies: Snobbery and Lady Shawford. I ought, perhaps, to have put her ladyship first, for it was she who gave my enterprise the fillip it needed, while Snobbery did the rest.

The theory I have already mentioned was based on snobbery. It was my considered opinion that the quickest way to sell a thing in a small country town was to offer it not at less, but at more, than the market value. The average provincial lady will willingly pay "through the nose" provided that she is certain that other people notice her doing it. Mrs. Smith will pay without a word of protest twenty-five per cent, more than current prices, as long as *that woman,* Mrs. Jones, has seen her make the purchase or will hear of it afterwards. Mrs. Jones immediately proceeds to outdo Mrs. Smith and comes under the envious gaze of Mrs. Robinson. And so it goes on.

So when I started my business, which I intended to be more of a lending-library than a bookshop, I covered all my books—no reprints or publishers' remainders, but "mint" stuff, hot from the authors' typewriters—with dust-jackets of a striking orange colour, on which was printed in bold letters 'VOSLIVRES'. In this way I ensured that a glance would establish the origin of the books. But that was not enough. It was necessary that a woman should find it a matter for congratulation to be seen with an orange-coloured book projecting coyly from her shopping-basket. To achieve this, I charged an exorbitant rate of subscription. An advertisement appearing in one of my windows—orange metal letters clinging to a black magnetic background—announced that the yearly subscription was two guineas. It took me a long time to screw up enough courage to publish the figure so brazenly and, as I have said, for some months my shop was little patronized.

Then Lady Shawford appeared on my horizon.

I was sitting in the shop one midsummer morning, wondering moodily whether I should clear out and cut my losses, or reduce my charges to the "2d. per week and no deposit" level and admit that my precious theory was a wash-out, when a cream-and-black Rolls pulled up outside in the way that only a Rolls can, and her ladyship alighted, clutching an infinitesimal fragment of dog to her bosom. I recognized her immediately and ran to open the door. She passed through like a brigantine under full canvas.

"Good morning, your ladyship," I smiled politely, a little awed by her imposing presence.

"Oh, good morning," she answered, while the dog looked at me a trifle disdainfully. "You're Mr. Rutherford, aren't you? I've heard such a lot about you and your sweet little shop and your poor, dear mother. I was on a committee with her once. I can't remember what it was, but it was an awfully good thing. It must have come as a great shock to you. So sad!"

I thanked her for her interest and sympathy, and marvelling that my modest little story should have reached so far as the Grange, her house at Meanhurst, asked her what I could do for her.

"I think it's so nice to *do* something," she said, looking round approvingly. "If you can only *do* something, it makes all the difference. Lots of people I know are opening shops—hats and Cornish teas and things like that. They don't make anything out of it, of course, but they *do* feel that they are doing *something*. And that's what I like about all this. Such an original idea! Everybody reads books and I shouldn't be a bit surprised if you make a *profit*. I used to play tennis with your dear father at the vicarage. Such a delightful young man! What a tragedy it must have been for your mother. Everybody said that she was simply *wrapped* up in him. You must visit us at the Grange. My husband says he gets so tired of seeing the same old faces. Now I came in here for something what was it?"

By this time, we were both a bit breathless. In fairness to the compositors, I ought to add that her ladyship delivered that last sentence exactly as it is printed.

"Oh, yes," she went on after an almost imperceptible pause, "I want to take out one of your lending-library subscriptions. Two guineas a year, isn't it?"

I opened my mouth to agree with her, but she went on:

"And if you don't mind, I'll take a book with me now. One with at least one murder in it if you have one. I've a bridge tea on this afternoon and I always find a murder story so soothing after a bridge tea."

I supplied her with the latest in thrillers, complete with orange wrapper and when she had thanked me with a radiant smile and two hundred more words, she went out to her car, where the chauffeur stood holding the door.

By the next morning's post I received a cheque for two

guineas signed: "Shawford." His lordship had "parted".

Snobbery did the rest. The word must have flown round that Lady Shawford had patronized "that funny little bookshop on the corner of the Square" and before the next day was out, I had collected five new customers, who were careful to ascertain that her ladyship was already a subscriber before they laid down their money. After that, my vivid oriflamme was to be seen all over the town. Any woman who could persuade her husband to foot the bill, swooped down upon number twenty-four, High Street and left, a few minutes later, with a book displayed to the best advantage somewhere about her.

Further down the High Street, there were two coffee-shops. They were equally comfortable and clean; their coffee and afternoon tea were identical; they stocked the same quality pastries and cakes. Yet the 'Cozey' did indifferent business, while the 'Green Tea-pot' was always full of chattering women.

'Voslivres', like the 'Green Tea-pot', had become a Fashion.

★ ★ ★ ★

There is one other thing that I must mention before resuming the story of Police-constable Johnson. A little over a week before I found that unfortunate man's body, I was coming home from Southmouth in my little commercial van, which was painted to match my hook-jackets and hanging-sign and had 'Voslivres' in the form of handwriting inscribed diagonally across each side. In the early evening there had come down a heavy ground fog, which had been bad enough when I left Southmouth, but which, by the time I had got through Lulverton, grew so thick that I almost despaired of getting home and had visions of leaving my van tucked up for the night in a ditch.

Doing a steady five miles an hour, I climbed Cowhanger Hill, which avoids a steeper gradient by wriggling cunningly between the Downs, and then crawled down the other side, playing a dismal solo on my electric horn. As I got to the sharp bend to the right at the bottom of the hill, something shot—or rather, seemed to shoot—out of the fog, and the radiator of a car finished noisily up against my off-side mudguard.

It really wasn't much of a smash, as we had both been travelling at little more than a walking-pace, but I stopped my engine and jumped out.

"I'm most awfully sorry," a girl's voice called out, "but I didn't think I was anywhere near the corner."

"My fault, I'm afraid," I said gallantly. "I don't think there's much harm done. Your radiator's a bit scratched, but that's about all."

"Haven't I creased your mudguard?"

"No, I think you got the worst of it."

"I'm so glad," she said. "I had the shock of my life when your lights suddenly sprang out of the fog. Is it very bad on the other side of the hill?"

I said that I feared it was.

"It was quite clear at Littleworth and it was only just the other side of Paulsfield that I ran into it. How on earth I'm going to get to Southmouth, I don't know!"

I was by this time standing at the window of her car—it was a saloon, a biggish six-cylinder affair—peering at the shadowy figure inside and wondering if this was the most attractive face I had ever seen or whether the fog was just playing tricks with me. But the fog couldn't enhance the charm of her voice and at this last despairing cry, all the deeply buried Sir Lancelot stuff within me popped up like a cork through water.

"Can I help you at all?" I asked.

"Thank you very much. It is very kind of you," she answered and I wished, rather foolishly, that she would say it again. "I don't see what you can do, though. I must get to

Southmouth tonight."

"Why not take your car back to Paulsfield and catch a train from there to Southmouth? The fog probably reaches, by this time, to the sea and it will take you hours to get to Southmouth."

She thought for a moment: then she said:

"Yes, I *could* do that."

"I know every inch of the road," I said, "and you can tail on behind me."

"Are you sure you don't mind?"

I made some remark in the not-at-all class and after a bit of manoeuvring, we managed to get the cars sorted out and pointing in the right direction. It was a matter of three miles to Paulsfield, but it took us half-an-hour; and all the way, as I sat hunched over the wheel, I looked forward to hearing her say "Thank you" again. When we got to Paulsfield, I stopped at the first garage we came to, to put up her car. In this, I admit, I was guilty of a certain low cunning, for this was at the southern end of the part of Paulsfield that had sprouted since they cut the new road, whereas the railway station was away to the north-west of the town.

When the car had been duly housed for the night and she had made arrangements for a man to take it to Southmouth in the morning, I said:

"Can I offer you a lift to the station? That is, if you don't mind travelling in a van?"

"Oh, I'd love to!" she said. "It's a dear little van. Thanks awfully!"

I liked the way she accepted my invitation without an extravagant show of maidenly hesitation.

The fog in Paulsfield was far lighter than it had been round Cowhanger Hill, but it still made driving a bit difficult. Perhaps that is why it took us so long to get to the station. As I drove along the new road, waited for the traffic-lights by the garage with the vile lighthouse petrol-pumps and then turned sharp left into the road that led, past the railway station, to Meanhurst and the Grange, our polite exchange of small-talk—remarks about the fog and the recent ghastly weather and even, I believe, the imminence of Christmas, served one useful purpose. It endorsed the opinion I had formed at the bottom of Cowhanger Hill. This was the most charming voice I had ever heard. It lilted like a tango. To hear it was like getting into an old and valued pair of slippers. Even when she said a brutal word like "Fog", it was like the sweet sound that breathes upon a bank of violets. It was like the first breath of night air, after three hours in a stuffy cinema. It was like—but my rhapsody was cut short here by the mournful discovery that I had driven past the station.

When I had backed into the yard, I displayed more diplomacy, for when she had jumped out of the car, her thanks had been said and good night was just on her lips, I said:

"I think you'd better have my address, hadn't you, in case you want to make a claim against your insurance company?"

"Yes, perhaps I had," she answered; and I wondered if she realised as well as I did what little damage her car had suffered. I found out later that she did.

I gave her one of my cards and then stood waiting awkwardly, my diplomacy having deserted me—unless an amateurish sort of cough comes under that heading. But she soon relieved the situation by saying that I had better have her card as well, at which suggestion I jumped with a greater eagerness than politeness demanded.

Then she went into the station and I turned the car round and drove home through the wispy fog, with a friendly smile for the traffic-lights and a cheery word for the lighthouse petrol-pumps. I felt that a song would not be out of place, but as the only tune that I could remember was "Men of Harlech" which hardly seemed to do justice to the occasion, I hummed an impromptu composition of my own. The long and the short of it was that I was in love. I, John Rutherford, a staid old bachelor of thirty-and-something, in whose life no perfervid flame of passion had ever burnt, had fallen in a November fog for a girl with dark shingled hair under an impudent little hat, an incontrovertibly tip-tilted nose, big brown eyes and a voice like—but I have been into all that before.

III. ENTER GEORGE

The morning after Johnson was murdered, I arrived at the shop to find George preparing for the day's business, to the accompaniment of a most unmusical whistle.

George was my assistant. He made himself useful about the shop and drove my little van, which I had bought to assist in my free-delivery service—drove it, despite his mild, almost insipid, exterior, with the wild abandon of the Valkyries rushing into battle. He was also an expert on detective fiction, was George. My stock of thrillers was usually pretty large and I was constantly adding fresh books, but George managed somehow to keep pace with them. This, in its way, was quite useful to me, for he was always in a position to discuss with a customer the relative merits of two books and could give, at a moment's notice, a brief, concise epitome of any particular yarn, leaving out just enough of the details to whet the intending borrower's appetite.

George had one of those blank, rural faces so reminiscent of a mangel-wurzel—red and expressionless. His eyes, which were of some neutral colour, were as placid as a cow's and his lavishly greased hair was parted in the middle, from where it slid oilily down his scalp and then left it quite unexpectedly and rose sharply in two little waves, one on each side of his head. In a moment of confidence he once admitted to me that this capillary waywardness caused him a lot of worry, as no amount of brushing could prevent it. This confession relieved me somewhat, as I had always feared that he did it purposely.

The vast number of books George had devoured, both before and after coming to me, had had a marked effect on his speech, for he had managed to garner from their pages words from which his native speech was free. It was amusing to hear correctly used polysyllables coming from the son of a man who ploughed for Farmer Kidd, out Burgeston way.

He had come to me just after Lady Shawford's timely visit had changed my fortunes. I had advertised for a handy lad and he had answered with an almost magical dispatch. His apparent lack of intelligence urged me to turn him down before he opened his mouth, but five minutes' chat with him made me change my mind, for it was not until he spoke to you that you realized you were not in the presence of the Village Idiot incarnate.

George had his failings, of course. He thought that to be well-dressed one had to be over-dressed. When actively engaged in my behalf, he certainly kept his appearance unobtrusive—sombre, one might almost have said; but in his hours of leisure, unrestrained by convention, he let himself go. Plum was his favourite coloured suiting and he loved boots that were not so much brown as a devastating yellow. After he had been with me a few months, he had become of so much use to me that I don't know how the business would have fared without him. At the end of the first month, I doubled his salary—George would never admit that he worked for such common things as wages—and at the end of the third month, I doubled it again. He was always polite to customers and made no trouble too great to oblige them. With me, he managed to maintain a manner that was obedient without being servile and friendly without being familiar. He was never ill or late. At the time of which I write, he was just nineteen. He smoked a terrifying quantity of those small cigarettes that sell at thirty for the shilling. His other name was Stubbings.

As I came into the shop, George turned from dusting a row of books and greeted me with a smile. I had long before entrusted him with a duplicate set of keys and he had always opened the shop by the time I arrived. I was, in fact, rather like a senior partner, who did very little of the work and trousered most of the takings.

"Good morning, sir," said George.

It was his usual greeting, but behind it I sensed suppressed excitement.

"Good morning, George," I replied. "A wretched day."

He agreed with me, but his tone did not suggest that vagaries of the weather held any great interest for him. He seemed in the process of consumption by an inner fire and made the dust fly from the shelves with wild sweeps of his feather duster. Just as I was about to suggest a little more restraint, he said:

"I was outside the police station last night, sir!"

"If you go on using that thing like that," I retorted, "you'll be inside by tonight."

He usually laughed at the poorest jest of mine, but this time not a suspicion of a smile crossed his features. He went on as if he had not been interrupted:

"And I saw them taking in Johnson's body. Is that right about you finding it, sir?"

"Quite right, George."

"Was he horrible to see, sir?"

"He wasn't very pretty."

"I've heard his head was bashed in—" he sank his voice an octave—"like an egg. Was it Murder, sir?"

You could hear the capital letter.

"I don't know, George, but it looked like it."

"And will they want you at the inquest?"

I nodded.

"Gosh, it must be great to be at an inquest! The cynosure of all eyes! Aren't you thrilled, sir?"

"Not awfully."

He looked at me as if I was some freak of nature.

"You'll get into the papers," he said, as if for that, it least, I should be grateful.

"I'm afraid so," I said.

"Prominent Paulsfield Personality Finds Body of Murdered Constable," declaimed George sonorously.

"The alliteration is good," I laughed and walked to the staircase, but George's next remark made me pause.

"Mr. Trench sat on my aunt," he said solemnly.

"Who did *what?*" I asked.

"Mr. Trench, sir, the coroner. My aunt fell down the stairs."

"Oh, I see," I said, and ran quickly up to my office before George could see my face.

In a quarter of an hour, I had cleared up what little business there was to do and at half-past nine I fixed the cover over my portable typewriter and went down again into the shop. George had finished his dusting and was now deep in the pages of a book, a new one that had come in on the Saturday before. This apparent waste of time had my full approval and it was without a trace of embarrassment that he looked up as I came down the stairs and said:

"This'll go well, sir. The man knows his job. He doesn't try to thrill you with mechanical devices."

"No trap-doors or false whiskers, eh?"

"That's right, sir. I hate trap-doors. They show faulty technique. They're nearly as bad as skeletons."

His docile eyes looked gravely out at me from his bumpkin face, but I did not laugh. I understood George and valued his opinions.

"George," I said, "I'm going to Southmouth to-day on business. I'll be back after lunch and you'll have to wait for yours till I arrive. If Mrs. Knowles comes in, tell her the book she wants is out of print temporarily, but I hope to have it in by Thursday."

"Right, sir; and don't forget about *Muffin Murder.* You said you'd see about it when you went to Southmouth next."

I promised him that I would give the matter my attention.

I had intended to go early into Southmouth, but at about ten o'clock P.C. Chandler came into the shop. His country face, very like George's in many ways, was without expression and I found it difficult to associate him with his outburst of the previous evening. He seemed too stolid and unemotional to be stirred into saying more than "Ay?" at the saddest of tidings or "Ah" at the most tragic of happenings. Which only went to prove that it doesn't do to judge by appearances.

"Detective-inspector Charlton presents 'is compliments, sir," Chandler intoned, as if he had learnt the speech by heart on his way to the shop, "and will you do 'im the favour of stepping along to the police station. 'E would like a few words with you."

George stood in the background with his mouth open.

"Certainly," I replied. "I'll be with him in five minutes."

After Chandler had left, I got my hat and coat and walked to the police station, leaving George in charge of the shop. When I was shown into a room at the back of the building, Inspector Charlton stubbed out a cigarette end in the ashtray on the desk and rose to his feet.

"Good morning, Mr. Rutherford," he smiled, holding out his hand across the desk. "I hope I'm not inconveniencing you. Sit down, won't you?"

I took the chair by the side of the desk and the Inspector went on:

"I want to talk to you about this unfortunate business of Johnson. I have here the prints of the photographs that were taken last night, with a certain amount of diffidence, by Mr. Hopkins. Was the body in that position when you found it?"

He passed one of the photographs over to me.

"Yes," I said, after a short examination.

"You notice the cap lying on the bank to his left?"

"I put that there," I admitted.

"Ah!" he said in a satisfied tone. "That's what I wanted to know. Where was it before you moved it?"

"It was on the road just there."

I pointed with my finger to a position close up to the

44

bank just below where Johnson's hand lay on the grass above.

"The peak was nearest the bank," I added.

"Did it lie on its crown or on its brim—or rather," he smiled, "where the brim would be if there were one?"

"It lay on the crown, Inspector—like this."

I placed my own soft hat in the same position on the desk.

"I see," said the Inspector. "thank you very much. I don't know whether you are very busy this morning, Mr. Rutherford," he went on, "but I shall be extremely obliged if you will run out with me in my car to the place where Johnson was killed."

"As a matter of fact," I said doubtfully, "I had intended to go into Southmouth this morning. . . . But it's early yet. Yes, Inspector, I'll be pleased to come."

"Good," he said, "we'll go now." Fortunately, the rain had stopped, but the sky was still overcast and sullen. I found that I did most of the talking during our drive. The Inspector had that rare quality of being a good listener, and before I really realized it, I was telling him about 'Voslivres' and Crawhurst and how I came to be lodging with Mrs. Hendon. In fact, practically the only thing I didn't tell him was about the girl I had met in the fog—and I should probably have enthusiastically enlarged on even that theme if our ride through the dripping, depressing countryside had been longer. I am not usually too keen on talking about myself, but that morning I was, I am afraid, the most crashing of bores. At last I had the grace to say:

"But all these personal details can't possibly interest you, Inspector."

"To the contrary," he smiled, "I am interested in everything—particularly in details. Some time ago, I saw a baby girl lying on a rug. I suppose she was about eleven months or so old. She had picked up a tiny strand of wool—or whatever it was—and was silently examining it with cross-eyed concentration. She took it in one hand, then she took it in the other hand, then she took it in both hands. She pulled at it, pushed at it, bent it and tasted it; and in two absorbed minutes, she knew, within the limits of her comprehension, all there was to know about it. To me, it was just a scrap of wool—a mere detail; but it was far more than that to her. I was hampered by the knowledge that it was a scrap of wool and accepted it *in toto,* while she brought to it an open mind and probably discovered quite a lot of exciting things about it!"

It suddenly struck me that the car had been standing still for some time and that we had reached our destination. The big car blocked the narrow lane and there was only just room to enable us to open the doors on each side.

"Now, Mr. Rutherford," said the Inspector, "I want you to show me exactly where and how that bicycle was lying when you found it last night. This is where Johnson was."

He had walked a few paces along the road and now pointed to the grass bank on the left-hand side of the road.

"It was immediately opposite him," I explained. "Just here. You can see where the handle-bar has scored the grass."

The Inspector bent down and examined the marks on the edge of the bank, which was about eighteen inches high. Then he pulled out of his pocket a circular bakelite case, from which he extracted a flexible steel rule. After marking off with his thumb a length of approximately three feet, he laid the rule so that his thumb coincided with the mark on the bank and from the point where the end of the rule touched the road, he measured the distance to the base of the bank.

"That, I suppose," I said, "was the position of the bicycle before it was allowed to fall?"

The Inspector was busy jotting down these particulars in his note-book and his only reply was a non-committal grunt.

His next step was to measure the width of the lane, and it was while he was doing this that he suddenly pounced on something almost hidden in the grass on top of the bank, a foot or so from where the bicycle had scraped it. It looked like a scrap of pink-coloured paper to me, but it was in the Inspector's pocket before I could be sure.

"Well, Mr. Rutherford," he smiled, "I think that's all that concerns us here for the moment. We'll just have a look at that footpath, if you don't mind."

We drove the short distance that separated us from the footpath. The Inspector laid a hand on my arm.

"Don't trouble to get out, Mr. Rutherford," he said. "I shall only be a few minutes."

He opened the door of the car and jumped out. As he entered the footpath, he stopped and carefully examined the ground. Then he turned to me.

"I may be more than a few minutes," he said. "Do you mind waiting?"

"Not a bit," I answered, and he went off down the footpath, glancing at the ground and the trees and undergrowth to each side of him.

When a bend in the path hid him from me, curiosity got the better of me and I climbed out of the car, to see what it was that had changed the Inspector's mind so suddenly. I don't think I have mentioned before that whereas the road to Burgeston was tarred, this particular lane had a macadam surface, which, of course, does not register very readily such things as footprints. But when I scanned the footpath, which was composed chiefly of mud and dead leaves, I saw clearly marked in it the track of a bicycle, the curving contour of which suggested that a machine had been ridden into the footpath from the direction of Paulsfield or *vice versa.*

It was over a quarter of an hour before the Inspector got back to the car.

"So sorry to keep you waiting," he said.

"Not a bit," I answered. "It naturally takes longer to walk along the path than to ride a bicycle."

The Inspector looked at me quickly.

"*Touché*" he smiled. "I must admit that those tracks interested me."

"Do they go the whole length of the footpath?" I asked.

"They run intermittently," he said, "right through to the Burgeston road, where they disappear completely. The wheels must have been a bit muddy by the time they reached the road, but the rain has washed away all traces."

"I'm afraid I'm not sufficiently experienced," I admitted, "To tell from the tracks which way the cyclist went."

"He had been riding along this road from the direction of Paulsfield and turned into the footpath here. He was in a great hurry. No other bicycles have been ridden along the footpath in either direction but there are traces of a good many different footprints. The tyres on the machine were 'Runlock Roadsters' and were both pumped up hard, besides being comparatively new. Pick the bones out of that, Mr. Rutherford!"

He walked over to the other side of the road, where a gate gave access to a field, in which, fifty yards or so from the road, was a pond with a couple of trees growing on its cattle-trampled banks. He stood gazing reflectively at the pond for a few moments and then said, turning quickly to me:

"Were you wearing those brown, rubber-soled brogues last night?"

I said I was.

"They looked like the same pair," he said, "Which is rather fortunate, because we can check up your footprints on the footpath. That will dispose of some of the tracks."

"And will also help to prove," I said, but only to myself, "That I wasn't lying when I said I walked along that path last night!"

As I got out of the car, there was a distant explosion.

"Two minutes' silence," murmured the Inspector, and we took off our hats.

When the second maroon marked the end of the

Armistice Day ceremony, I said:

"My father died on Passchendaele Ridge."

"He was a great chap," the Inspector said quietly.

"Did you know him?" I asked.

"Yes," he answered, and then went on hurriedly, "Now, let's test those footprints. I've wasted enough of your time already!"

Experiments with several imprints, which fitted my shoe perfectly, seemed to satisfy the Inspector and we got back into the car. The lane was too narrow for us to turn, so the Inspector drove on towards Hazeloak, where we could turn to the right and get back to Paulsfield through Burgeston.

"This is all very interesting," I said. "I've never been mixed up in a murder case before."

"I expect it is," the Inspector replied. "Crime detection must have a great deal of fascination for the layman, judging from the popularity of detective-stories; but I can assure you that for those of us who earn our bread by it, there's precious little romance about it! It's hard work, that demands our attention at all hours of the day and night."

"I expect you cursed yesterday evening?" I said.

The Inspector shrugged his shoulders.

"They kept me tomfooling about yesterday over some poor girl at Lulverton, who thought a gas oven was the quietest way out; and then as soon as I had got home, had some food and changed into my slippers, Sergeant Martin rang me."

"I suppose you are attached to Lulverton police station?" I asked.

"Yes, officially. Paulsfield, of course, is in my section. The Chief Constable of the County is at Whitchester. As I was saying, a month's work sometimes goes for nothing, and a night's watching in the rain results in no more than a chill. After sifting endless evidence and sorting out the grain from the chaff, and after following up assiduously the slightest of clues that may lead us to Edinburgh or the West Indies, we build up against a man a cast-iron case; and then some solitary, sentimental nit-wit on the jury, who's fallen for the culprit's honest blue eyes, sticks out against a conviction.

"No, Mr. Rutherford, a detective's life is not a bed of roses, on which he gracefully reclines and languidly acknowledges the plaudits of the adoring populace. The only praise he's ever likely to get is some raucous, drunken voice shouting out, 'Good old flat-feet!' To be a detective, you've got to have the patience of Job, the wisdom of Solomon, the indifference to discomfort of a Stoic, the hide of a rhinoceros and the constitution of a horse! Can I drop you anywhere?"

At my request, he dropped me at 'Voslivres'.

★ ★ ★ ★

When I passed the word round that I was going that morning to Southmouth on business, I had not stuck strictly to the truth. I was not going on business. I was going to see the Fog Girl. A week had gone by and I could still remember what she looked like, which proved that this was no ephemeral infatuation. I could have kicked myself for being such a sentimental fool. She was probably engaged or in the process of becoming so. If she wasn't, I thought, the male population of Southmouth sadly needed the attention not only of an optician, but also of an aurist—particularly of an aurist, for any normal man must surely realise that, although he will not have to *look* at his wife-to-be any oftener than he wishes, he will not be able to avoid *hearing* her, unless he puts his fingers in his ears, which would savour of ostentation.

I *did* know that she wasn't married. That was something. Her card had told me that: "Miss Molly Arnold". A pretty name, I decided; and although I should have outgrown such foolishness, I tried, one evening, to write a poem about her. But as the only words I could think of to rhyme with

"Molly" were "jolly", which was a bit too boisterous for my gentle Muse, and "folly" and "melancholy", which made the situation even more depressing, I gave it up and did the crossword puzzle in my newspaper.

But on the Sunday afternoon I had made up my mind. I would call upon her. After all, I told myself—arrant self-deceiver that I was—it was only the polite thing to do. Perhaps I should meet her fiancé and give my *amour propre* the jolt it well deserved.

That was why I caught the 11.35 train from Paulsfield that morning and some time later walked along Northern Avenue, Southmouth, looking for a house called Holmedene. I was not long finding it—a two-storeyed, four-square residence, standing, as an F.S.I. would have it, in its own grounds, with a garage built on to one side of it. I went up the path and encouraging my lagging spirits with such truisms as "faint heart . . ." and "he who hesitates . . .", I pressed the bell.

My ring was answered promptly—or perhaps I only thought it was promptly—by a smart little maid, of whom I enquired if Miss Arnold was at home. She said that if I would be good enough to step inside, she would find out; and after showing me into a handsomely furnished front room, she bore off my card. I was closely examining a fine sea-scape, which might have been a fire-escape, for all it meant to me, when Molly came in.

"Good morning, Mr. Rutherford," she smiled.

"Good morning, Miss Arnold," I smiled back. "I hope I haven't come at an awkward time, but I was in here on business this morning and ..." I stumbled a bit here, but she helped me out.

"It's very nice of you to call," she said. "As a matter of fact, I have wanted to see you again to thank you for what you did on that simply dreadful evening. Won't you sit down?"

We took a couple of chairs by the fire and she went on:

"Did you get back home without banging into anything?"

"Yes," I laughed, "I came through without a scratch."

That seemed to dispose of that. After a silence that was just beginning its fourth year, she said:

"Please smoke if you want to."

Cigarettes are not my strong point, but I had bought some that morning to meet this eventuality. I offered Molly my case.

"Do you usually smoke cigarettes?" she asked, after I had given her a light.

"Not as a rule. I smoke a disgusting pipe, which, if I dared to light it here, would get me forbidden the house!"

"Please don't mind me," she said. "I'm completely smoke-dried. Uncle's double-strength gaspers would knock the fussiness out of anybody and he doesn't mind very much where he puts the ends. Anything with a hole in the top is an ash-tray to Uncle Harry!"

I gave a hearty laugh and discovered when I stopped that I had nothing to take its place. I was just considering the advisability of giving another hearty laugh, when Molly said:

"Do you often come to Southmouth?"

"Yes," I said. "My business brings me in here quite a lot. I run a bookshop in Paulsfield, you know. I used to live in Southmouth."

"At Crawhurst, in the Glebe," Molly added.

"Who on earth told you that?"

"I didn't have to be told," she laughed. "I knew. I lived over the road."

"I'm afraid I don't remember you," I admitted. "How long ago was it?"

"About twenty-two years. That makes us both seem very old, doesn't it?"

I was still at a loss, but here, at least, was something to avert another chunk of silence.

"You seem to know all about *me*" I laughed, "but I can't, for the life of me, reconcile you with the Glebe."

"Oh, but you must do—you used to tease our cat! Your mother got so cross about it, too. And once you let me come in and play with your soldiers. Don't you remember how you had to make the ones that were kneeling down with fixed bayonets march up to the front line? And how I nursed the wounded and fixed on their heads again with bits of match-stick?"

This was harking back a bit, but when she mentioned my soldiers, my memory stirred.

"Good heavens, yes—I remember now!" I said. "You were a long-legged kid with a pigtail and we used to quarrel terribly!"

"I'm afraid the description fits!" Molly laughed. "I was a truly awful child."

The going became much easier after that and the silence took itself off, probably in high dudgeon. After all, it does break the ice a bit when The Girl reminds you that she once poured a bottle of ink over your head. For nearly an hour we chatted of those old days. I heard how her father had gone down in the Dardanelles with the ship he commanded, leaving her an orphan. Her mother had died when Molly came into the world. She told me how, in 1916, she had come to live with her uncle, who was her mother's bachelor brother. I, in my turn, told my story.

"Heavens!" I said suddenly. "I must make a move!"

"I'm sorry I can't ask you to stay to lunch," Molly said, "because, to be perfectly frank, there isn't any. Uncle has gone off on a case and when he's not here I usually go out somewhere."

"Then why not go out somewhere with me?" I suggested. "This reunion after all these years should surely be celebrated?"

"I'd love to!" said Molly.

"Where shall we go?"

"What about the Metropole?"

This was a bit of a facer. The Metropole was the real name of the hotel I have previously mentioned as the Frightful, which I had left under what may safely be called a cloud. For all I knew Molly's uncle might be an important shareholder, which might make things a little awkward.

"Have you ever been to Saletti's?" I asked.

That was safe enough, for Saletti's was even more expensive than the Metropole.

"No," Molly admitted, "but I don't see why that should stop us!"

So we went to Saletti's and it wasn't until three o'clock that we got back to Holmedene. I refused Molly's offer to come in, as I was very late already, and suggested a visit to a theatre later in the week. Molly seemed to think this a good idea and we fixed it for Friday.

"Well," I said at last, "your doorstep is a delightful spot, but I must really go."

"Good-bye, Mr. Rutherford, and thank you for lunch."

"Was it 'Mr. Rutherford'," I asked, "when we lived in the Glebe, Miss Arnold?"

"No—and it wasn't 'Miss Arnold' either, John!"

And with a delightful little gurgle of laughter, she gently closed the door.

★ ★ ★ ★

It was nearly four o'clock before I got back to 'Voslivres'. When I pushed open the door, George looked up from the book he was reading by the fire, in the most comfortable chair in the shop. There was a reproachful light in his eyes.

"Hullo, George!" I said. "Sorry to be late, but I was kept. Had your lunch?"

He looked at me like a faithful dog that has been unreasonably spanked.

"No, sir."

"You must be hungry by this time!"

"I'm starving, sir!"

"'And his chief beside, smiling the boy fell dead,'" I quoted. "Well, you'd better pack yourself off home for the highest of high teas, to make up for it. Offer my apologies to your mother for interfering with her domestic arrangements."

"Right, sir."

"Everything gone smoothly?"

"All in order, sir. I finished *The Corpse in the Copse* and passed it on to Colonel Hawtrey. He said that the man who wrote the last book he had knows as much about the Punjab as his wife's tabby cat."

"Oh, I expect India's changed a lot since Kipling and the Colonel graced it with their presence. Now then, off you go!"

He put on his mackintosh and trilby hat, but at the door he turned back.

"Did you see about *Muffin Murder*, sir?" he asked.

"No, George," I admitted, "I forgot all about it."

"Oh," was all he said as he went out, but his previous look of reproach was nothing to that which was now in his eyes. And it was really only a trifle. A customer had seen—or so he said—a book in a Southmouth shop window, but I had been unable to trace a story with that title. So I had promised George that when I went next to Southmouth, I would inspect the window in question. That was all, but George went away as if I had committed a heinous crime. He was like that. As a matter of fact, the book eventually turned out to be called *The Crime at Crumpetts*, but that is by the way.

For the next hour I pottered about the shop, with not much of my attention on what I did. I was thinking more of the events of the day. I marvelled that such a girl as Molly should still be unattached. Perhaps, I thought, she didn't go out much. She seemed to act as her uncle's chatelaine. He was probably a doctor or a veterinary surgeon, for she had spoken of his being engaged on a case. Possibly he was a lawyer or a solicitor. How the discovery that we had played and squabbled as children had helped! That kind of thing usually only happens in novels. I must fix up those seats for Friday. *Trailing Clouds of Glory* was on at one of the Southmouth theatres. That was a good show. Ran for a year in London. Or would Molly like something a little lighter? I ought to have asked her.

I was still mooning about when George came back from his long-postponed meal.

"Well, George," I asked, "was the tea high enough for you?"

"Yes, thank you, sir. It was a kipper."

His perfectly serious expression denied any suggestion of a *double entendre*.

"Seen the notices up about the murder, sir?" he went on.

I was quite sincere in my question:

"Which murder, George?"

"Why. Johnson, sir!" said George, looking surprised.

"Oh, yes, of course. I'd forgotten about it."

The strange part of it was that I really had. An odd expression came to George's face. It seemed almost as if he understood.

"No," I continued, "I haven't seen any notices."

"The police," said George, "are advertising for anyone who can tell them anything about the affair."

"I don't think they'll be very lucky," I said. "I saw nobody about."

"No, sir; but you don't know how long the body had been lying there before you found it."

"Oh, yes I do—approximately. Before I got to Deeptree Corner, Johnson and Didcott passed me on bicycles. That was about five-and-twenty to nine and I found his body at five-past. He was killed during that half-hour."

"I didn't know that," said George. "did you recognise Johnson when he passed you?"

"No."

"Then how did you know, sir, that it *was* Johnson?"

"I was told afterwards that it must have been."

"That's not proof, sir."

I had to admit that it was not. But the Sergeant had said that Johnson and Didcott went that way at that time every Sunday evening. I told George that.

"Well, sir," he conceded, "that makes a bit of difference, but it doesn't prove that Johnson was one of the men you saw and it doesn't prove that Didcott was the other. It's only circumstantial evidence, isn't it?"

"Look here, George," I protested good-humouredly, "I shall have quite enough questions to answer at the inquest. Let's drop the subject until then."

George looked crestfallen.

"Sorry, sir. Perhaps I shouldn't have catechized you like that, but I'm awfully interested. It's the first real murder I've ever experienced."

"How do you know it was murder?" I asked swiftly, giving George a dose of his own medicine.

"I don't," he said with a broad grin, "but I hope it was."

"You cold-blooded young devil!" I laughed.

Business that evening was far from brisk: the rain, which had reconsidered its decision to stop, kept people indoors. It was therefore with a sigh of relief that I eventually left George to lock up the shop and, pulling the collar of my raincoat round my ears, walked back home to Thorpe Street. On the notice-board outside the police station, prominently displayed among the "Losts", was one of the broadsheets George had mentioned, but I was in too much of a hurry to give it more than a casual glance. While I was rubbing my shoes on the hall-mat, Lizzie came out of her kitchen.

"Bless your 'eart, Master John," she said, "but where 'ave you been to. Surely it isn't the police again?"

She had called me "Master Johnny" at first, just as she had at Crawhurst, but I had tactfully suggested that "John" was more in keeping with my maturer years.

57

"I humbly plead forgiveness," I smiled, "but I went to Southmouth this morning and had lunch there."

"And me keeping a lovely steak and chips 'ot for two hours for you!"

I repeated my apologies and asked her if there were any letters.

"Yes," she said, "One came this evening and I put it on your mantelpiece. Mighty official, it looked."

"It's the sub-poena, I expect," I said and went upstairs.

I was right. The communication in the buff envelope required me to attend at eleven in the forenoon of the next Wednesday, to give evidence before the jury which had been convened to enquire into the death of P.C. Johnson of the Downshire County Constabulary; this enquiry to take place in the Horticultural Hall, Paulsfield.

IV.   I ATTEND A PUBLIC ENQUIRY

Ten minutes before the appointed hour on the following Wednesday morning, I walked across to the Horticultural Hall, having left George, in the depths of despondency at not being able to attend the inquest, to mind the shop.

The Horticultural Hall, usually the home of flower-shows and displays of local histrionic, vocal and terpsichorean talent, was on the north-west corner of the Square. There were a couple of dozen sightseers hanging about outside, and when the constable stationed at the door had let me through, I found that about forty members of the public had been admitted. They were occupying chairs at the back of the Hall, the space in front having been cleared. Just in front of the curtained stage were the coroner's table and chair, and at right-angles to the stage were the seats for the jury. Three-quarters of the way down each side of the Hall were five or six more chairs and in those to my left as I walked forward, gentlemen of the Press sat ready with their note-books. On the other side, Dr. Weston was pacing impatiently up and down. I walked over to him and after exchanging greetings, which were, as far as he was concerned, perfunctory, I sat down.

A few minutes before the hour, the coroner's clerk came through a door to the side of the stage, carrying a handful of papers, which he placed on the desk. He was followed by the jury, an ill-at-ease band of nine strong; and at eleven o'clock precisely Mr. Trench, a little man, dressed in dark grey, wearing gold-rimmed spectacles with extraordinarily thick lenses on his large nose, took his seat at the table. The jury were sworn by an impassive constable—like the man at the door, he was a stranger to me—and sat down in the chairs provided for them.

For a minute or two, Mr. Trench sorted out his papers, peering short-sightedly at each. Then, when he had arranged them to his entire satisfaction—his every action marked him a meticulous man—he said:

"Have the jury inspected the body?"

The foreman, a draper from the High Street, rose to his feet and said, "Yes, sir."

"Gentleman of the jury," said Mr. Trench, "during the evening of Sunday last, the tenth of November, the dead body of Police-constable Johnson, of the Downshire County Constabulary, was found approximately half-way between Deeptree Corner and Hazeloak village. I understand that you are all acquainted with that particular strip of road. After listening to the evidence to be given in this court, it will be your duty to decide how Police-constable Johnson met his death."

He paused for a few moments. Then he said:

"Call Doctor Weston."

Almost before he had spoken, the Doctor had jumped from the chair he had taken. He marched up to the coroner's table and took the oath in a clear, definite voice.

The coroner consulted the papers before him.

"You are Henry Arthur Weston, a registered medical practitioner?"

"Yes, sir."

"You live at Trevona, Hill Road, Paulsfield, and are in practice here?"

"Yes, sir."

"And you are also police surgeon for this district?"

"Yes, sir."

"On the evening of Sunday last, you made an examination of Police-constable Thomas Johnson, of the Downshire County Constabulary?"

"That is so."

"And what was the result of this examination?"

"When I examined him, Police-constable Johnson was dead. I found the face of the deceased covered with partially dried blood, with traces of rain and mud mixed with it. These stains were more pronounced on the left side of the face than on the right. I found also a lacerated wound on the scalp, extending from just above the left eye, and another deep scalp wound behind the left ear."

The Doctor paused.

"Was that all the injury the head had suffered?" asked the coroner.

"No. I found also a depressed compound fracture of the skull. The frontal bone was broken on the left side and the crack extended backwards through the temple bone. Several small pieces of bone had been driven into the brain, which was severely lacerated."

"Were there no other signs of injury?"

"No, sir."

"Were there any signs of disease?"

"No, sir."

"Your opinion then is that the injuries to the skull were responsible for the death of the deceased?"

"That is my opinion, sir."

"And would death be instantaneous?"

"Possibly, but with a healthy man such as the deceased, death would not be likely to follow until a few minutes after the blows were struck."

"You speak of blows, Doctor. Might it not be that the deceased came by these injuries as the result of a fall?"

"A fall from a considerable height, yes."

"Or a fall from a push-bicycle?"

"No, sir."

"Can you give the jury any reason for this decision, Doctor?"

"Yes. No man could fall, in ordinary circumstances, from

a push-bicycle with such violence as to injure his skull so severely."

"Even if he were hit by a fast-travelling car or motor-cycle?"

"The injuries were too local to suggest such a possibility. Had the deceased been involved in a collision of that sort, there would have been other signs of the impact."

"Then how do you suggest the injuries may have occurred?"

"It is my opinion that the injuries were the result of at least two blows on the head with some blunt, heavy implement, heavily used."

Excited whisperings burst out here from the back of the hall and it was several moments before quiet was restored.

"You are convinced of this, Doctor?"

The coroner's voice was very grave.

"I am. No other explanation could account for such injuries as the head received."

"And could these blows have been self-inflicted?"

"It would be impossible for a man to hit himself with such violence as to cause injuries of this nature."

"From the position of the wounds, can you form any theory as to how these blows you are suggesting were delivered?"

"I suggest that the first blow was struck on the bare head with considerable violence by a right-handed person standing immediately in front of the deceased. This blow landed on the left side of the skull and, as the deceased staggered backwards, turning slightly to his right, a further blow was struck, which landed to the left side of the skull, just above the ear. This may have been followed by further blows on the side of the head, possibly as the body lay on its side."

"Thank you, Doctor: I think that is all for the moment. I may have to recall you."

The Doctor bowed sharply and came back to his chair.

Mr. Trench fiddled with his papers. Then:

"John Rutherford."

Feeling as I did when I once had to go up for a prize at school, I rose from my seat and walked to the coroner's desk. I don't think it is necessary to record my examination by Mr. Trench. It took very much the same course as my conversation with Inspector Charlton on the previous Sunday evening. The evidence of Police-constables Harwood and Chandler told the jury nothing fresh. They had driven out to where Johnson lay and after making certain that he was dead and that nothing could, therefore, be done for him, Harwood had returned on his motor-cycle to the police station, leaving Chandler to look after the body. Mr. Trench asked Harwood what steps he took to prove that Johnson no longer lived, and Harwood explained how, when he came to examine Johnson, Johnson's eyes were dim and glassy and the eyelids were partially closed. His jaws were clenched firmly on his tongue, the exposed parts of the body were cold and his fingers stiff.

Inspector Charlton was the next to be called. I need quote only one part of his testimony.

"You found," asked Mr. Trench, "no implement or stone or any object by means of which the deceased may have come by his injuries?"

"No, sir," the Inspector answered.

"No low-hanging bough of a tree?"

"No, sir."

Police-constable Didcott followed the Inspector. He was a well-built man of thirty-three or four, with fair hair, light blue eyes and a large, healthily coloured face. His voice was rather high-pitched, and he looked as if he took himself very seriously. A markedly different type from gay, debonair, curly-headed Johnson. When the usual formalities had been gone through, the coroner said to Didcott:

"At eight-thirty precisely on the evening of last Sunday, you left Paulsfield police station in the company of Police-constable Johnson?"

"Yes, sir."

"You were riding bicycles?"

"Yes, sir."

"Your departure was in accordance with your customary routine?"

"Yes, sir."

"Please tell the jury what happened after you left the police station."

"We rode together, sir, along the old main road, as far as Deeptree Corner, where we separated, Johnson to go to Hazeloak and me to Burgeston."

"What time did you get to Deeptree Corner?"

"I do not know exactly, sir, but I should say that it was about two minutes after five-and-twenty to nine."

"And you met nobody on the road?"

"During the first part of our ride we met a few pedestrians."

"What exactly do you mean by the first part of your ride?"

"The outskirts of Paulsfield, sir."

"And after you had reached what we may call the open country?"

"At a point approximately a quarter of a mile this side of Deeptree Corner, we caught up and passed a pedestrian."

"Did you recognize this pedestrian?"

"No, sir."

"Was it a man or a woman?"

"A man, sir."

"Can you tell the jury anything about him—how he was dressed?"

"Yes, sir. He was fairly tall and was wearing a belted raincoat, and a soft hat, pulled down at the front. His hands were in the pockets of his raincoat, which had the collar turned up. Under 'is right arm was a walking-stick. I only saw him, sir, by the light from our bicycle-lamps."

"Would you be prepared to say that this man was Mr. Rutherford, a previous witness?"

"It might have been him, sir."

"We are not concerned with 'mights,' " said Mr. Trench sharply. "You have seen Mr. Rutherford in this court to-day. Was he the man you rode past last Sunday night?"

"I cannot say, sir."

"Can you call to mind anything else you noticed about this man?"

"Yes, sir. The lowest part of his coat at the back was stained, like as if it had oil on it."

That was a nasty one. It's a bit thick when the disreputable old motoring coat, which you had decided was good enough for a night like that, is brought into the full glare of publicity at a coroner's inquest!

"You saw nobody besides this man until you left Johnson at the Corner?"

"I saw no one else, sir."

"And when you parted with the deceased at Deeptree Corner, that was the last time that you saw him alive?"

"Yes, sir."

"During your ride, did you find the deceased in his usual spirits? That is to say, was his behaviour normal?"

"He seemed quite normal to me, sir."

"There was no suggestion in his manner of excitement or fear or any emotion that would not be natural in the circumstances?"

"No, sir. He was a bit bad-tempered, but that was at being out in the rain all night."

"Were you and the deceased armed in any way on this night duty?"

"Not with firearms, sir. We each carried a truncheon."

"Thank you," said Mr. Trench. "You may stand down."

By this time the people at the back of the hall were beginning to get a bit restless. The coroner's questions seemed to be boring them. They fidgeted and coughed and there were swiftly checked whisperings. Mr. Trench looked over his papers. Then he said:

"Frederick Benson Walker."

A man whose presence in a chair behind me I had only sub-consciously realised rose to his feet and walked up to the desk. He was a tall man of about my own age, with already iron-grey hair, mouth a trifle weak, thin, haggard as if from worry, clean-shaven and neatly dressed in grey. His hands showed signs of hard work, but he had a general air of refinement.

"You are Frederick Benson Walker?" asked the coroner.

"Yes, sir."

"You are the proprietor of the Hazeloak Garage, over which you reside?"

Of course—I recognized him now.

"Yes, sir."

"On the evening of Sunday last, you were walking along the Hazeloak road in the direction of Paulsfield?"

"Yes, sir."

"Will you please tell the jury whom you met between Hazeloak and Deeptree Corner?"

Everybody was now sitting forward eagerly. We felt that we were going to hear something.

"I met two men, whom I took to be constables, riding bicycles."

There was a general gasp of surprise. Here was excitement at last! Johnson had left Didcott to go along that lane alone, and now we were told that not one, but two, had cycled that way.

"They were riding in the direction of Hazeloak?"

"Yes, sir."

"You are certain that you met them on the Hazeloak side of Deeptree Corner?"

"Yes, sir. They had left it about half a mile behind."

"Did you recognise either of these men?"

"No, sir. Their lamps were shining in my face until they

had gone by, but I did see that they were both wearing policeman's caps and black waterproof capes."

"Did you hear their voices?"

"They were not talking as they passed me. One of them drew in behind the other to leave me room. The lane is not very wide. I do remember that after they had passed me I heard a loud, high cough, rather like the neigh of a horse. I recollect thinking at the time what an unpleasant noise it was."

"At what time did you meet these men?"

"I should put it, sir, at just after twenty to nine. I remember looking at my watch when I got to Deeptree Corner and it then said eight-fifty."

"You met nobody else on the road?"

"No, sir."

"Thank you, Mr. Walker. You may stand down."

Mr. Trench now recalled Harwood.

"You have heard," he said, "the last witness's description of a cough given by one of the men who passed him. Can you identify this cough?"

"Yes, sir. The deceased used to cough like that."

"Thank you . . . John Rutherford?"

I had been expecting this summons.

"The witness, Police-constable Didcott, has described to the jury certain details of a man past whom he cycled last Sunday evening. Will you please tell the jury that you were wearing during your walk a . . ."

Mr. Trench referred to his notes.

". . .a belted raincoat, stained at the back, probably with oil, and a soft felt hat pulled down at the front, and that you were carrying a walking-stick."

"Yes, sir," I answered, "that is so."

"You can produce, if called upon, the raincoat for the examination of Police-constable Didcott?"

"Yes, sir."

"Thank you, Mr. Rutherford."

As I returned to my seat, Mr. Trench said:

"Have the jury any questions to ask the witnesses?"

A juryman in the back row leant forward and murmured into the ear of the foreman. The foreman stood.

"We should like to hear, sir, from the doctor who examined the body, whether he has formed any opinion of the nature of the blunt, heavy implement that he suggests was used."

Mr. Trench frowned slightly.

"Dr. Weston," he said, "Will you please step up here?"

The Doctor stepped up.

"The jury have asked, Doctor," said Mr. Trench, "whether you have formed an opinion of the implement used upon the deceased. Will you please tell them."

"Other than that it was blunt, sir", the Doctor replied, "I cannot say definitely what it was. It was certainly not a hammer or an axe or a sword or anything of that kind. It may have been made of wood—I found, by the way, no splinters in the wound—or a piece of lead piping or a length of steel rod with a rounded end. Farther than that, I cannot go."

The foreman rose to his feet.

"We should like the witness to tell us, sir," he said doggedly, "whether the injuries could have been caused by a constable's truncheon."

"Such a question," said the coroner sharply, "Is not admissible in this court. You are here to decide how the deceased met his death. You have been told that he received blows on the head by a blunt implement. That is sufficient for this enquiry. Dr. Weston, you may stand down."

The foreman opened his mouth, thought better of it, and sat down. Mr. Trench collected together the papers on his desk, sorted them out and placed them in a neat pile before him. Then he sat back in his chair with his hands clasped.

"Members of the jury," he said, "you have now heard all the *relative* evidence and it rests with you to decide how the deceased came to his death. But before you consider your verdict, let me remind you of the main features of this case:

"At eight-thirty, Police-constables Johnson and Didcott left Paulsfield police station on their bicycles. Johnson was in his usual spirits, except for a justifiable exasperation at the prospect of a night's exposure to the weather. They cycled together as far as Deeptree Corner, where they separated, Johnson to go to Hazeloak and Didcott to Burgeston. But Johnson never reached Hazeloak. At just after twenty minutes to nine, he was seen by Mr. Walker cycling along the Hazeloak road in the company of another person, who was clad in the cap and waterproof cape of a police-constable. At five minutes past nine, Johnson's dead body was found by Mr. Rutherford. I say 'dead' body as I think we can take it, from what Mr. Rutherford has said, that by that time Johnson had expired. Between those times, Johnson met his death.

"You have heard the medical evidence: that the deceased was probably killed with two or more blows from a blunt, heavy implement, heavily used. From Dr. Weston's examination of the corpse, he has drawn the conclusion that the injuries were not the result of a fall or a collision with a vehicle, and that the wounds could not have been self-inflicted. The only other alternative, gentlemen, is that the deceased came by his death through some human agency. In short, that he was done to death.

"We have no evidence as to the identity of Johnson's companion after he left Deeptree Corner behind. This person was seen only by one witness and he can give us no information as to this person, except that he was dressed in a constable's cape and cap.

"It is not for me, gentlemen, to influence your verdict, but I beg you not to allow the more singular features of this case to influence you. We do not yet know who this person was who travelled with the deceased. Please, therefore, do not base your verdict on hastily formulated theories. The decision you have to make is just this: how did the deceased meet his death?"

That was all he said to them—and it was enough. When the jury returned after five minutes, their verdict was:

"Murder against some person or persons unknown."

"Thank you," said Mr. Trench.

★ ★ ★ ★

As I was leaving the Hall, Inspector Charlton stopped me.

"Can you give me a few minutes, Mr. Rutherford?" he asked.

"More than that if you like, Inspector," I smiled.

We walked round the corner to the police station together. Sergeant Martin was alone in the charge-room.

"Good morning, sir. Morning, Mr. Rutherford," he greeted us. "What was the verdict?"

"Murder," the Inspector answered briefly.

"Some person or persons unknown?" Martin said slightly too casually.

"Yes, and if it hadn't been for Joe Trench, Martin," said the Inspector, "It might have been—anything."

"I thought, myself, it was going to be a bit risky—but you know best, of course, Inspector. A coroner's inquest, if you don't mind my saying so, is like going for a moonlight walk with a young woman—you never know where it is going to lead to."

"With your wider experience, Martin," smiled the Inspector, "you are able to speak on that point with greater authority than I could."

"There's not much I don't know about inquests," said Martin, engaging, at the same time, in the complicated manoeuvre of winking at me without moving his eyelid.

I followed the Inspector into the back room. He threw his hat on top of a filing cabinet and motioned me to a chair.

"Well," he said, as he dropped into his own seat and held

out his cigarette-case to me, "Mr. Trench's job ends where mine begins."

"Walker's evidence," I said, taking a cigarette,—"thanks very much—Walker's evidence came as rather a surprise—to me, at any rate."

"He'll be here in a few moments," said the Inspector. "I want to have a chat with the two of you."

"When you spoke to me last Monday about the exact position in which I found Johnson's cap," I said, changing the subject, as it was clear that the Inspector did not wish to discuss Walker's evidence, "I really ought to have apologized to you for having moved it from the road. I carefully considered the advisability of moving the bicycle, but I'm afraid that I picked up the cap and threw it on the bank without giving it a thought."

"Don't mention it," he smiled. "Fortunately, you remembered precisely where you found it."

"Forgive my bluntness," I said, "but I still can't see why it really matters."

"Didn't the position of the cap suggest anything to you, Mr. Rutherford? Didn't it seem to you that it had dropped from Johnson's hand, as he fell backwards over the bank? Or, as Dr. Weston suggested, possibly sideways?"

"Yes, I suppose so," I admitted, "but I hadn't thought of it like that. I imagined that the cap had dropped off Johnson's head in the struggle."

"Which struggle, Mr. Rutherford? Dr. Weston said there was no struggle and I have never known him to be mistaken. He said also that the first blow was struck on the bare head."

"Perhaps the murderer snatched the cap off Johnson's head before he delivered the blow?"

"That possibility is denied by what you have told me. If the cap dropped from Johnson's hand, it was he himself who removed it from his head. Can *you* think of any reason for Johnson to take off his cap, so that the murderous attack might be facilitated?"

"To scratch his head?" I suggested tentatively.

"And did the murderer, when making his plans, assume that at the right moment Johnson would be overtaken by the desire to scratch his head? Bear this one point in mind, Mr. Rutherford: the attack would probably not have met with such fatal results if Johnson's skull had been protected by his cap, and it was of vital importance to Mr. A. that his victim's head should be bare just long enough for him to get in that first blow. Were you acquainted with Johnson, Mr. Rutherford?"

"I knew him sufficiently," I said, "to pass a word or two about the weather when I met him in the street. Everybody knows everybody else in a small town like this. The only member of the Paulsfield force that I know *well* is Sergeant Martin."

"So he has told me. The good man's devotion to you is quite—marked."

"We get on very well together," I said.

"He's an excellent fellow in many ways," said the Inspector. "Conscientious, honest, with a sense of humour—and no fool. It was men like him who got us through the War."

There was a tap on the door.

"Come in!" called the Inspector.

The knob turned and Harwood appeared.

"Mr. Walker to see you, sir," he said.

"Oh, yes, Harwood. Ask him to come in, will you?"

When Walker entered, he smiled pleasantly, but with the weariness that seemed characteristic of him.

"Ah, Mr. Walker," said the Inspector, "it is kind of you to come. This is Mr. Rutherford—I don't know whether you have met before?"

Walker smiled.

"Our meetings have always been of a business nature," he said. "Mr. Rutherford has visited my garage at Hazeloak, although I didn't know until this morning what his name was."

"Well," I said, "let us regard this as our first official introduction!"

We shook hands—I thought for the first time, but I was wrong.

"Please sit down, won't you?" the Inspector invited us. "I have asked you both here this morning, because I feel sure that you will be able to give me valuable assistance in the clearing up of this case."

Walker said he would be delighted to help in any way and I concurred.

"Thank you," said the Inspector. "now let me begin our chat with a homily. A murder-case is like a jigsaw puzzle—and I don't pretend that the simile is original! In the completion of a picture-puzzle, the only satisfactory method is to take a piece that you recognize—a part of a man's face or a section of a bicycle—and use it as a starting-point. The bits of sky and so forth, you can always do afterwards. If you have the handlebars of a bicycle, you know what to look for next—the front wheel or the saddle; but if you try starting with a piece of sky, the only thing you have to go on is that two or three of your remaining fragments of sky—and you may have twenty or thirty of them—will possibly fit round your original piece. The same thing applies in the detection of crime.

"In this case that I have taken over, I have two such starting-points. One is you, Mr. Walker, for you were the last person—except the murderer—to see Johnson alive. The other is Mr. Rutherford, who was the first person—except the murderer—to see Johnson dead. I base this statement, of course, on the evidence that is at the moment available. Mr. Rutherford has already supplied me with some valuable information. He has thrown a good deal of light on a mystery that was attached to a bicycle."

"A bicycle?" asked Walker.

I might have put the same question. I couldn't recall any illuminating comments of mine on such a point.

"And you, Mr. Walker," the Inspector went on, as if Walker had not spoken, "Have been equally helpful with your story of Johnson's mysterious companion. Had it not been for you two gentlemen, I should have been confronted with a problem even greater than the one it is now my duty to solve."

The Inspector smiled.

"It is fortunate for me," he continued, "that you both decided not to allow the rain to deter you from your evening rambles. If Mr. Rutherford had not discovered Johnson, the body might have lain there all night before it was found."

"I should probably have come across it," said Walker. "As I have already told you, after meeting the two constables, I walked on past Deeptree Corner into Paulsfield. When I had had a drink at the 'Roebuck', I set out for Hazeloak— and I must surely have noticed either him or the bicycle."

"Very likely," the Inspector agreed, and turned the conversation to more general topics.

V.   WHICH INTRODUCES MAGGIE WOOD

At half-past eight that evening, I pushed open the door of the 'Queen's Head'. Half a dozen men sat at the long cigarette-scarred table, two more stood against the bar, while a couple played skittles with a little swinging ball. All of them had pint tankards within easy distance of their hands, with the exception of Bob Coombe, Paulsfield's only bookie, who was drinking whisky, with his bowler hat in danger of falling from the back of his head. As I came in, one of the sitters slammed down his empty pot on the table. He was a gamekeeper from Meanhurst Grange.

"I says," he said decisively, "as 'ow Didcott done it."

One of the players stood stooping with the skittle-ball in his hand, but paused before releasing it.

"And I says," he said equally decisively, "As 'ow Didcott never done it."

A strange, dark little man, this, with a straggling moustache and big, beautiful, intensely pathetic eyes, who haunted the golf-course and seemed to live by the illicit sale of the balls he found in the gorse and ditches. Through the haze of smoke he caught sight of me and wished me a good evening. As the ball swung from his hand in a gentle curve and six proud skittles were laid low, all the others greeted me in their turn. I hadn't the vaguest idea who some of them were, but they knew me all right—and all my history as well, I expect!

I returned their salutations and as Agnes, the daughter of Tom Pettitt, the proprietor, drew me a pint from the wood, said what a lovely day it had been, which restarted the conversation that my arrival had stopped. There seemed to be the makings of a fine slander action in their discussion, but that didn't appear to worry them.

"What's your opinion about this murder, Mr. Rutherford?" asked his lordship's gamekeeper.

"I don't think I've reached an opinion," I answered.

"D'yer think Didcott done it?" was his next blunt question.

"No," I said, "I don't think he did. He doesn't seem to have had any motive."

The gamekeeper laughed.

"No motive! Did you 'ear that?"

He turned to the others and then brought his heavy gaze back to me.

"Ain't you never 'eard of Maggie Wood, sir?" he asked.

I shook my head.

"'Aven't you, now," he said and buried his face in the tankard that Agnes had refilled for him. After a while he emerged and having wiped his mouth on his sleeve, went on:

"Maggie Wood used to be a maid up at the Grange. She ain't there no longer. She left a couple of months ago and now she's behind the bar in a pub down near the 'arbour at Portsmouth. As pretty a girl as ever walked, though some might 'ave called 'er plump. She came to the Grange it must have been about last June and soon afterwards Didcott came around after 'er. Several times I caught them chatting at the Lodge gates and they were seen about the lanes together, 'im being in ordinary clothes. It was plain that she'd made a hit with 'im, but though 'e's a pretty good-looker, I think she only fell for 'is lovely uniform."

He dived into his mug again. Then continued:

"Things went on nicely for a couple of months and we all thought the banns would go up any Sunday. Then up pops Master Johnson, bless 'is little 'eart! 'E was a snatcher, if ever there was one! It didn't take young Maggie long to throw Didcott over and take up with 'andsome Tom.

Didcott was fair cut up about it."

He drained his tankard and passed it over to Agnes. I don't know how he dealt with poachers, but he certainly made a pint of beer look silly. After a generous sip, he went on with his tale.

"It must 'ave been about the end of August—an 'ot, 'eavy evening—that I was down near the Lodge gates, prowling about on the look-out for them as was up to no good. I went across the drive to go through the spinney on the other side, when I caught sight of two figures standing by the gate. It was nigh on dark, but I saw that they were Maggie Wood and her new copper. I wasn't going to take much notice of them. I'd seen 'em at it before and it weren't no business of mine. But just as I was going into the spinney, I 'eard an angry voice. 'Didcott!' I says to myself at once, and stayed where I was."

He paused dramatically.

"The two coppers began to chuck angry words at each other and I 'eard Didcott say something about 'stealing other men's girls, you swine.' Then Maggie gave a bit of a scream and I 'eard 'em scuffling on the gravel. I've never found out to this day whether they 'ad much of a fight, because I left them to it. 'You ain't going to do any good butting in,' I says to myself. 'Let 'em fight it out.' After all, as I said before," he ended virtuously, "It weren't no business of mine."

The little man with the sad eyes had been waiting patiently for the end of the gamekeeper's story. Now he said:

"And just because you once saw two men 'aving a row about a girl, you say that when one of them is murdered, the other must 'ave done it!"

"Yes, I do!" said the gamekeeper, banging the table with his hairy fist. I had begun to dislike the man.

"Well, I don't," said the little man and turned his attention to his game.

"Didcott's got a wicked temper," observed Bob Coombe solemnly. He had a solemn voice.

"'Oo told you that?" asked another man. "I ain't never seen no sign of it. Placid is what I should call 'im."

"It's a bookie's job to know all about the police," said Coombe.

"And it's the police's job to know all about the bookies!" the other retorted, and there was a general laugh, in which Coombe joined.

"What do *you* think about it, Bob?" asked the gamekeeper.

Coombe pushed his hat still further back.

"I don't know," he said. "All the evidence seems against him, but I can't somehow see Didcott cracking Johnson's 'ead in—unless 'e did it in a fit of rage. 'E doesn't look one to 'arbour a grudge. If 'e'd done it when 'Enery 'ere saw the three of them at Meanhurst Lodge gates, I could 'ave understood it, but I can't see Didcott storin' the malice up in his 'eart for two months and then doin' Johnson in."

"P'r'aps," suggested the gamekeeper, "Johnson began to twit 'im last Sunday evening about Maggie. That might 'ave sent 'im raging."

"But what was Didcott doing on the wrong road?" asked another man. "That doesn't look like flying off the 'andle. 'E must 'ave 'ad a well thought out plan if 'e did it at all, which I myself doubts."

I intruded myself into the conversation.

"How did the two men behave towards each other," I asked, "After the rough-and-tumble outside the Grange?"

"Didcott must 'ave realized what Maggie Wood was like," said the little sad-eyed man, "And left 'er to Johnson. 'E couldn't 'ave thought of a better revenge on 'er—or on either of them, if it came to that!"

This gentleman was decidedly pro-Didcott and anti-Johnson. Most of the town was, I had discovered.

"Then Maggie went to Portsmouth," he went on, "And the 'ole thing seemed to blow over, as you might say. Probably Johnson wasn't borne no ill-will by Didcott, 'oo likely saw 'e was well out of it. 'Im and Johnson 'ave been quite friendly ever since."

"Love's a funny thing," ponderously observed the gamekeeper, and they all sagely wagged their heads.

I felt a gust of cold air from behind me and turned just as the door swung back behind Sergeant Martin.

"Evening, Sergeant," was the general greeting.

Martin nodded to them, then caught sight of me standing against the bar.

"Good evening, Martin," I said. "What will you take?"

"Good evening, Mr. Rutherford. I'll have a pint of B. and B. if it's all the same to you. Thank you, Agnes. How's your mother. Better? That's good."

Martin was in mufti tonight: brown suit and overcoat and a cap. But even without his uniform, his presence immediately changed the subject of our talk.

"'Ow's your old dog, Sergeant?" one man asked.

"Oh, I think he's better, thank you, Mr. Brown. He had another fit on Tuesday of last week, but I got the vet to come and have a look at 'im. He gave me some potassium bromide for 'im, and it seems to be doing 'im good."

"I 'ad a dog once what was subject to fits," said Bob Coombe in his solemn voice, "And it was all on account of worms."

And so the conversation went on from dogs to cows, from cows to Southmouth's chances for the Cup; until I suggested a game of billiards to Martin. Agnes turned on the lights in the back room and we left the others to their talk.

Martin was pretty good at billiards, but I managed to put it across him by a narrow margin.

"You're in form tonight, Mr. Rutherford," he said, as we replaced our cues in their stand.

"Flukes, I'm afraid, Martin," I laughed. "when luck and I get together, we're unbeatable!"

The Sergeant pressed the bell for Agnes and joined me on the faded red plush settee. Agnes knew our needs and brought in two fresh tankards. When the door had closed behind her—not too late for me to hear the gamekeeper reiterating that Didcott done it—Martin said:

"Well, Mr. Rutherford, what's it feel like to be mixed up in a real murder, after lending out so many of the other kind?"

I had not intended bringing up the matter, but this was a definite lead, so I said that it was certainly an experience, if not an entirely pleasant one. Martin looked round a trifle furtively, but the low drone of voices coming through the door assured him that we were not overheard. For all that, he spoke almost in a whisper.

"The Inspector has been finding out a thing or two," he said.

"I'm glad to see the taxpayers' money is not being wasted," I smiled. "Is it a secret, Martin?"

"With anyone else, Mr. Rutherford, yes; but I know I can trust you like I trust myself. Seeing that you seem to be occupying a stall in this little vaudeville show, you might as well know what's going on back-stage. I warn you, though, that if Inspector Charlton finds out that I've been opening my heart to you, I'll be back on the beat in twenty-four hours!"

"I won't breathe a word," I promised, "but don't tell me if you don't want to."

"I do want to," Martin said rather pathetically. "I've got to talk to somebody about it. They're beginning to get me down—all these suspicions and queer goings-on. Things aren't too rosy at the station, what with one thing and another. Didcott's going round as if he's not suspected of murder, like a dog pretending 'e 'asn't noticed the tin-can tied to his tail; while Chandler and Harwood are trying to treat 'im as if nothing had 'appened. It's a bit difficult, Mr. Rutherford."

I agreed that it must be.

"Last Monday morning," said Martin, "The Inspector

went to Burgeston and made a few discreet enquiries—and
nobody can make discreet enquiries like the Inspector can!
When you think you've been 'aving a chat with him about
the weather, you find you've told him why you did it and
where you've put the body!"

Martin chuckled and refilled his pipe.

"What do you think he found out?" he asked, but gave
me no time to reply. "Didcott didn't get to Burgeston till
five-past nine last Sunday."

"Later than usual?" I asked.

"Yes. The men usually reckoned to reach Burgeston soon
after eight-fifty—nearly a quarter of an hour earlier than 'e
got there on Sunday."

I whistled.

"They put their bikes up for the night at the 'Porcupine',
as I seem to remember telling you last Sunday, and old man
Rawlinson, who runs the pub, told the Inspector that he
didn't see Didcott until gone nine. He said that Didcott was
a bit breathless and what you might call 'arassed. Looked as
if he'd been hurrying."

"There's probably nothing in that," I said. "he may have
had a puncture."

"Funny you should've suggested that, Mr. Rutherford.
Rawlinson pulled Didcott's leg about being late and asked
'im what the girl's name was. Didcott looked a bit shirty at
first and then laughed it off and said 'e'd had a puncture."

"Well," I laughed, "I'm willing to believe that Inspector
Charlton is an adept at making discreet enquiries, but I'll bet
the whole of Paulsfield and district know that Didcott was
late on the one occasion when punctuality was vital!"

"I don't think they do," contradicted Martin. "Rawlinson
told the Inspector that, when 'e heard about the murder,
he decided that 'e better keep 'is mouth shut; and, as far as
we know, nobody else noticed what time Didcott got to
Burgeston."

The Sergeant went on to tell me how, when the Inspector

got back to Paulsfield, he asked Martin to show him the bicycle that Didcott had ridden the night before. Didcott had finished his night's duty at Burgeston, ridden back to Paulsfield soon after six o'clock in the morning, replaced his machine in the shed at the back of the police station and gone home to bed. When, therefore, the Inspector came to examine the bicycle, it was just as Didcott had left it. Alone with Martin in the shed, he turned the bicycle upside down and removed both covers with a tyre-lever. Neither of the inner tubes had a patch on it.

"And there it is, Mr. Rutherford," concluded Martin, "For what it's worth."

"Which isn't much, to my mind," I said. "It seems to me that Didcott told Mr. Rawlinson the first thing that came into his head. I should probably have said the same thing in his position. I don't know Mr. Rawlinson, but he may be one of those people one has to lie to in sheer self-defence. It was nothing to do with him that Didcott was late, whatever Didcott's real reason was, and Didcott may have just said it to keep Rawlinson from asking any more questions. If Didcott *was* guilty, why, when he knew that the murder would delay him, didn't he think of a more convincing alibi than the obviously last-minute makeshift one of an imaginary puncture?"

"Just what I think," Martin agreed. "I'm dead sure that the man Walker saw with Johnson wasn't Didcott. I believe Didcott is as innocent as the day. That funny business of the bicycle you rode . . ."

He cut himself short in mid-sentence.

"What funny business, Martin?" I asked, in mild surprise.

"Nothing," said Martin quickly, "nothing, Mr. Rutherford. Didcott, I was going to say, is a good steady chap. Been under me for several years and I ain't got much against him. Made a bit of a fool of 'imself over a girl last summer, but constables are human, ain't they?"

"The charming Maggie Wood?" I asked innocently.

"Who told you that?" Martin asked sharply.

"A little bird, Martin!" I smiled.

"Too many little birds in this part of the world," he snorted. "Anyway, a proper little so-and-so Maggie Wood turned out to be. I 'ad a word or two with her ladyship's butler about her some time ago and he said her goings-on got that bad, he 'ad to send her packing. After the affair at the Lodge gates—did some little bird tell you about *that*?"

I said I had heard of it.

"I'll bet you have!" he grunted. "When there's a bit of scandal in Downshire, everybody knows it! Well, after that business, Didcott came to me and made a clean breast of it—said he'd been carried away by 'is feelings and that he'd have nothing more to do with the wench. I told 'im to find some nice plain girl to get married to—they always make the best wives. Then I had a word with Johnson, who said he was sorry about it and it wouldn't 'appen again. I didn't believe him, but I made sure that him and Didcott made it up. I'll stake my Bible oath Didcott didn't bear Johnson any malice!"

Sergeant Martin was pro-Didcott, too.

"Mind you, Mr. Rutherford," he went on, "I'm not saying Didcott isn't a quaint kind of chap. He's reserved as they make 'em. Doesn't talk much—until he loses 'is temper and then he's quite chatty. Five minutes later he's quiet again, like a pond when you've chucked an 'alf brick into it. Though sometimes I'm not quite sure . . ."

"That the brick isn't still in the pond?" I suggested, and Martin nodded.

"But that doesn't mean," he said, "that he'd do murder—not for Maggie Wood, at any rate! I don't think he finished up with any delusions about that young woman!"

"What sort of a man was Johnson?" I asked. "I remember him, of course, as a pleasant-mannered, decently spoken chap, with a rather attractive smile, but I know very little of his character."

"I don't rightly know what to say about him," Martin admitted. "He was a nice chap and good at 'is job. I'm not much good at figures of speech, Mr. Rutherford, but imagine a steep hill, with Johnson and my other two men, Harwood and Didcott, at the bottom of it. Harwood'd fix his eyes on the road and plod along, slowly but surely, until he got to the top; Didcott would start out in the same way, but would fix his eyes so firm on the road, that he'd take a wrong turning, leading him back to where he started from: and Johnson would sit down, light a fag, wait for a bus to come along—and be on his way down again, after a nice cup of tea, by the time Harwood had reached the summit."

He paused to sip his beer.

"You couldn't help liking Johnson," he went on. "He had a way with him. 'E and young Ted used to get on well together, and the missus liked 'im. All the women did—— and that was the trouble. He was a good-looker and with the gift of the gab. Spoke like a gent and when 'e was in mufti, looked like one. The girls used to run after 'im—and that's bad for a young chap. Not that 'e didn't do a bit of running himself. He 'ad what you might call an itch. He was a born—what's the word?"

"Philanderer?"

"That's it—a born philanderer. Let a man philander, I say. It gives 'im valuable experience. Half-a-dozen love affairs don't do any real harm, as long as he doesn't get any of the girls into trouble. It's part of a man's education. But Johnson's education was a bit too—extensive. All open and above-board, as far as I know. The only real trouble I heard about was that set-to with Didcott and there wasn't anything really nasty in that."

Martin was silent for a moment or two and meditatively sucked at his pipe.

"That's what been worrying me, Mr. Rutherford," he said at last. "Johnson's been playing with fire, and when you do that, you stand a chance of getting burnt—even to death. Forgetting Didcott and Maggie Wood for a minute or two, do you think there's somebody else who killed Johnson because 'e went too far?"

"Perhaps he was murdered, not because he was a Lothario, but because he was a policeman. You people must make a good many enemies."

"I wish I could think that, Mr. Rutherford," said Martin sadly, "but I can't, some'ow. I've tried to kid myself that Johnson was killed by somebody who was convicted through his agency. The Inspector's been following up Johnson's career in the Police. His mother and father live in London—Catford way. Father was a clerk in an Insurance Company. Retired now. Gave his son a pretty good education at one of the schools near there and then put 'im in a bank. After a year, Johnson said e'd 'ad enough of it: that thumping an adding machine in one of the Head Office Departments and carrying bundles of cheques to and from the Bankers' Clearing House wasn't his idea of making 'is name in the world. He was going to be a policeman. A Chief Constable was something better to work up to than a chief clerk. Ma and Pa hummed and 'awed a bit, but finally gave in, so Johnson sent 'is notice in to the bank—one of the Big Five, it was—and, not liking the idea of the Metropolitan Police, applied to the Chief Constable at Whitchester, passed 'is tests and became an 'umble member of the Downshire County Constabulary. He was sent to Padgham, away to the west of Whitchester, and was there for some years. He came under me at Paulsfield something like two years ago."

Martin relighted his pipe.

"During all that time, Mr. Rutherford," he went on, "Johnson never got anybody into prison. When I say prison, I mean a long stretch. Of course, he's apprehended a good many law-breakers in 'is time—poaching, burglary, vagrancy, dangerous driving and so on; but nothing that seems to justify anybody killing him to get even. Everything points, Mr. Rutherford, to it being *Mr.* Johnson and not *Police-*

constable Johnson who was murdered."

"Coming back to the question of the uniformed cyclist Walker saw with Johnson," I said, "I venture to suggest that if it *was* Didcott, he was very foolish to murder Johnson after having been seen with him. Walker said that one of the cyclists drew in behind the other to let him pass, so they must both have noticed him. Then, after killing Johnson, for Didcott to arrive fifteen minutes late at Burgeston with the flimsiest of excuses—why, he must have been crazy!"

"Most murderers are, if it comes to that," said Martin sententiously.

"Perhaps Didcott is involved in another little intrigue," I suggested, "and doesn't want you to know about it. He may have had a clandestine meeting with a girl last Sunday night, which made him late."

"Let's hope he's got the sense to admit it," said Martin. "It's better to be choked off than swung off."

After this macabre pleasantry, Martin took a long swig at his beer.

"Mr. Trench's jury," I said, "Took a great interest in the implement that was used to kill Johnson. Would it be asking you to open your mouth too wide if I enquired about the truncheons that Johnson and Didcott carried?"

"Johnson's was still in 'is trouser-pocket when he was found and Didcott produced his when I asked him for it. Neither of them was badly marked like they would be if they'd been used on Johnson's skull."

"Does every constable have his own particular truncheon?" I asked. "Or are they interchangeable?"

"Each man has 'is own and it's numbered. I had a look at Harwood's and Chandler's, but they weren't any more helpful than the other two."

My next question was a crafty one.

"You say that the Inspector examined the inner-tubes on the bicycle Didcott rode. If he actually did have a puncture and, by some means or other, the tubes were changed between that time and the occasion of the Inspector's examination, did the condition of the outer covers endorse Didcott's story of the puncture? Were they in good condition?"

I had in mind, of course, those tracks on the footpath.

"They were practically new," said Martin. "We've got five bikes at the station and every so often, we have 'em all fitted with new tyres. They were all of them fitted with new inner-tubes and 'Runlock Roadster' outers somewhere round the middle of last month."

That was rather interesting. The footpath tracks had been made by 'Runlock Roadsters'.

"There weren't any pieces of flint stuck in the covers or anything to suggest that an inner tube had been punctured and afterwards been replaced by a new tube?"

The Sergeant shook his head. Just then the door opened and Agnes poked her head through.

"Time, please, gentlemen!" she smiled, and Martin and I finished our drinks and rose to go.

When I arrived home, after leaving the Sergeant at the corner of Thorpe Street, I found two letters waiting for me. One enclosed two tickets for the next Friday evening's performance at the "Princess's". The other was from Molly, saying she had got my letter and was glad I was booking for *Trailing Clouds of Glory,* which she very much wanted to see. She signed herself "Molly" and I felt immensely pleased.

The fire was invitingly bright and it seemed too early to go to bed. One last pipe, I thought, and half-an-hour with a book. I took down *Jane Eyre* from the shelf, opened it at random and, for the twentieth time in my life, fell under the spell of the sweet, wry courtship of Jane and Mr. Rochester. But tonight the spell was short-lived, for when, after ten minutes reading, I laid the open book on my knee while I relighted my pipe, it stayed there and I lay back watching the smoke-clouds, with my thoughts on Johnson and Didcott, Martin and the Inspector, Walker and Didcott's sad-eyed little champion in the 'Queen's Head'.

I ran through the case, from the time I left Paulsfield three evenings before, to my chat with Martin that evening. Apart from the main mystery of Johnson's uniformed companion on the Hazeloak road, there were two other little problems that interested me. Firstly, that piece of pink paper that the Inspector had picked up: had it anything to do with the murder? Had it been dropped by the murderer? If it had, what was the significance of it? Would the Inspector be able to trace it back to the person who had dropped it, or had it been idly thrown aside by somebody who was in no way connected with the crime? Secondly, the secret of the bicycle. The Inspector had told Walker and me that I had thrown a good deal of light on a mystery that was attached to a bicycle. The mystery of which bicycle? The one Johnson had ridden? But there was no mystery about that. The one that the other man had ridden? But I could not recall giving the Inspector any information about that. Certainly, there were interesting tracks along the footpath, but the Inspector had discovered those without any assistance from me. "That funny business of the bicycle you rode," Martin had said, and had then avoided saying any more. He had been very frank about Didcott, but the truth about the bicycle was apparently not for my ears. One fact that emerged from my talk with Martin gave rise to speculation. He had told me that all the machines used by the Paulsfield police were fitted with 'Runlock Roadsters'. That meant that the machine Didcott had used on the previous Sunday evening could well have accounted for the tracks on the footpath.

My thoughts turned to the men who were concerned in the case. Sergeant Martin, a good fellow and a friend of mine, with the acid wit of a Londoner—rather like a Gordon Harker characterisation, but not quite so unpolished. Detective-inspector Charlton, with his easy, consoling manner and a smile that was childlike and bland—

both, I had come to realize, a part of his stock-in-trade, but immensely engaging, for all that. Frederick Benson Walker, a man who, in 1919, would have been dubbed one of the "New Poor" with past sorrows in his lined face and the hint of present sorrows in his eyes. Didcott, big, fair, and healthy looking, like a Newfoundland dog, and very slightly smug. Chandler, Downshire born and bred, seemingly more fitted for Lord Shawford's stables than Paulsfield police station, but, like Caliban, with an unexpected depth of feeling. Harwood, a big-nosed, earnest, serious man, whose sharp, decisive manner marked him as capable of dealing, adequately, if not brilliantly, with an emergency, and in whose spare, muscular figure and thin face reliability was manifest.

I don't quite know when it was that I fell asleep, but I did not wake until nearly one o'clock. My pipe and *Jane Eyre* shared the hearthrug, the fire was nearly out, and I was very cold.

VI.   I TURN ARITHMETICIAN

The next day's papers were full of the inquest. "The Downshire Killing", as they chose to call it, was the first interesting case they had had for a month and they made the most of it. Large headlines announced "DRAMATIC EVIDENCE AT INQUEST" and asked "WHO WAS THE MYSTERIOUS CONSTABLE?" Photographs of the dead man stared from front pages, editors wrote columns and columns of magnificent hyperbole, sub-editors dished up the Gutteridge case and drew entirely fanciful parallels, while already the correspondence pages contained letters asking what the police had done, were doing and were going to do, about it.

Personally, I was getting rather sick of the whole affair and I hinted as much to George when he wanted to discuss it at length. He had read a full report of the inquest over his breakfast and met me at the shop with all the available facts at his fingers' ends. The previous afternoon I had flatly refused to discuss the case with him, but that morning I might just as well have tried to stem the Thames in its course.

"Things look black for Didcott, sir," he said after our morning greetings had been exchanged.

"Do you think so?" I said.

"You know, sir, I don't think he did it."

"No, George?"

"No, sir."

"Oh?"

I was purposely not encouraging, but that didn't trouble George.

"No, sir. In the first place, he's not the sort of man to do a murder. I'd as soon believe you did it, sir."

"Thank you, George."

"And even if he had, he would have given the show away long before this. Didcott is not a very intelligent man, sir."

"No, George?"

"No, sir. He once caught me poaching on Lord Shawford's estate and, although I had a ferret in a bag, he swallowed the story I told him and let me go."

"That probably says more for his kind heart than his lack of intelligence," I suggested.

"And a man with a kind heart doesn't batter a fellow-creature's head in, sir!"

George had a ready tongue.

"If you were in Didcott's position, sir, and you wanted to dispose of Johnson, would you choose a time when you and he were known to be alone together? And if you knew you had been seen in his company—for Johnson and his murderer must have noticed Walker when he passed them—would you select that time for effecting his demise?"

"Effecting his demise is good, George."

"It is, isn't it, sir? I got it out of *The Corpse in the Copse*. But you wouldn't, would you, sir?"

"No, I don't think I should."

"Of course you wouldn't. You'd do it when people were least likely to associate you with it and you'd arrange a cast-iron alibi."

"Suppose that Didcott did it in a sudden fit of rage?"

"If it was sudden, sir, why did he go a mile along the wrong road before it came over him?"

"He may have been so angry that he didn't notice."

"Yes, sir, perhaps so; but surely Johnson would have noticed?"

"They may have been quarrelling, so that neither of them noticed."

"If they had been quarrelling, Walker would have heard them, sir."

"George," I said sternly, "have you finished your dusting?"

"No, sir," said George.

"Well, kindly do so, while I finish my paper."

He took up his feather brush and attended to the shelves for a few minutes. Then he said, a bit doubtful as to how I would take it:

"I believe, sir, that Johnson's Sinister Companion was not a policeman, but a man dressed in a policeman's uniform."

I looked at him.

"Stubbings," I said, "take a week's notice."

George looked really scared. Then a slow smile spread over his face.

"Certainly, sir," he said.

"Impudent little oaf!" I said, and hid my face behind the *Daily Standard*.

At about eleven o'clock a young woman came into the shop. I got up from my chair.

"Are you Mr. Rutherford?" she asked.

"Yes," I answered. "How can I help you?"

I knew her well by sight: a slight woman, little more than a girl, with the insipid prettiness of the heroines illustrated on the covers of threepenny novelettes, but showing in her face signs of premature age. Her clothes were not shabby, but she was dressed like the wife of a three-pounds-ten-a-weeker.

"Mr. Rutherford," she said with a weak sort of eagerness, "I want to speak to you."

She glanced at George, who was dusting a row of books so carefully that I knew he was listening hard. I took the hint.

"George," I said, "just pop down the road and get me an ounce of tobacco, will you?"

He turned from his work.

"I bought you some first thing this morning, sir," he said. "It's on your desk upstairs. I'll get it for you."

I stopped him at the foot of the stairs.

"Yes, George," I said, "I know about that lot, but I want some more."

"But, sir . . ." he began.

"An ounce, please, George," I interrupted him and gave him half-a-crown. He took the coin, but stopped at the door.

"The usual kind, sir?" he asked innocently, but as the brand I favoured was "Bachelor's Choice", I suspected a double meaning.

"Now, Miss ..." I began, as the door closed behind George.

"I am Mrs. Stevens, of Burgeston," she said.

"Won't you sit down, Mrs. Stevens?" I suggested.

She sat on the edge of one of my easy-chairs, with her handbag clutched nervously in her cotton-gloved hands. For a moment she hesitated: then she said quickly:

"It's about Johnson. I'm at my wit's end to know what to do. Do, please, help me!"

"Why, certainly!" I smiled encouragingly. "Tell me about it."

"They believe Jack Didcott murdered Johnson!" she said.

"Oh," I protested, "It's not so bad as that!"

"They do!" she almost sobbed. "I know they do! Mr. Walker said he saw another policeman with Johnson just before he was murdered and Jack didn't get to Burgeston until nearly five-past nine!"

"I shouldn't worry about that," I smiled. "all sorts of things may have detained him. I expect he has been able to give Inspector Charlton a satisfactory explanation."

Her pale eyes grew wild with fright.

"Inspector Charlton knows he was late?" she asked.

"If Didcott was late, the Inspector must have discovered it by this time," I said.

"But Jack couldn't tell him why he was late, because he promised me he wouldn't!"

I wondered if that would stop Didcott, but I misjudged him.

"I must go to the Inspector and tell him what I know. If I don't, they'll hang Jack! Oh, I must tell him at once! But I daren't!"

As I pondered on this sudden contradiction, she fumbled in her bag and dabbed her eyes.

"Please don't disturb yourself," I urged her. "Perhaps if you will confide in me, I can advise you what to do."

"Thank you," she said simply, and then, after getting a hold on her feelings, went on:

"Jack Didcott was late at Burgeston because he met me."

I was prepared for this.

"You knew him—well, that is?"

"Too well for Jack Didcott! Do you know my husband, Mr. Rutherford?"

"No," I replied, "I haven't that pleasure."

"Pleasure," she said, "is the last word I should use."

She paused and bit nervously at the corner of her handkerchief. Finally she said:

"Well, I don't see why you shouldn't know the whole story. Most of it's common property, anyway! Mr. Rutherford, my husband is one of the biggest blackguards in Christendom!"

"I'm sorry to hear that, Mrs. Stevens," I said, rather inadequately.

"I married him in a registry office in Brighton when I was a sloppy, sentimental kid—and I've regretted it ever since. If I'd had anywhere else to go, I should have left him a long while ago, but I daren't—and he knows it, the beast! He once told me I hadn't got the guts to run away—and it's true!"

I began to feel a little uncomfortable.

"You were going to tell me about Didcott?" I prompted gently.

"I met Didcott for the first time a few months ago—some time in August," Mrs. Stevens said. "One afternoon, Frank—my husband—came home from the 'Porcupine'—

one of his favourite haunts, where he treats the slut of a barmaid better than he treats his wife—disgustingly drunk. Heaven knows it's a common enough thing with him, but this time he was extra bad. I put up with him for about ten minutes and then snatched my hat and coat, and bolted, leaving him to sober down a bit. I had a shilling or two in my bag, so I decided to go to Southmouth and try to forget things for a few hours. When I got there, I had some tea and then went for a look round the shops. In Clarendon Street I met Jack Didcott. I don't quite know how it happened. . . I felt sad and desperately lonely. . . .I think he felt the same . . .He looked a . . . friendly sort of person . . . who would talk to me . . .I longed for someone to talk to me nicely . . So I . . ."

"I don't think you need go into that, Mrs. Stevens," I helped her out. "You struck up a friendship with Didcott— let us leave it at that."

"Yes," she said gratefully, "and we went to a cinema."

"He was, of course, in plain clothes?"

"Yes. I didn't think for a moment that he was a policeman. He was so kind and sympathetic."

I don't think she meant this spitefully.

"And he didn't know who you were—and that you were married?"

"No. I told him I was in domestic service in Southmouth."

"And after that?"

"Oh, we met each other several times in Southmouth. I managed to slip away from my husband and Jack used to get evenings off. He never told me what he was or where he worked. I knew his name, but that didn't mean anything to me. Then, one day, I saw him on point-duty in Paulsfield and when I saw him next at Southmouth, I told him I knew who he was. And like a fool, I told him I was married."

"What did he do?"

"He said we must never . . . see each other again . . . That it wasn't right and if he was found out, would get him discharged from the Force. After that, he refused to have anything to do with me. I tried to see him . . . to speak to him . . . but he avoided me. Then my husband got to hear about it. Some beast must have seen us together in Southmouth. Why can't people mind their own business? It was the only chance I ever had of happiness!"

Up went the handkerchief. A pathetic spectacle, but a little trying.

"Come, Mrs. Stevens," I said. "you won't do yourself any good—or Didcott, either."

"No," she said, "I must try to be brave for Jack's sake. When Frank told me he knew that I had been going out with Jack, I thought he was going to kill me. After he'd quietened down a bit, he swore—and he was perfectly sober, which is when he's most dangerous—he swore that if he ever caught Jack and me together again or heard that we'd been seen together—he'd beat the life out of me and then go after Jack. I tried lying about it, but he laughed at me . . . For weeks he laughed at me and jeered at Jack . . . Called him my boyfriend and my pretty copper."

Taking into consideration that Mrs. Stevens was a woman with a grievance, Mr. Frank Stevens really seemed a most unwholesome specimen.

"This last week," Mrs. Stevens went on, "he's been unbearable. He refuses to leave the house, but just sits drinking whisky, which I have to go out and buy for him. Where he gets the money from, I don't know: he never does a stroke of honest work. He just sits there, hardly saying a word and looking at me with a strange ugly smile on his face. This morning he said to me with an awful leer, 'What about your sweetheart in blue now?' and sometimes he plays with a doll that bounces when he drops it to the floor."

I let this little eccentricity pass without comment and callously steered the conversation back to Johnson's murder.

"I knew Jack was due to come along the Burgeston

road last Sunday evening," she said, "and I walked out to meet him. Frank was safe in the 'Porcupine'. I thought I might soften Jack's heart and persuade him to take me away somewhere from Frank . . . Anywhere—I didn't mind, so long as I escaped from him. Oh, I'm so unhappy!"

She sobbed weakly.

"Mrs. Stevens," I pleaded, "you must pull yourself together. Where did you meet Didcott?"

"Just by the footpath that runs through Phantom Coppice."

"He saw you and got off his bicycle?"

She looked at me queerly.

"No."

"What, then?"

"When I met him, he was pushing his bicycle out from the footpath into the road."

"He was doing *what?*" I almost shouted.

"Pushing his bicycle out from the footpath into the road," she repeated dully.

"That leads from the Hazeloak road—where Johnson was killed," I said.

"I know," she said, "and when I asked him what he was doing, he said that was where he had come from."

"He told you *that?*"

"Yes, but he couldn't have . . . done it . . . in the time. He couldn't."

"What time was it when you met him?"

"Ten to nine. He couldn't have got round in the time, could he?" She looked at me entreatingly.

"I don't know," I said. "It is difficult to tell. You spoke with Didcott for some little while?"

"Yes. He looked startled when he saw me and when I tried to talk to him, he wouldn't listen . . . said he was late and tried to get on his bicycle. . . . I hung on to him. . . . Almost went down on my knees in the rain, but he was like iron. . . . he walked along the road, pushing his bicycle.

I argued with him, pleaded with him. . . . and it was all no use. His love for me must have died."

I fancied that his love for her had never lived. Pity he *may* have felt for her, but not passion. I saw him as a man in an extremely awkward position; and the thought of this rather precise constable doing a midnight flit with another man's wife was funny.

"At last I had to let him go, after we'd gone about a quarter of a mile," she went on, "but before he got on his bicycle, I made him promise—for his sake and mine—not to tell anybody of our meeting. He was ready enough to do that!" this with a wry smile that turned suddenly into floods of tears. She was a definitely humid young woman. "If Frank ever finds out that we met each other again," came between the sobs, "I don't know what will happen to me!"

"Don't you worry about that," I said soothingly. "There's no reason why your husband should ever know."

It did not occur to me until afterwards that if a customer had come in just then and caught this remark out of its context, my reputation would have been torn to rags! It did, however, stem the tears of Mrs. Stevens, who looked at me with red, enquiring eyes.

"What I suggest that you do," I said, "is to go to Didcott and urge him to tell the whole story to Inspector Charlton. If you don't want to see him, you can send him a letter. If Didcott is innocent—and I don't for one moment doubt it—he will be only too glad to do so. If he is guilty—but don't let's think too much about that!"

This seemed to buck her up considerably and she gave me a feeble smile.

"I don't know how to thank you, Mr. Rutherford," she began, but luckily enough George came in and cut her short.

We both rose to our feet and she left the shop, presumably to seek out Didcott. Whether their meeting would later reach the ears of the appalling Frank did not, fortunately, concern me. I hold no brief for bar-haunters and agree that Stevens's going-on were deplorable, but after fifteen minutes or so with his wife, I was inclined to think that there was a certain amount to be said for the 'Porcupine'. She looked like the heroine of *A Mill Girl's Tragedy,* and she behaved like her; and on reviewing our conversation, I had to admit that most of my remarks had been in the best "Chapter V—A Friend in Need" tradition.

I looked at George severely. I was, in fact, really cross with him.

"The next time I give you instructions, George," I said, "Please carry them out without argument."

"I'm very sorry, sir," he answered, "but I thought you actually wanted some tobacco."

"George," I demanded, "Is that the truth?"

"No, sir."

His innocent red face and gentle, submissive eyes were too much for me. I burst out laughing.

"I'm awfully sorry, sir," he said, "but I *did* want to hear what Mrs. Stevens had to say. If I'd thought it was really a private matter, I shouldn't have *dreamt* of listening."

I knew that George meant that.

"But," he went on, "I knew Didcott had been friendly with Mrs. Stevens and . . ."

"Tell me, George," I interrupted him, "Are everybody's private affairs public property in this part of the world?"

"Very nearly, sir."

"You'll have to mind your step."

"I have always been discreet, sir."

I don't know how I should have got along without George.

"I felt sure, sir," he said, "that Mrs. Stevens wanted to tell you something about the murder."

"As usual, George," I said with mild sarcasm, "you are only too right—and what's more, young fellow, you're not going to hear what it was!"

"I thought perhaps it was she," he said in an off-hand way, "who made Didcott late at Burgeston."

"What makes you suggest that?" I asked, hiding my feelings as well as I could.

"Nous, sir."

"Why should you think Didcott was late at Burgeston?"

"Because they didn't ask him what time he got there at the inquest," said George with a knowing wink. "Mr. Trench kept that point well in the background. He obviously considered that an inquest should not degenerate into a murder trial—and very rightly so, sir."

"It is a bad practice, George," I reproved him, "to base one hypothesis upon another. Now what about your lunch? It's close on your time."

"Right, sir. It's going to be steak-and-kidney pudding to-day." he dived into his pocket and held something out to me. "Your half-crown, sir," he said.

I took it without a word and he went off to his steak-and-kidney pudding.

Mrs. Stevens's visit had left me rather thoughtful. She had said that Didcott was late at Burgeston because he had met her; but it seemed to me that he would have been delayed in his arrival even if she had not hindered him. I got a sheet of paper and a pencil and applied myself to a few calculations. Walker's meeting with the two uniformed cyclists was the obvious starting-point. Walker had estimated that to be just after twenty minutes to nine. Say nineteen minutes to. I wrote down:

"8.41. Walker met Johnson and X."

Their meeting-place was about half a mile from Deep-tree Corner and the murder took place a mile from the Corner. The cyclists, therefore, travelled approximately half a mile before they dismounted. At what rate would they travel under such conditions? Seven miles an hour? A bit faster than that? Say eight miles an hour. Half a mile at eight miles an hour. That was one-sixteenth of sixty. Fifteen over four. Three and three-quarters.

" 8.44¾. Cyclists dismount."

How long would it take X to murder Johnson? A couple of minutes?

" 8.46¾. X leaves the body and rides off."

Mrs. Stevens had said that she met Didcott coming from the footpath at 8.50. That left three and a quarter minutes for Didcott, assuming that he was X, to cycle a hundred yards along the Hazeloak road and half a mile along the footpath. Eight hundred and eighty plus a hundred. Nine hundred and eighty divided by three and a quarter. I worked out the sum. Three hundred and one and seven-thirteenths. Call it a half. Three hundred and one and a half yards in a minute. Multiply by sixty. 18090. Divide by 1760. Say ten and a quarter.

Ten and a quarter miles an hour along a narrow footpath on a black, wet night. Was it possible? The path was comparatively straight, so there would not be any tricky bends or corners to negotiate. I wondered what sort of a lamp Didcott had had on his machine. An electric or acetylene lamp would have made it easier. The machine that I had ridden had been fitted with an oil lamp. Had Didcott's been the same? I might have asked the Sergeant.

Suppose that Mrs. Stevens had not gone out to meet Didcott. Could he have arrived, by hard pedalling, at Burgeston at his usual time? When was it Martin had said was his usual time? Soon after eight-fifty. But surely it was not so exact that it didn't vary a minute or two either way? Somewhere between ten and five to nine. Mrs. Stevens saw Didcott emerge from the footpath at, or so she said, eight-fifty. That was a mile from Burgeston and Didcott would have had anything up to five minutes to do it in, on an empty, fairly level road. Twelve miles an hour, not forgetting that as he drew nearer to Burgeston he would have to reduce his speed to a dignified, unhurried progress.

The conclusions I drew from my calculations were firstly,

that Didcott could have killed Johnson and still have met Mrs. Stevens at eight-fifty, and secondly, that Didcott could have killed Johnson and still have arrived at Burgeston so near to his customary time that nobody would have noticed any delay. So my original premise had been wrong. *If* Didcott had murdered Johnson, he would not have been late at Burgeston, had not Mrs. Stevens stopped him. "Jack Didcott was late at Burgeston because he met me," Mrs. Stevens had said; but that was no alibi for Didcott. Her evidence did, in fact, go against him, for had she not seen him coming from the footpath that led almost direct from the spot where Johnson lay? How was he going to explain that? One interesting thing was that, when Mrs. Stevens came upon him, Didcott was wheeling his bicycle, not riding it. From what I remembered of the entrance to the footpath, there was no occasion for a cyclist to dismount when emerging from it.

For all that, I was beginning to alter my opinions about Police-constable Didcott.

VII. THE PROVIDENTIAL BARKING
OF A DOG

At six-thirty the next evening I pressed the bell and stood waiting on Molly's doorstep. I did not wait long and in a few moments was in the room where Molly and I had swapped our childhood memories. The maid greeted me with a radiant smile. Whether any inference was to be drawn from the fact that on my previous visit her face might have been made of marble, I could not decide. I put my crush-hat on the table and dropped into an easy-chair, with the thought that Molly's uncle certainly knew the meaning of the word comfort. I was leaning forward, warming my hands in front of the fire, when I heard the door-bell ring and scarcely a minute had elapsed before the door of the room in which I sat was opened and somebody came in. I looked up from the fire to glance at my fellow visitor.

It was Inspector Charlton.

I am afraid I gaped rather rudely as I got to my feet.

"Hamlet, I am thy father's spirit!" he smiled.

"Good evening, Inspector," I answered, taking a grip on myself. "Forgive my amazement, but you were the last person I thought to see!"

"It is laid down in the Police Code," he said with one of his deep chuckles, "that it is the duty of a policeman to be where he is least expected."

I sat down again and the Inspector plumped down into another chair. He produced his cigarette case and held it out to me. I smiled and shook my head.

"I wish I had your strength of character," he laughed. "Cigarettes are a pernicious habit. Sometimes when I am smoking one, I promise myself I'll give them up and I chuck the wretched thing away—and then light another!"

He leant back in his chair and blew a cloud of smoke from his nostrils. Then he said casually:

"Weren't you surprised to receive a visit from Mrs. Stevens, that attractive young woman, at three minutes past eleven yesterday morning?"

I jumped. I hadn't thought that Mrs. Stevens would tell him of her talk with me.

"You are well-informed, Inspector," I parried.

"Usually, yes; but in this case, no. With my own two eyes I saw her enter your shop."

"A very simple explanation!" I laughed.

"Perhaps I shouldn't have told you," he said "another illusion is probably shattered!"

"Surely there is nothing unusual in her coming into my shop?" I asked. "A good many people do, you know."

"Quite; but they can afford your—forgive my saying so—exorbitant charges: and Frank Stevens's wife never had two pennies to spend on amusement, let alone two guineas!"

He drew at his cigarette.

"It was," I said, "the most uncomfortable quarter of an hour I have had for some time. She came to me—Heaven knows why—for advice."

"And the advice you gave her was good."

"You know what I told her?"

He nodded.

"I have been wondering how you would feel about it," I admitted, "although I really couldn't help myself. I had it more or less thrust upon me."

"You did the right thing, Mr. Rutherford. Had you suggested that she came straight to me, she would probably have gone scuttling off home in a blue funk, whereas she actually went to Didcott and released him from his promise. He brought her in to me."

"And she told you the whole story?"

"Only the part she knew of it. The rest of Didcott's story I have known for some time."

"You have?" I asked in surprise, and he nodded.

"Stevens seems a nasty piece of work, from what his wife told me," I said, seeing that the Inspector was not prepared to discuss the other matter.

"Yes," he agreed, throwing his cigarette-stub into the fire. "In his palmy days Frank Stevens—he called himself Jimmy Stevano then—was one of the most popular comedians on the south coast. His pierrot troupe, 'The Bantams', used to fill every pier pavilion. I saw Stevens myself some years ago at Bognor and I must admit that he had me laughing as much as anybody."

"I don't think I have ever seen him," I said.

"He's not much to look at: less than middling height, with short legs out of proportion to his big body, and a large face that he can twist about in a remarkable way. When he was on the stage, one minute he'd be a babbling old dotard, the next a love-sick, stammering swain, and then he'd be a round jolly man, singing a song about rhubarb or dumplings."

The Inspector paused to light a cigarette.

"Then," he went on, "soon after his marriage—to an orphan girl he picked up somewhere, an insipid little thing, as you know, with about as much personality as a pint of luke-warm water—after his marriage, he went all to pieces. Suddenly lost his touch. Went sour. Nerves chiefly, I think. Professional funny men go like that sometimes. Couldn't raise a laugh—except when he fell over his feet, which is always popular with the G. B. P. Then he took the daughter of the vine to spouse, and has been going down the hill ever since."

"And giving his wife a hell of a time," I added.

"Don't you be too sure about that," said the Inspector enigmatically.

"How does he get a living?" I asked.

"Oh, the chap who took over 'The Bantams' sends him a charitable fiver now and then; and he still gets a few royalties on songs he composed when he was in his prime. Have you ever heard that great classic: 'The Week That Aunt Eliza Came To Stay'?"

"I believe I have," I said.

"Mrs. Stevens helps to keep the pot boiling," the Inspector went on, "by doing what is called 'plain-sewing' for her neighbours. Do you know Carnation Villas, Burgeston? Well, that's where they live. Number five. A single row of nasty little modern houses in an otherwise pleasant little old-world village. Our friend, Harwood, took his wife to number eleven, when he married her last year and he tells me—Harwood, that is—that there's a good deal to be said for and against both sides in the Stevens household."

I pulled back the sleeve from my watch.

"You'll enjoy the show," the Inspector said casually, "I saw it when I was in London last year."

Just then Molly came in, looking positively ravishing and making me think, quaintly enough, of thick black stockings and a pigtail.

"Good evening, John," she smiled as I jumped up. "I hope I haven't kept you waiting too fearfully long?"

"Not at all," I said. "Inspector Charlton and I have been keeping each other amused."

Molly turned to him.

"Good evening, Inspector," she said.

"Good evening, Miss Arnold," he answered with a bow. "before Mr. Rutherford bears you off to the gay frivolities of Southmouth's night-life, can you spare me a few minutes?"

"Of course!" she said. "Mr. Rutherford won't mind waiting—will you, John?"

"Not at all," I assured her; and they left me alone, a little thoughtful.

I wandered about the room for some time and finally picked up a copy of the current number of *Punch*. Lying on the table underneath was an unframed photograph: a studio portrait of a moustached young man in the early twenties. As I looked down at it, I had a feeling that I knew the face and picked it up to take it nearer to the light; but a step in the hall outside made me throw the photograph back on the table and hurriedly replace the *Punch*. Which was, when you come to think of it, thoroughly disgraceful behaviour.

The Inspector came back into the room.

"Now, Mr. Rutherford, if you're ready," he said. "I have suggested to Miss Arnold that I run you down in my car. You never see a taxi in this part of the town."

"Much obliged to you," I said, but I was not too sure that I was.

I found Molly sitting in the back of the Inspector's car and jumped in beside her, while the Inspector climbed into the driving-seat.

"Where would you like to go?" he asked, and I turned enquiringly to Molly.

"Saletti's, please," she smiled, and the Inspector drove us there.

I don't think I had ever enjoyed an evening quite so much before, in spite of the distressing little thoughts that crept now and again into my head. The dinner was good and so was *Trailing Clouds of Glory;* and Molly was a perfect companion. It seemed to me that before we had settled ourselves down, we had to stand again for "The King."

We came out under a sky of brilliant stars and I looked round for a taxi.

"No, John," Molly said, slipping her arm into mine, "Let's walk. It's a marvellous night!"

So we walked. I can't remember what we talked about, but it doesn't really matter. I do know that my heart was singing inside me. A ridiculous expression, I know, but if you have ever been in love, you'll understand—and smile a little, perhaps. We reached the gate of Holmedene and I opened it for Molly.

"Will you come again?" I asked her softly.

"If you are very, very good," she smiled.

"I got a prize for good conduct at school."

"But that was a long time ago."

"I haven't changed much."

"No," her voice came gently, "you were a wickedly lovable little urchin."

By the bushes to the side of the gate, it was invitingly dark, and Molly was very close to me.

"When you nursed my soldiers, did I ever kiss you, Molly?"

"No, John, you were too busy fighting battles."

"The general is home from the wars, Molly. May he kiss you now?"

"I shall be cross if he doesn't," she said very low.

It might have been ten minutes later that she said:

"John, I must go in. Uncle must be getting worried about me. He fusses, the silly old dear."

"What will he say—about us, I mean?" I asked her.

"You'll have to ask *him* that!" she answered mischievously.

"He knows?"

"Knows? Of course he knows! You can't keep much from Uncle Harry!"

"When shall I see him?"

"Soon."

And with that I had to be content.

★ ★ ★ ★

I caught the last train from Southmouth and it was well after midnight when I came out of Paulsfield station. The solitary sleepy porter took my ticket and I heard him locking up the station as I walked down to the crossing, where the traffic-lights were fixed in favour of the main road traffic, unless some belated motorist chanced to come the other way. I turned to the left at the crossing and walked along the London road to the point where there branched off to the right a road that led across Paulsfield Common and connected up on the other side with Thorpe Street, where, as you will remember, I lived.

The few inadequate lamps along Common Road were alight, but beyond the tiny oases of illumination, the road and the gorse-covered Common were dark. The sky, as I have said, was clear and thick with stars, but the moon was only an emaciated phantom in the early stages of its first quarter. Most of Paulsfield went early to bed and as I strode along, humming a popular dance-tune of the moment, there was no other living person to disturb the solitude.

On previous occasions, when returning late from the station, I had frequently thought what a fine stretch that was for gentlemen of the road to ply their calling, but on that particular night I was too elated to bother with such sombre imaginings. Timorous folk would have probably preferred to reach Thorpe Street by the longer but more civilized route that led them from the station straight across the main road and along into the High Street, where a sharp turn to the left by the 'Queen's Head' would take them into the road that ran along the eastern boundary of the Common, bisecting the junction of Common Road and Thorpe Street on its way.

Half-way across the Common, and about fifty yards from the road, was a stretch of water, which was euphemistically called the Lake. On its bank was a boathouse, where, during the summer, it was possible to hire a skiff for a shilling an hour; but now, of course, they were all snugly locked away. I was drawing level with the Lake, which lay to my left, and had just passed into the yellow beam from a lamp, when, from the direction of the Lake, I heard a voice cry out.

I paused in my stride, wondering whether I was imagining things. The cry came again, a high-pitched sound, that might have been made by a woman or a child. It was not loud, but it was very distinct and seemed an urgent plea for help. I stood for a moment irresolute, then turned off the road and hurried towards the Lake. The cry was repeated, this time more pressingly and accompanied by the noise of splashing water. Somebody seemed in desperate straits in the Lake and I broke into a run along the roughly formed footpath through the gorse. When I had nearly reached the banks of the Lake, my foot caught into something and I stumbled and fell; then, as I was about to pick myself up, everything was suddenly blotted out.

★　★　★　★

It must have been the shock of the cold water that restored me to consciousness. My mouth was full of it . . .I was choking. . . .I lashed out with my arms, then instinctively realized where I was and relaxed myself. I came up to the surface of the Lake and drew in a gasping breath; but something rammed me cruelly between the shoulders and I was driven under again. From the confused jumble in my mind one thought sprang out: I was being systematically drowned. I tried to use my arms and legs to swim under the water away from whoever waited with devilish expectancy above, but my limbs only functioned for a few strokes. When I once more reached the surface and eagerly drew in the air, I saw him—a shadowy figure in a boat, with an oar poised menacingly, like a harpoon. He lunged savagely at me and I tried to avoid the thrust, which was clumsily delivered and missed me. Summoning all my strength I struck out and swam like a maniac. Behind me I heard the hurried squeak of oars in the rowlocks. My pace grew slower and slower— and then he got me again. An agonizing stab in the small of the back sent my head below the water. Everything was nearly over. I felt that there was just enough life in me to bring me to the surface once again, but another submersion would utterly finish me. I made a few weak strokes to take me as far away from him as possible and then came up. But this time I received no blow. I shook the water from my eyes and saw that the boat was being rowed away from me. I could just see that the oarsman was wearing something that concealed his face. My head was singing and I was only just conscious, but I had the presence of mind to roll over on to my back to float for a while until my strength returned. Through the quiet night there echoed the frantic and persistent barking of a dog.

At length I began to swim, I hoped towards the nearest bank—a nightmare task in my dress-clothes and overcoat. After what seemed hours of slowly weakening endeavours, I crawled up the sloping bank—and then passed out completely.

When I regained my senses, my face was being nuzzled by a dog. I pushed him away and painfully got to my feet, to stand swaying, while everything seemed to swirl up to me and away again in nauseating waves. After a while, things steadied down a bit and I was able to see that I had clambered from the Lake at a point quite near to the footpath that led back to the road.

How I got back to Thorpe Street, I don't know, but I seem to remember the dog frisking playfully around me all the way. My first idea had been to lie down again on the ground and pass quietly away, but I solemnly decided that I was damned if I would. I must have been rather funny to watch. When I got to number eighteen, I beat a drunken rataplan on the knocker and collapsed on the step.

Fortunately, Mrs. Hendon and her daughter were awakened by the hubbub, and in a quarter of an hour I was in bed with half-a-dozen confoundedly hot water bottles. After settling me down and asking me six or seven times if there was anything more they could do for me, the good souls left me and took their dressing-gowns back to their bedrooms.

I don't quite know why, but as I lay thinking of my unpleasant experience, one thought kept drifting back into my mind: the photograph I had noticed in Molly's house. Where the dickens had I seen that face before? You know how it is when you can't remember somebody's name or a tune the B.B.C. broadcast yesterday evening? That was how I felt. I knew that face, but whose was it? Then suddenly it came to me.

It was P.C. Johnson.

Saturday, November 16th.

VIII. TEA FOR THREE

The amazing thing was that when I awoke some six hours later, apart from a bruised back and a morning-after-the-Old-Boys'-dinner head, I was little the worse for the previous night's gymkhana. A bout of pneumonia would not have been surprising, in the circumstances, or, at any rate, a chill; but when Lizzie knocked early on my door, it was with a healthy shout that I told her to come in. The good woman's solicitous manner was tinged with a certain amount of disapproval.

"Well, Master John," she said, "I 'ope you've slept it off?"

There was no doubt that Lizzie had formed her own conclusions about my condition when she had found me on the doorstep. I deliberately misunderstood her.

"I think the hot-water bottles have driven the chill out of my system, thanks to you, Lizzie," I said; then thinking that some sort of explanation was due, went on: "I fell in the Lake."

"Did you now," said Lizzie; "And how did you come to do that?"

"I'm not too clear on that point," I said, deeming it politic to endanger my reputation with Lizzie, rather than tell her the truth, which I decided was only for the Inspector's ears.

"I thought you were going to the theatre with a *lady*," she said severely, with marked stress on the last word.

"So I did, Lizzie. I fell in the Lake on my way home."

"I didn't smell it on your breath," she said darkly.

"Now, Lizzie," I said wheedlingly, "be a sweet, gracious thing and go down to get my breakfast ready, while I struggle into some clothes. Didn't I understand you to say yesterday that you proposed to devil me some kidneys this morning?"

"Will you be *wanting* anything for breakfast?" she asked in a surprised tone. "My poor dear husband never didn't."

"Lizzie," I said earnestly, "get one thing out of your head: I was *not* drunk last night. Something happened that I can't tell you about. If anyone speaks to you of it, say I met with a slight accident."

Lizzie looked scared and left me a few moments later. I lay back looking at the ceiling, and pondered on the autocracy of the old family servant. There was a P. G. Wodehouse story I remembered, in which an O. F. S. locked up in a cupboard a young man and woman, over whom she had domineered in their childhood; and in the same way as they had obediently immured themselves in the dusty interior of the cupboard, so did I suffer Lizzie to bully me.

I had finished my breakfast and was just filling my pipe, when Lizzie came puffing up the stairs.

"There's a policeman at the door," she said between the gasps, "and he says, 'Sergeant Martin's compliments and are you all right?' "

"Show him up, please," I told her. "I'll speak to him."

It was Harwood. He came into the room with his cap in his hand.

"Good morning, officer," I greeted him. "Sit down and help yourself to a cigarette."

I pushed the box over to him.

"I'm very glad you're all right, Mr. Rutherford," he said. "We were a bit worried about you."

I said nothing, but looked enquiringly at him.

"One of the common-keepers was doing his rounds this morning and he found your pocket-book on the edge of the Lake. There was an opera-hat lying under a gorse-bush a little way away and the Lake boathouse had been broken open and a skiff taken out, which he found drifting about, with the oars floating about on the water."

"I *was* mixed up in the jolly little frolic, Harwood," I said, "but I came out of it, fortunately, with no more injury than a few bruises."

"I'm very glad to hear it, sir," said Harwood in a relieved tone. "We were afraid—afraid that something had happened to you. The Sergeant has 'phoned Inspector Charlton and he's coming straight over."

"That's good," I said. "I'd like to tell the Inspector exactly what happened."

In which polite way I gave Harwood to understand that I did not propose to tell *him*.

"Was there any money in your wallet, Mr. Rutherford?" was Harwood's next remark.

"Five pound notes and two or three ten-shilling ones."

"There was nothing in it when the keeper found it," he told me.

"Bang go six months' profits!" I laughed. "It looks as though our friend is prostituting his talent with a sandbag in the cause of Mammon."

"Were you attacked, then, sir?"

I nodded and relit my pipe.

"Does Inspector Charlton want me to go round to the station, or will he come here?" I asked.

"If you'll take my advice, sir—not wanting to give offence—you'll take things easy. I'll say you told me to ask him to be good enough to step round here."

"That is kind of you," I said; and he left me a few minutes afterwards.

I rang George up at the shop to tell him that I felt a bit off colour, but would try to get along by his lunch-time. The telephone, which was in my living-room, I had had installed when I came to live at number eighteen.

Five minutes later, Lizzie came up again.

"What do you want me to do with the dog, Master John?" she asked. "The one you brought home with you last night."

"Is it still here?" I said.

"He slipped past us when we were getting you in and

we didn't know whether you'd bought him or what, so we gave him a box in the kitchen. He's in the garden now and a pretty little thing he is, to be sure."

"He isn't mine, Lizzie," I told her, "but I should certainly like to have a few words with him. I've a feeling that he saved my life at twenty minutes to one this morning."

So I went down into the garden and had a few words with him. He was a chummy little fox-terrier and seemed very pleased to see me. I had a look at the "Tail-Waggers' Disc" on his collar and learnt that his owner was a Mr. Marling, of Chesapeake Road, which was just round the corner. I mentioned it in the previous chapter as running along the eastern boundary of the Common. I went back into the house and the dog followed me.

"Lizzie," I said, "this little fellow belongs to a Mr. Marling round in Chesapeake. I'd better take him back now— they'll probably be getting anxious about him. Got a piece of string?"

This was duly produced from a drawer in the dresser (Is there *nothing* that a housewife cannot produce from a drawer in the dresser?) and after I had told Lizzie that if the Inspector called while I was gone, she was to show him upstairs, we set off.

Mr. Marling was charming. He was extremely grateful, he said, and felt sure that his wife would wish him to join her thanks with his.

"Spot," he said, "ran out last night and disappeared. We call him Spot because of the black spot on his head. My wife's idea entirely. Very apt, don't you think?"

"Extremely original," I agreed, thinking of the millions of fox-terriers who, for the same reason, have been given that name.

"I gave him to my wife as a birthday present," Mr. Marling said. "She really wanted a Cairn, but I couldn't get one anywhere; and now that we've got Spot, a friend of mine has offered me a Cairn puppy. Annoying, isn't it?"

The result had seemed inevitable right from the beginning. Even on the way round, I had been thinking that I should have to buy him a proper lead, as I couldn't very well go on using a piece of string; and now Mr. Marling was joining in the conspiracy.

"The trouble is, I suppose, that you have grown fond of Spot and don't want to get rid of him?"

"Yes, in a way," said Mr. Marling, "although we've only had him a month. My wife and I wouldn't mind disposing of him, as long as we knew that he was going to a good home."

"I was wondering," I said tentatively, "if you would sell him to me?"

"That all depends," was his doubtful reply, "on what my wife says. She may not want to lose him. But if you took Spot," he went on with a sudden eagerness, "We *could* have the Cairn."

The end of it was that I went back to number eighteen the richer by Spot and the poorer by thirty shillings. Lizzie met me in the hall and asked me if nobody had been in at the Marlings. I told her that they had been in all right, but that I had bought the dog from Mr. Marling.

"What are you going to call him?" she asked. "What about Spot, because of the black spot on his head?"

"That's a splendid idea, Lizzie. We'll call him Spot."

So I called him Spot, not because he had a black spot on his head, but because I should probably have had to face social ostracism if I hadn't. Humpty Dumpty boasted that, when it came to words, he could manage the whole lot of them. Impenetrability was what he said on that topic. But Humpty Dumpty was never suddenly called upon to name a fox-terrier with a black spot on his head!

The Inspector came at about eleven. He looked very grave, and did not greet me with his usual smile.

"I'm sorry to hear what happened last night, Mr. Rutherford" he said. "Perhaps you will let me have your account of it. I understand from Harwood that you were attacked."

"Sit down, won't you?" I invited him; and trying to avoid making a wry face, I let myself down into a chair. My back felt as if the myrmidons of the Inquisitor General of Spain had just laid down their implements and gone off to lunch, to return later to finish off the job of flaying me alive.

"I came back to Paulsfield by the last train, Inspector", I went on, "after seeing Miss Arnold to her door, and went along Common Road."

"Do you always go that way, when coming home from the station?"

"Almost always."

"So that anybody who saw you catching a train from Paulsfield earlier in the evening could reasonably assume that you would return later along Common Road?"

"Yes; and if they noticed that I was wearing dress-kit, they could also reasonably assume that the evening would be well advanced before I came back."

"That is perfectly true," the Inspector agreed. "but please go on with your story."

"As I was saying, I walked along Common Road. When I reached the street lamp about half-way along the left-hand side, I heard a cry for help coming from the direction of the Lake. . . ."

"It wasn't until you had walked into the area of illumination that the cry was given?"

"No. I stopped when I heard it and then when it came again, I hurried towards the Lake. When I caught the sound of splashing water, I thought somebody must be drowning and started running, but I hadn't gone very far before I tripped over something and fell . . ."

"A piece of stout cord fixed across the footpath about six inches from the ground," said the Inspector.

I told him the rest of the story and how I had eventually reached home with Spot.

"It looks," I said, "as if I am indebted to Spot for my

life. He must have been wandering about the Common and discovered that something exciting was going on on the Lake. My attacker couldn't be sure, when Spot started barking, that he wasn't accompanied by his owner, and decided that he'd better get away while the going was good. I don't know what to make of the affair, Inspector. Why was I set upon? The chap wasn't just after my money, because, although he rifled my pocket-book, it was his obvious intention to murder me. Do you think it's something to do with the Johnson business? Is there a homicidal maniac abroad in Paulsfield?"

"I don't know," the Inspector admitted. "There is one rather interesting thing, however. You say that this chap wasn't *just* after your money. I have proof that he wasn't after your money at all. He took it out of your wallet and burnt it. I found charred scraps of the notes on the banks of the Lake. They were doubtless removed from your wallet to give the impression that robbery was the intention, and then destroyed, for fear they should be traced. Can you tell me anything about this man in the boat?"

"Nothing, except that he appeared to be masked. I can't even vouch for the gender. It may even have been a woman."

"Was he tall, short, fat, thin? From the strength of the blows on your back, would you say they were dealt by a strong person?"

"I have only the sketchiest recollection of him," I said. "You'll understand that I wasn't in a particularly happy position to recognise my aggressor. As to the blows, they were sufficiently powerful to drive me under the water. That suggests fairly hefty muscles."

"I expect your back is painful," said the Inspector sympathetically. "Is it badly bruised?"

"It does hurt a bit," I admitted, "but no serious damage has been done."

"Have you been examined by a doctor?" was his next question.

"No. It hasn't seemed necessary. It's a little short of miraculous that I'm not laid up this morning with a first-rate chill."

"As you say," said the Inspector, "little short of miraculous."

I looked at him as he drew at his cigarette. I was beginning to have the uncomfortable suspicion that he did not believe a word of my story. I got up.

"Perhaps you'll excuse me for a few moments?" I said.

When he nodded, I went into my bedroom and stripped myself to the waist. Then, after having slipped on a dressing-gown, I returned to him. He examined my back without a word.

"Thank you," he said at length, and I went and redressed myself. When I came back to the living-room, the Inspector was smiling.

"You jumped to rather hasty conclusions, Mr. Rutherford."

"Am I not still one of the Johnson suspects?" I smiled in my turn.

"Frankly, no," he replied, "but I *did* want to see those bruises. In my profession, Mr. Rutherford, nothing must be taken for granted. You know," he continued with a boyish laugh, "this case is beginning to interest me!"

He sat back in his chair and stroked his left palm with the second finger of his right hand.

"You may be surprised to hear, Mr. Rutherford," he said, "that the bicycle you rode to Paulsfield last Sunday evening and the one that Johnson used on that last journey of his were not the same machine."

I jerked bolt upright in my chair, which hurt me quite a lot.

"But that's nonsense!" I said sharply.

"Why?" he asked calmly.

"Sorry, Inspector," I said sheepishly, lapsing back again, "but you rather startled me."

The Inspector smiled.

"Your own evidence supports it," he said. "Didn't you find the body and the bicycle on opposite sides of the road?

When that bicycle fell, it was something less than three feet from the right-hand side of the road—the right-hand side, that is, if one were facing in the direction of Hazeloak. Why did it fall? Because its previous rider relaxed his grip."

"But Johnson might easily have staggered backwards across the road from his standing position by the machine."

"And if he did do that, where do you suppose his machine would fall? It would fall against the man who delivered the blow that sent Johnson staggering backwards—not against the bank!"

"He may have been standing sufficiently in advance of the bicycle to avoid it as it fell."

"Dr. Weston said in his evidence that the first blow was struck by a right-handed person standing immediately in front of Johnson. If the murderer stood, as you suggest, in advance of the machine Johnson was holding, Johnson would have been facing more or less in the direction of Hazeloak, so that when that first blow fell, he would have had to stagger sideways across the road, in order to fall across the bank right opposite those marks we found on the other bank. Would a stricken man stagger sideways like that, Mr. Rutherford?"

I admitted that it did not seem feasible.

"Imagine this scene, Mr. Rutherford," said the Inspector. "The murderer and Johnson stand facing one another. Between them is Johnson's bicycle, which he holds with his left hand as he removes his cap with his right. If the machine had been on the other side of him, he would have fallen across it and not back across the bank. Behind the murderer, held by his left hand, is his own bicycle. The blow is delivered. As Johnson staggers backwards, releasing his hold on his bicycle, but still clutching his cap, the murderer lets his own machine fall and, catching at Johnson's machine, deals him another swift blow on the side of the skull. Then, when Johnson has fallen across the bank, the murderer finishes the job with his weapon, after leaning Johnson's machine gently against the bank. Then, after satisfying himself that the job has been well and truly done, the murderer rides away on Johnson's machine, which was fitted with tyres coinciding with the tracks along the footpath."

"A very foolish move," I suggested.

"Or a very clever one," said the Inspector.

"Now," I said, "you've only to find out where the second machine came from—and there you are!"

"I do know where the second machine came from," said the Inspector.

"You're full of surprises this morning!" I laughed.

His only reply was to slip something from his jacket pocket and hand it across to me.

"Recognise this?" he asked.

It was the photo of Johnson I had seen the night before.

"It might be a picture of Johnson," I said after a few moments' examination, "taken several years ago."

"Six, to be precise," he agreed, "In Padgham."

I read out what had been written in the bottom corner: " 'Yours ever, Tom.' "

"His moustache altered his appearance a good deal," said the Inspector. "This was taken some little time after Johnson entered the Force, although he's wearing mufti. I came by it in rather unusual circumstances. Have you ever seen it before?"

I felt like a mouse at the mercy of a charmingly courteous cat.

"I don't quite know," I answered evasively.

"They tell me," said the Inspector with a disarming smile, "that *Punch* is very amusing this week."

For the second time at that interview I sat up sharply.

"Inspector Charlton," I said, "you are playing with me! For God's sake tell me—has Miss Arnold anything to do with this damnable business?"

He looked at me steadily. He was not smiling now.

"This is Saturday morning," he said. "by this time on

Monday you will know."

His face broke suddenly into a smile.

"And now," he said, "I must go and have a chat with Mr. Marling."

★ ★ ★ ★

George and I shared Saturdays—that is to say, each of us had every other Saturday afternoon off. Wednesday was early-closing day and George, of course, had that to himself, but I did not want to deprive him entirely of the enjoyment of his *grande passion*—Football, to which even Literature had to yield first place.

The afternoon following my talk with Inspector Charlton was George's 'watch,' Much to his gallantly suppressed annoyance, for at two-thirty the Paulsfield eleven were to meet Abbotsbridge—and Abbotsbridge had beaten Paulsfield on their own ground for five years in succession— not a thing to be lightly borne.

George, I knew, would have foregone a week's wages to be there, to cheer his team on to their long-delayed victory; and when I strolled along to the shop later in the morning, with Spot on a brand new lead, I offered to 'trade' the next Saturday afternoon with him. He looked very wistful, as he said:

"But if I have this Saturday off, I'll have to be on duty next Saturday—and I'd rather not do that, sir, if you don't mind."

"But Paulsfield are playing away at Whitchester next Saturday," I reminded him.

"I know that, sir," was all he said.

"Just as you please, then, George," I said, and there the matter rested.

I introduced George to Spot, but although George made friendly overtures, Spot didn't seem at all disposed to cement their friendship. I won't say he growled menacingly or bared his teeth, because he didn't; but he certainly backed away with his ears down and a let's-get-out-of-here look about him. Perhaps he didn't like the way George's hair curled up. I said nothing to George of the previous night's affair, as the Inspector had asked me to keep it to myself. The only other people who knew about it were the common-keeper and the men at the police station, but upon them the Inspector had enjoined silence.

At twelve o'clock I sent George off to his lunch and when he came back a few minutes before one, I gave him a few necessary instructions and then prepared to leave 'Voslivres' in his care. As I was putting on my overcoat, with a difficulty I tried hard to disguise, he said, in a tone that Sir Philip Sydney might have used to the soldier on the field of Zutphen:

"Why don't you go along to the match this afternoon, sir? It'll be a rare tussle."

"Not a bad idea, George," I agreed. "I'll think about it."

And after Lizzie had cleared away my lunch, I thought, "Why not?" I am afraid I have always regarded Soccer with a certain amount of humorous contempt. Quite apart from the professional side of it—playing for a weekly wage, that is—it has always struck me as being an ineffectual sort of game. Or do I mean ineffective? Anyway, as far as I am concerned, it lacks the fine sparkle of Rugger. I once read a book about a boy whose parents removed him from a school where they played Rugger to a school where Association obtained. I never sympathised with a character more than I did with that unhappy boy. There seems to be a very big difference between the crowds at, let us say, Wembley and Twickenham. Men who go along to see a Rugger match almost always play, or have played, themselves; but I'll wager that very few who pay to see an Association game have ever taken the field. I know it's largely a question of opportunity—and I know I am writing like an outrageous snob: but Soccer leaves me cold.

But for all that, I asked myself, "Why not?" It was a beautiful crisp afternoon and if the game did bore me stiff, there was always the crowd. A crowd is an interesting phenomenon, especially when feelings run high. A man in a crowd will say things he would never dream of saying anywhere else. It will bring out the worst in him—and sometimes the best.

So at a little before half-past two, I was in the three-deep press on the touch-line, where already wordy battles were raging between Paulsfield and Abbotsbridge supporters. A large gentleman in a bowler hat slightly too small for him, who stood next to me, said over his shoulder:

"We've done it five times and this afternoon the boys are going to make it 'alf a dozen."

"Don't you be so sure of that," answered a voice I thought I knew. "We're turning out some good men this year."

"We only turn out the bad ones in Abbotsbridge," said the man at my side with a hoarse laugh. "The good 'uns we keep."

"You just wait and see," said the other voice.

"Paulsfield ain't got a leg to stand on," said the big man loudly.

"Yes, they 'ave," said the other.

"No, they 'aven't," said the big man, still more loudly.

"I say they 'ave!" said the small insistent voice.

"I say they 'aven't!" The big man was getting heated.

"*You* say they 'aven't," persevered the other voice.

The conversation was beginning to have a familiar ring about it. It reminded me of another I had heard. I looked round to identify the tenacious controvertist and saw the little sad-eyed man of the 'Queen's Head', who had defended Didcott with such timorous persistence. He caught sight of me and respectfully touched his shabby trilby.

Just then, the referee's whistle blew and we turned our attention to the game. I don't propose to embark on a detailed description of the play. It was quite exciting in its way, its chief virtue being that, as the players were all amateurs, they wanted to win for the glory of winning and not to avoid relegation to a lower Division, with an ensuing loss in 'gate' money. The visitors pressed hard and by half-time were one goal up. The little man and the large Abbotsbridge supporter had drifted away somewhere and I was wondering whether to see the rest of the game, when a voice said:

"I didn't know you were a Soccer fan, Mr. Rutherford."

I turned round and saw that it was Walker.

"I'm not," I said.

"Neither am I," he said, shrugging his shoulders. "Usually, I avoid crowds like the pestilence; but this afternoon I felt as if a crowd would do me good. There's a certain tonic quality in a noisy, enthusiastic mob of people."

We saw the rest of the game together. A minute or two after the beginning of the second half, Paulsfield equalised; but to the chagrin of their adherents and the wild delight of the Abbotsbridge contingent, the visitors again found the net—as our newspapers put it—and the game finished with the score: Paulsfield 1. Abbotsbridge 2.

"Forgive me if I am thrusting myself upon you," said Walker as we left the ground, "but would you care to take a cup of tea with me?"

I said I should be delighted and we shouldered our way through the throng—most of them still arguing—and made our way towards the High Street. 'The Green Teapot' was, as usual, full, but in the 'Cozey' we managed to find a comfortable corner table. A radio loudspeaker with a restful depth of tone was supplying pleasant, unobtrusive music. A girl took our order and in a few minutes toasted scones and tea were put before us.

"Do you know," said Walker as I filled our cups, "That you and I have been jointly guilty of misrepresentation?"

"That sounds rather serious," I said with an answering

smile, as I pushed over the sugar-basin.

"No, thanks," he said, "not for me. Yes, we circumvented the law by leading Inspector Charlton to believe that we have never met before, except at my place at Hazeloak."

"And have we?" I asked.

"Do you remember," he said with that sad smile of his, "Many years ago at Mereworth, a little chap they used to call 'Smudger'? And do you remember once, down in the spinney behind the chapel, going to the rescue of 'Smudger', who was being put through it by a boy twice his size, for doing or not doing something or other—and giving the lout the thrashing he deserved?"

"I seem to have some hazy recollection of it," I said.

"It's as clear to me," said Walker, "As if it happened yesterday. I don't think I'll ever forget what you did for me that day."

"What I did for *you?*"

"Yes."

"Then you're. ...'Smudger'?"

"No, I was the other fellow. My name was Langdon, but I have changed it since. I won't go into that now. It's a long story and not very pretty. It suddenly came to me who you were, after I left you the other day, and when I met you this afternoon, I decided to tell you—but I hope you will forget that my name was ever anything but Frederick Benson Walker."

"Certainly, Walker," I said as he passed me his empty cup.

"This Johnson business is getting on my nerves," he said suddenly, drumming his fingers on the table-cloth.

"It's getting on mine a bit," I agreed. "It seems a strange mix-up. Here we have what is, on the face of it, a simple, straightforward crime—a primitive and seemingly unpremeditated killing—which, on investigation, presents a mass of contradictions."

"Contradictions?" Walker asked sharply. "It seems fairly clear to me."

It suddenly struck me that I was in danger of saying too much.

"I mean," I said, hedging hurriedly, "your seeing that other chap with Johnson, for instance."

"The other constable? Well, who could it have been but . . ."

I stopped him with my upraised hand. Nobody seemed to be taking the least notice of us, but it did not do to be to careless.

"By a coincidence," Walker went on in a lower tone, "I find myself on the Hazeloak road a short while before a brutal crime is done. I am met by two constables riding bicycles. A few minutes before, on the same stretch of road, you yourself had been passed by two constables riding bicycles. Isn't it safe to assume that the two pairs of constables were identical?"

"In a case of this kind," I said, "it is safe to assume nothing."

"Why didn't I look at them more closely," he said with exasperation. "The trouble was that they meant so little to me and those capes policemen wear, with high collars covering most of their faces, would have made it practically impossible to identify them, even if I had had my wits about me."

"But you identified Johnson's cough, didn't you?"

"Yes; but if it had been the other man's cough, it would have been more to the point."

"Strange," I said, "that you should have been on the road at that time."

"Nothing very strange about it," said Walker, abruptly for him. "Surely I've a perfect right to walk along a road at night?"

"I didn't know you were a poet, Mr. Walker!" said a familiar voice; and I looked up to find Inspector Charlton standing by our table.

"Why, good afternoon, Inspector!" I said. "What brings you here?"

"Thirst!" he said with a broad smile.

"Why don't you join us?" I suggested; and the Inspector looked enquiringly at Walker.

"Do, by all means," agreed Walker with a smile.

"You'll excuse my rudeness butting in as I did, Mr. Walker," said the Inspector, "but your last remark was rather—audible."

"Not at all," answered Walker. "I'm afraid I got a bit excited."

"You weren't at the football match, by any chance, Inspector?" I asked, changing the subject.

"No," he said. "I have been obeying the stern call of duty. I have been engaged in a little district-visiting in Blossom Street, Whitchester."

Walker's cup came down sharply in his saucer.

"And I thought" the Inspector went merrily on, "that a dish of tea would be a good idea. It was a pleasant surprise to find you two here when I came in."

I reserved judgment on the Inspector's veracity. I was beginning to realise that *Le Subtil Renard* was a puling infant by comparison with Detective-inspector Charlton.

"We met at the match," I said, when the girl had taken the Inspector's order. "I don't know whether you're interested, but Abbotsbridge won by two goals to one."

"There's nothing to beat a good game of Soccer," he said.

"I'm afraid Walker and I prefer Rugger," I laughed.

"What Old Mereworthian doesn't?" asked the Inspector blandly.

Walker drew in his breath sharply, but I managed to say, calmly enough:

"My respect for you increases every day, Inspector!"

"That is as it should be," he smiled.

"I know I'm risking a rap on the knuckles for speaking out of my turn," I said, "but how is the Johnson case going?"

"The outlook is decidedly promising," said the Inspector in a satisfied tone. "The police, as the saying has it, are following up a clue, which means, in most cases, that they are completely fogged, but in this case does not. I had a chat with a man this morning, who gave me quite an interesting little piece of information. He told me that he was motoring last Sunday evening along the old main road. He came along from Burgeston and got to Deeptree Corner at a couple of minutes or so after nine o'clock. As he neared the Corner, the headlights of his car picked out the figure of a man standing at the entrance to the Hazeloak Road. A tallish chap, the motorist said he was, wearing a raincoat and a cap. Now, if I can only lay my hands on that Lurking Stranger, he may be able to tell me quite a lot."

"I'm afraid you're going to be disappointed, Inspector!" laughed Walker. "That man the motorist saw was myself."

"Of course, it must have been!" chuckled the Inspector. "The laugh is on me this time, I'm afraid! There was I formulating all sorts of beautiful theories and now they're all completely busted!"

He chuckled again and drained his tea-cup.

"And why, Mr. Walker," he said softly as he put down his cup, "were you kicking your heels on the Corner? I understood you to say that you were out for a walk?"

IX   DIDCOTT ON THE CARPET

Walker's smile disappeared and his face straightened with a jerk.

"You trapped me into that, Inspector," he said slowly.

"Trapped you into what, Mr. Walker?" the Inspector asked mildly. "I merely enquired your reason for waiting at the Corner. It seems a little odd to me that you should kill time in such unpleasant surroundings."

"I beg your pardon," said Walker. "I shouldn't have spoken like that, but I expect you understand how keenly I feel my position. By sheer bad luck, I got mixed up in the business; and I've had the feeling ever since that I'm under suspicion. I do remember now that I paused in my walk at Deeptree Corner to refill my pipe; and it must have been during those few moments that the motorist went by."

"That seems very probable," said the Inspector, as if the subject no longer interested him. "Now, there's just one other little matter I should like to ask you about before I leave you, Mr. Walker. It concerns bicycles—not any particular bicycle, but the ones you have occasion to deal with in your business. When you repair a machine or re-enamel it, do you place on what is, I believe, technically called the 'head' a transfer of artistic and complicated design, which incorporates your name and address?"

"Yes," said Walker with a nod. "I come into possession of a good many machines through 'part-exchange'—a pernicious system that forces me to buy old machines for considerably more than they are worth, in order to sell a new machine to my customer. I try to do the best I can with these crocks, by fitting them up with new tyres, brake-blocks and so on, and giving them a lick of enamel. On these machines—and also, of course, on those I buy second-hand for cash—I put my transfers. They not only give the work a finished appearance, but also serve as an advertisement for me. I never put the transfer, of course, on a new machine."

"Thanks very much, Mr. Walker," the Inspector smiled. "And now, gentlemen, if you will excuse me, I must again apply my reluctant nose to the grindstone!"

"Rutherford," said Walker despairingly, when the Inspector had paid his bill and left the shop, "what *does* it all mean?"

"I understood you to say that it seemed fairly clear to you," I answered, rubbing it in rather cruelly.

"Why that question about my transfer?"

"Because the Inspector is following up a clue. Bicycles seem to be playing quite a big part in this case and the Inspector is trying to identify one of them."

"With me?"

"Not necessarily; but you will understand his interest when I tell you that the machine Johnson's murderer rode last Sunday night came from your shop."

"Good God!"

It was only a guess, in any case, and I hadn't really meant to tell him, but it was out now.

"What does it all mean?" Walker repeated.

"It only means," I said, "that you sold a bicycle to somebody, after imprinting on it your transfer, and the Inspector wants to get into touch with that somebody."

"Yes, that's what it is!" he said, looking at me eagerly. "It must be! There are dozens of bicycles in this neighbourhood with my transfer on them."

"As far as I can see," I said as we rose to go, "you have become mixed up in this thing in the same way as I have—by accident."

"I hope you're right," he said.

After I left him outside the 'Cozey', I went along to

'Voslivres' to see how George was getting on. I found him wearing the expression of a cod that has suffered a recent bereavement. I anxiously asked him the cause.

"Two—one," he answered sombrely.

"Cheer up, George," I laughed. "Paulsfield put up a good fight."

"They'd have put up a better one if I'd been there, sir. It was through me that they won last week."

"How did you do that?"

"Shouting, sir."

"Well, don't blame me, George. I offered to let you go— and what's one football match more or less, anyway?"

"*Sir,*" he said, as much aghast as if I had suggested that we should poison his mother.

"Anything happened this afternoon?" I asked.

"No, sir—except that Miss Dolden came in to complain that the last book we lent her had in it some questionable passages. A bit near the knuckle, sir."

"Have you read it, George?"

"Yes, sir."

"What's your opinion?"

"It *was* a trifle candid, sir."

"We'd better take it off our shelves."

"Can't do that, sir. Just after Miss Dolden left, Mrs. Morrison came in and borrowed it—and five minutes before, I had seen them through the window talking to each other outside Burnside's."

"From which we draw our own conclusions!" I laughed. "Well, George, I'll be in just before eight. Be a good boy!"

"Certainly, sir," said George.

As I was walking along Chesapeake Road, I met Mrs. Martin, the Sergeant's good lady. She greeted me with a wide smile: everything about her was wide.

"Good evening, Mrs. Martin," I smiled. "How's Ted?"

"Bonny, sir. Won't you step in and see 'im?"

I said I had business to do in the High Street, but I'd be round at their house within a quarter of an hour. They lived in a turning off Chesapeake Road. I wanted to buy some tobacco, I explained.

"Last time," she said, raising an admonishing finger, "it was a clockwork train."

"I like clockwork trains," I said.

A few minutes afterwards, I was in Burnside's the toy-shop, weighing up the relative merits of a box of bricks and a wooden crane. I finally bought them both and bore them off to 14, Handen Street. In the open doorway of that pleasant little house stood an imposing figure in a papier mache replica of a policeman's helmet. To his proud, blue-jerseyed chest a whistle was pinned and round his waist was a belt, in which were stuck two diminutive thumbs.

"Mr. Rutherford," said this personification of justice in a stern voice and with a solemn face, "I arrest you on this warrant"—he removed one thumb from the belt and extracted a tradesman's circular from his trouser-pocket—"For robbery with violence and I warn you that anything you say will be taken down in writing and may be used in evidence."

"Heavens, Teddy!" I laughed. "What a mouthful! Who taught you that?"

"Mr. Johnson—'im that was killed in an accident. I've arrested you."

"All right, officer. It's a fair cop." The arm of the law thereupon burst into a merry peal of laughter.

"Last time l saw you, Ted," I said, as we went into the gay little parlour, "you were a Red Indian. This is a surprise!"

Mrs. Martin came in just then and was apprehended with all due ceremony. The prisoner looked at my parcels suspiciously. I put on a bold front and suggested to the Constable that he should examine the stolen goods. His other captive, he could release on parole. Ted asked what that was and I explained that she would promise not to escape.

"That I don't," said Mrs. Martin, "with my man's supper to cook. Get along with you—you're both as bad as each other!" And she gave P. C. Edward Martin a playful push, which sent that keeper of the King's peace sprawling backwards on the settee, to his shrill delight.

She left us to open the parcels between us and in a quarter of an hour we had built a handsome police station—Teddy would have nothing but a police station—complete with lock-up. Teddy was the builder, architect and surveyor rolled into one, while I filled the part of consulting engineer, with short intervals as O. C. crane. We had just demolished the police station and had prepared the specification and bills of quantities for a church, when Sergeant Martin came into the room.

"Evening, Mr. Rutherford. Good to see you again," he said. "Well, you young rascal, what've you got there?"

"They're bricks and a crane and Mr. Rutherford gave me them and we've made a police station better'n yours and we're going to make a big church with a big steeple and out come all the people," was Teddy's expansive reply delivered in one breath.

We appointed the Sergeant clerk-of-works and built what might, by a stretch of the imagination, have been taken as a church. Then Mrs. Martin summoned the reluctant Ted into the kitchen. Martin followed him and returned in a few moments with a couple of glasses. The sideboard yielded a bottle of beer.

"I had tea to-day with Walker and the Inspector," I told him as he filled the glasses.

"There's something I don't quite like about that man, Mr. Rutherford," he said, frowning slightly.

"Who—the Inspector?" I asked, being mischievously dense.

"Good Lord, no!" said Martin with a horrified expression. "I wouldn't say a word against the Inspector. I'm talking about that other fellow Walker, 'im with the worn-out smile that looks as if 'e's picked it up after somebody else 'as thrown it away. Furtive's the word, Mr. Rutherford. What was 'e doing out there on the Hazeloak road?"

"The same as I was, Martin—taking a little constitutional. His best defence is that he came forward at the inquest and admitted to being near the scene of the crime at the time it was done."

"His best defence," repeated Martin significantly. "It was better for 'im to speak out when he did and say that he was there, than to 'ave somebody come along and say it for him. More natural, as you might say."

"I think that would be rather looking for trouble," I said, "and if that was why he did own up, why didn't he have a convincing reason for being there: something a little more powerful than, 'If you please, I was out for a walk'? I know that was all the excuse I had, but I was in a different position from a man who planned a murder. It's the same trouble as with Didcott's story of the imaginary puncture. It's too feeble."

Martin grunted and poked the fire viciously.

"There aren't many things more suspicious, Mr. Rutherford, than a snug little watertight, jewelled-in-every-movement alibi. It's like George Robey's egg: it looks all right. If Walker'd had a nice neat story with no loose bits, the Inspector would have torn it to pieces like a puppy with a pair of trousers. But he hadn't. He just said he went for a walk and even the Inspector can't pick any holes in that."

I thought to myself that the Inspector wasn't doing too badly.

"Assume," I said, "—only assume, mark you—that Walker did commit the murder. Where does the other constable come in—the one he saw with Johnson."

"The one he *said* 'e saw with Johnson," retorted Martin.

"You mean that he's trying to throw the blame on Didcott?"

"That's about the size of it."

"And what if something had not prevented Didcott from arriving to time?"

"That's what interests me, Mr. Rutherford—that something did. You know, there's been some 'anky-panky somewhere and funny 'anky-panky, at that."

"And another thing," I said, "where did the other bicycle come from—the one I rode, with Walker's transfer on it?"

"Why not from Walker's shop?" asked Martin.

"And you suggest that he was riding it just before he murdered Johnson?"

"Yes, and when he'd done Johnson in, 'e panicked and took away the wrong bike by mistake."

"Don't you think he would have seen his mistake as soon as he got on the machine? He'd been riding the other just a few minutes before. And even if, in the heat of the moment, he didn't notice it, what did he do with the bicycle almost immediately afterwards?"

"Probably hid it in the hedge."

"Why?"

"Because it wasn't his."

"So he put it in the hedge and walked on into Paulsfield, knowing full well that his own machine was still lying by the body? Wouldn't his one idea be to get back to the body with Johnson's bicycle and take his own away?"

"It had his transfer on it, but that didn't mean that it was 'is bike."

"I'm sure that he wouldn't look at it quite like that. If it was his machine, his one idea, I submit, would have been to get it back to Hazeloak. Besides, if his machine was found beside Johnson instead of the one upon which Johnson had been known to leave Paulsfield, where did the case against Didcott come in? The third bicycle would immediately complicate things. But why on earth have a bicycle himself? Why didn't he walk from Hazeloak to the point where he met Johnson and then, after getting his man, slip back again quietly to Hazeloak—and nobody any the wiser?"

"I still think it's funny," said Martin, unconvinced.

So did I, if it came to that, for all my specious arguments. As I had walked along Chesapeake Road, I had been doing a little mental arithmetic.

"I didn't tell you what Didcott said to the Inspector, did I?" Martin asked. "About why he was late at Burgeston? You remember I told you how the Inspector got out of Rawlinson, the chap who keeps the 'Porcupine' at Burgeston, that Didcott didn't arrive to time last Sunday? Well, when the Inspector got back to the station that morning, he 'ad Didcott in to a private confab. Didcott told me about it afterwards: last Thursday, as a matter of fact, the morning after we 'ad our chat at the 'Queen's Head'.

" 'Didcott,' says the Inspector, as if he was talking to 'is own son, 'what time did you get to Burgeston last Sunday evening?'

" 'About five-past nine, sir,' says Didcott, looking scared.

" 'A good deal later than your usual time, Didcott?' says the Doctor."

"The Doctor?" I interrupted Martin.

"We call 'im that in the Force. An old lag the Inspector once took up at Whitchester said after 'is conviction that he wouldn't 'ave given 'imself away like he did if the Inspector hadn't led him on with his bedside manner. And it's kind of stuck. A chap once said of the Doctor that when you come up against 'im, he starts by laying all his cards on the table—and it isn't till it's too late that you discover that they weren't out of the same pack as you were using."

As I laughed at this, Martin relighted his pipe. "Where was I?" he asked, throwing the match into the fire. "Oh, yes—the Inspector says to Didcott, soft like: 'A good deal later than your usual time, Didcott?'

"'Yes, sir,' says Didcott awkward

" 'It was a nasty night for a lady so frail as Mrs. Stevens to be out, wasn't it?' asks the Inspector as sweet as a cooing dove in a little pink velvet waistcoat."

Martin burst out laughing.

"I wish I could've seen Didcott's face, Mr. Rutherford! I bet funny wasn't the word! After several tries, 'e managed to say, 'I only happened to meet 'er, sir.'

" 'I don't suggest for a moment you did otherwise,' said the Inspector, 'and you probably chatted with 'er long enough to make you late at Burgeston.'

"Didcott looked a bit less like as if he had a hot potato in his mouth and said 'No, sir. If I 'adn't met her, I should still have been late.'

" 'How's that?' asks the Inspector." 'As I was riding along before I met Mrs. Stevens, sir,' said Didcott, ' I heard a noise in Phantom Coppice, that sounded like a pistol shot.'

" 'That's interesting,' says the Inspector. 'Tell me about it.'

" 'I'd nearly got to the footpath that leads off through the Coppice,' says Didcott, ' when I 'eard what I thought was a pistol or gun shot come from the Coppice. I immediately got off my bicycle to investigate, thinking something funny might be going on—a wet November night 'ardly being the time for shooting rabbits. I wheeled my bike down the footpath where the shot seemed to have come from and leant it against a tree ..."

" 'A beech tree to the right of the path,' the Doctor butts in, and Didcott looks startled.

" 'It *was* on the right, sir,' he said, 'but I don't know what sort of a tree it was. I walked a bit further along the path, listening for any sounds; but I couldn't hear anything.'

" 'How close did the shot seem to be?' asks the Inspector.

" 'Quite close, sir—less than fifty yards, though it's difficult to say for certain. I gave up after a bit and pushed my bike back into the road.'

" 'How long did this delay you?'

" 'I should say five minutes,' answered Didcott. 'As I was wheeling my bicycle into the road, I met Mrs. Stevens.'

" 'And what time was that?'

" 'About ten to nine.'

" 'That makes the time of the shot approximately 8.45,' said the Inspector."

Martin then went on to tell how Mrs. Stevens had 'phoned Didcott at the station after her talk with me on the following Thursday, and had been urged by him to come round and tell the whole story to the Inspector. She had repeated to the Inspector what she had previously told me, but without going so fully into her matrimonial troubles or her exact reason for going out to meet Didcott. The Inspector had asked her whether she heard a pistol shot some little time before she met Didcott and after an appealing glance at Didcott, who told her to tell the Inspector all she knew, she said she had heard no pistol shot. The Inspector had then let her go.

"What a singular business," I said to Martin.

"Yes, Mr. Rutherford; but I've got a sort of feeling that Didcott was telling the truth. It's like what you said about Walker's alibi. If it wasn't the truth, it was a pretty wet sort of story. I believe that somebody fired off that shot to attract Didcott's attention, so as to make 'im late at Burgeston, which would've been suspicious."

"But that shot was fired only a few yards from Didcott and the murderer couldn't have been anywhere near there at a quarter to nine. An accomplice would complicate things."

"Not a bit of it, Mr. Rutherford. It would simplify things. Two are easier to catch than one."

"How do you account for Didcott telling Mrs. Stevens when he met her that he had just come along the footpath from the Hazeloak road?"

"Who said he said that?" demanded Martin. "That's what she told me."

"Well, she didn't tell the Inspector that."

"Perhaps it was just another of Didcott's naughty little fibs," I smiled.

"And why not, Mr. Rutherford, if it comes to that?" said Martin. "Didcott told me on Thursday about 'is affair with her, and there's no doubt about it that 'e wasn't too darn pleased to see her last Sunday evening. He wanted to be shot of her—not only for keeps, but there and then. What would she have done if he'd told 'er that he'd just 'eard somebody firing off artillery? She'd 'ave clung to him like a wet night-shirt and made 'im take 'er back to Burgeston hand in hand."

"There's something in that," I conceded. "After all, if he did murder Johnson, the last thing he would surely do would be to tell the first person he met that he's just come from where the body was lying."

"If Didcott killed Johnson," said Martin with immense conviction, as he knocked out his pipe on the grate, "I'm the Queen of the Fairies."

"I should hate to imagine either possibility," I laughed.

Mrs. Martin came in just then and our chat was brought to an end. I glanced at the clock on the mantelpiece and said that I ought to be getting back to the shop. After refusing a pressing invitation to stay to supper, I hurried off to release George from his long imprisonment. I sent him off home and attended myself to the steady stream of customers who poured in until well after closing time for their Sunday reading matter. After the door had been closed on the last of them, I set myself to a task I had been meaning, for some time, to ask George to do. The books in the cases round the walls of the shop were divided into sections: Detective, Adventure, Romance and so on; and it had been my custom thitherto to keep some of the detective novels in the two narrow bookcases to the sides of the door. This meant that, as books of this kind were in the greatest demand, borrowers congregated round the door and made things difficult for those who wished to enter or leave the shop. That evening, therefore, I cleared the thrillers from the two bookcases I have mentioned and replaced them with books from the

General section. This took me the better part of half an hour and it wasn't until nearly nine o'clock that I got back home to number eighteen.

There was a letter from Molly waiting for me there. Would I care to take tea with her the next afternoon, when her uncle would be pleased to see me? She hadn't given me much time, she said, but she did hope I could come.

She needn't have worried!

X. UNDERNEATH THE GRATE

The fine dry weather held. The crisp brilliance of the next morning was irresistible, especially to an old—or, at any rate, not so young—fogey such as I, who prefer Shanks's immemorial mare to any of your motor cars. At ten o'clock, after my leisured Sunday breakfast—the most wonderful meal of the week—I took my hat and stick—who would insult the sun with an overcoat?—and started out with Spot on a tramp—five, ten, twenty, a hundred miles, for all I cared, so long as I was at Southmouth by tea-time!

The remnants of the night's frost still glistened bravely in the sun and the cold cleanness of the air seemed to rid me of "That perilous stuff, which weighs upon the heart." To quote *Macbeth* again, at the risk of being dubbed a tedious fellow, I had supped full with horrors. The business of Johnson was beginning to prey upon me. My thoughts kept returning to it like a tongue to a bad tooth. That other little affair on the Lake, when I must have come nearer to death than I had ever been before, had left its mark on me. I wouldn't have admitted it to anybody, but the fear was for ever in my mind that although, through Spot, the first attempt on my life had failed, next time it might be successful. But that morning I had forgotten that Johnson had ever existed or that I had ever seen his photo in Molly's house—or almost forgotten. I went up past the railway station to Meanhurst, the little village under the protecting wing of the Grange. The High Street was a dead street and the door of the 'Gardeners' Arms' was closed as fast as the gates of the temple of Janus in times of peace. The tiny pub seemed so forsaken that it might never offer its hospitality again; and I thought of the tavern in "The Deserted Village":

"Low lies that house where nut-brown draughts inspired,
Where grey-beard mirth and smiling toil retired,
Where village statesmen talked with looks profound,
And news much older than their ale went round."

"Why not have a Whitney?" asked a sign in the window of the bar-parlour. "But not just now," the quiet building seemed to answer sadly.

The road I was on led twistingly to the other village of which I have written so much—Burgeston. I don't think I have explained before that the South Downs intervened between Paulsfield and Burgeston in the shape of one particular hill, which was called the Romp. The autocratic railway line was not to be diverted and tunnelled its way under the Romp, to emerge again into the open a couple of hundred yards north of Burgeston village; but the old main road was more amenable. After leaving Deeptree Corner, it gradually drew nearer to the railway and eventually ran parallel with it for fifty yards or so; but after that short distance, at the point where the footpath through Phantom Coppice ran into it and where Burgeston tunnel began, the road swung sharply to the left and described a rough half-circle round the base of the Romp, to cross the railway by means of a bridge a short distance from the tunnel's southern mouth.

The road from Meanhurst was of sterner stuff than the Burgeston road, for it climbed bravely over the top of Carvery Hill, the Romp's western neighbour, and wound round to Burgeston. The new arterial road made its ugly concrete way to the coast between Carvery Hill and the Romp.

I passed the old windmill atop Carvery Hill and strode on down the other side. I crossed the arterial road and approached the railway bridge, on the other side of which the road became, for a very short distance, Burgeston High Street. In Burgeston, there was the Sunday quiet that had pervaded Meanhurst. A couple of small boys, apparently cowed by the prevailing silence, sat on the edge of the horse-trough, their big country boots dangling. As I went by with Spot, I heard one of them whisper urgently to the other:

"That's the guy 'oo found the cop!"

"Coo!" was the other's expressive reply. Such was fame, I thought, as I walked on; and such was the influence of American talking-films.

I carried on along the Burgeston road until the houses and shops were left behind and reached the fork that took me off the Burgeston road and led me to Hazeloak. In Hazeloak things seemed to be a little brisker—I might almost say lively. Women were at doorways and men in their slippers stood at gates. There was a good deal of shouted questions and unintelligible answers. Something was obviously afoot. A procession of people, some of them hastily dressed, was making off down the High Street in the direction of Deeptree Corner and Paulsfield.

As much from idle curiosity as anything, I followed them. Behind me came others. The last building on the left of the High Street was a shabby shop with HAZELOAK GARAGE written on its hanging-sign. That was Walker's place. Why it was called a garage was difficult to say, because Walker dealt only in push-bicycles. Possibly, the sign was left behind by the previous tenant and Walker had adopted the title. I once tried to buy some petrol there, I remembered.

As I walked on, I heard somebody say:

"In the pond by the road, in Farmer Rushton's five-acre meadow."

One word leapt to my mind: Johnson. Something had been discovered in the pond. I recollected how the Inspector had stood looking over the ancient oak gate, when I had been there with him the previous Monday morning. When I arrived, a crowd had already gathered. At the gate was stationed Harwood, who had his hands full, trying to keep them from entering the field. Through a gap in the hedge I could just see the pond, with its overhanging trees. Standing by it was a figure I recognized: Inspector Charlton. I heard the clatter of an old engine and, when I had pushed my way through the crowd to the gate, I saw the Paulsfield fire-engine, with a pipe running from it into the pond. The harassed Harwood caught sight of me and bade me good-morning. I asked him what all the bother was about.

"The Inspector's carrying out an investigation," he explained.

"I thought as much," I said with mild irony.

"'E's found a bicycle in the pond," said a small voice at my elbow; and I turned to find my little sad-eyed friend, whose name, I had discovered, was Milke—a pretty piece of nomenclature. "'Alf a dozen nippers from 'Azeloak was skating on the ice this morning and one of them fell through and landed on a bicycle lying on the bottom. It ain't three foot deep."

There was to be no respite for me. There I was, back in the thick of it again!

"That's the bike, like as not," said Milke, "that Johnson's murderer rode. Why the p'lice ain't looked 'ere before's a mystery to me."

"Now, then," broke in Harwood, "that's enough of that talk."

"Sorry, Mr. 'Arwood," he said apologetically. "No offence, I'm sure." And he was no longer with us.

The crowd had thinned a good deal. Some enterprising fellow had found a passage through the hedge a little way down the road.

"One of the boys, Mr. Rutherford," said Harwood, "had the sense to run into Paulsfield and tell Sergeant Martin, who rang up the Inspector at 'is home. The Inspector wasn't satisfied with just the bike, so 'e routed out the fire-brigade—and weren't they pleased! They broke the rest of the ice and are pumping out the water now."

"He's hoping to find the weapon, I suppose?" I suggested.

Harwood did not answer, but shouted to Chandler, who was standing over by the Inspector. A dozen or so people were coming across the field from the direction of the newly discovered gap. Chandler left the Inspector and hurried to head them off. After some friendly expostulation and good-natured chivying, he managed to get them through the gate that Harwood guarded, into the road again.

The Inspector had looked over to us when Harwood had called to Chandler and a few moments after Chandler had rejoined him at the pond, the Inspector sent him across to the gate.

"Inspector Charlton's compliments, sir," he said, "and would you care to join him?"

Harwood allowed me to pass through the gate and I walked with Chandler to where the Inspector stood.

"Good morning, Mr. Rutherford," the Inspector greeted me. "This is a pleasant way to spend the Sabbath morning!"

"Isn't it?" I laughed. "I started out this morning with my mind free of this bothersome affair; and now I'm mixed up in it again!"

I noticed a weed-covered, dripping bicycle standing against a tree.

"Johnson's?" I murmured.

As he nodded a man called out to him:

"Nearly empty, Inspector."

We stepped to the edge of the pond. The water, filthy with the mud stirred up, was getting very low, and the pipe to the engine was beginning to bubble like a straw when the lemonade is almost gone. With a few lingering spits, the engine lapsed into silence.

"She won't take any more, Inspector—getting too thick," said the man who had previously spoken. "We'll 'ave to try a bucket."

Two men wearing long rubber boots stepped into the slime and began to scoop out the thick brown water, passing the filled buckets to other men, who emptied them in a nearby ditch. After a while, the rim of a bucket grated on something in the pond. The man sank his hand into the mud.

"Something 'ere, Inspector," he called out.

"Have it up," the Inspector instructed him; and the man pulled out a rusty iron poker with a brass handle.

"Anything else?" asked the Inspector.

Down again went the man's hand and groped around. This time it came up holding a piece of fire-grate—the front bars of the old-fashioned style of grate.

"There was something underneath this," said the explorer. "Feels like an empty sack. This was 'olding it down."

He passed his last find to a man on the bank and reached down again into the mud. I was glad he was doing it and not I! He brought up a sodden mass of cloth, which, after he had wrung it out, took some sort of shape.

It was a constable's jacket.

The white-metal buttons of it were dull and its blue cloth was soiled with thick mud and green slime, but there was no doubt what it was. It was passed to the Inspector, who examined it carefully and then laid it on the bank.

"Carry on," he ordered. "You may find a cape, a greatcoat, a cap and possibly"—he smiled—"a pair of trousers."

They found the cap and trousers, but protracted search produced nothing more than a leather belt from the pond.

"Interesting booty, Mr. Rutherford," said the Inspector in a satisfied tone.

"It certainly puts a different complexion on the case," I said.

"Possibly," was his reply.

He had the clothes put into a sack and taken to his car, which stood in the road. He asked me if he could take me back to Paulsfield, but I said that I had come out for a walk and I might as well have one. I walked across the field to the gate, where a knot of people still lingered. One man in the crowd I thought I ought to know: a shortish fellow, with a large white, clean-shaven face, wearing a plus-four suit of extravagant cut and pattern, and a cap to match. He was asking Harwood in a rather thick, heavy voice what all the excitement was about. Near him I caught sight of another face: a familiar rubicund dial. George's.

"Hullo, George," I greeted him. "I might have guessed *you'd* be here! Are you walking back with me?"

As he marched along by my side, I said:

"You seem to know everybody, George. Who was that standing near you in the crowd just now? The fellow with the gin-and-fog voice in the gents' natty sports suiting?"

"That was Frank Stevens, sir," said George promptly. "The Great Jimmy Stevano. The man with the Rubber Face. The Man Who Could Make a Cat Laugh. The ..."

"Thank you, George," I said politely. "You have told me enough to enable me to identify him."

"Do you remember, sir," said George, "what I said to you in the shop the other day: that I believed the man Mr. Walker saw with Johnson wasn't a real policeman, but somebody dressed in a policeman's uniform?"

"Yes, I think I do."

"Isn't it beginning to look as if I was right? May I tell you my theory, sir? Well, let's suppose that the murderer, whom we'll call A ..."

"Make it X, George," I interrupted with a laugh. "It's more usual."

"X, sir," said George reprovingly, "is always where the body was found."

"I thought that was a cross, but have it your own way."

We both always enjoyed these little passages. "Mr. A knew," George went on, "all about Johnson and Didcott going to Hazeloak and Burgeston every Sunday evening and that if he waited somewhere between Deeptree Corner and Hazeloak, Johnson would be along round about a quarter to nine. So he dressed himself up in a constable's uniform, which he had got from somewhere, and hid with his bicycle in the hedge a little way from the Corner on the Hazeloak side of it. Then when he heard Johnson and Didcott say good-bye to each other at the Corner—he could if he didn't go too far down the road—he came out of the hedge and waited in the middle of the road for Johnson to come along." George paused.

"I'm with you so far," I encouraged him. "When Johnson came up level with him," George continued, "Mr. A said that his lamp had gone out and had Johnson a match to spare. Johnson got off his bicycle and brought out his matches. While Mr. A was relighting his lamp, he told Johnson some story of how he got where he was. Perhaps he said he had cycled from Whitchester—and in case Johnson knew everybody there, added that he was a fresh arrival. He might have said that he was on his way to visit friends in Hazeloak."

"Visiting friends in uniform?" I queried. "Would Johnson have swallowed that?"

"He probably would, sir. He'd no reason to suspect foul play. But there are dozens of other reasons that Mr. A could have given. Then they both got on their bicycles and rode on side by side. In a little while, they passed Mr. Walker, which was what Mr. A wanted—somebody who would come forward afterwards and say he had seen two constables together on the Hazeloak road. Whichever way you look at this case, sir, there is one thing that sticks out a mile: it was the murderer's prearranged plan to implicate Didcott. After Mr. Walker was well out of the way, Mr. A suggested a cigarette and they both dismounted. Then, when Johnson had taken off his cap for a moment ..."

"Why do you suggest he did that?" I broke in.

"I was wondering if you would pick me up on that," George admitted. "I've thought about that point quite a lot. Perhaps Mr. A said Johnson looked the sort of man who would go bald quickly and Johnson took off his cap to prove that he wasn't. He was a bit proud, you know, sir, of his looks."

"Far-fetched, George, but I'll pass it."

"Anyway, sir, when Johnson took off his cap, Mr. A pulled out a weapon and smashed in Johnson's skull. When, after a few more blows, he decided that Johnson was dead, he rode his bicycle along to the pond and there took off his constable's kit. His own clothes he had left, rolled in a mackintosh, in some safe place nearby. When he had changed, he threw the uniform into the pond and weighed it down with some old iron that was lying about. Then he threw in the bicycle and slipped off home as fast as he could. There, sir, what do you think of that?"

"Quite good, George, and it seems to cover all the points," I said, thinking it better not to tell George about the transposed bicycles.

"It struck me as a better story than the case against Didcott," said George complacently, "even before the uniform was discovered; and now that's come to light, it practically clinches it, sir."

"Practically."

"Well, ask yourself, sir; what other construction is it possible to put upon it?"

"If the murderer wore that uniform, why hasn't he removed it since from the pond?"

"Because he's fled the country, sir. He's probably in America by this time."

And so George rambled on, all the way to my very doorstep in Thorpe Street.

* * * *

At four o'clock I was saying good afternoon to Molly. We were both full of questions. How was she? How was I? What had we been doing with ourselves? Had I kept her out too late on Friday? No, Uncle Harry had waited up for her. Had I got home all right? Oh, yes. That was not the moment to tell her of my natatorial exploits in the lake.

"You didn't mind coming at such short notice?" Molly asked.

" 'I would climb the highest mountain . . .' " I quoted with a dramatic gesture. Molly laughed—and to hear that, I think I really would have had a shot at any old mountain. How sardonically one smiles at the mewlings of lovers and at their ridiculous caperings—until the son of Venus scores an inner!

"Only Uncle's not often at home, even on Sundays, and to-day's a good opportunity for you to see him. He's out at the moment, but he won't be long."

"How long?"

"Oh, about ten minutes."

"That will be ample."

"For what, may I ask?"

"For me to have a little chat with you about your future plans."

"Anyone would think I was a film-star!" laughed Molly.

"Heaven forfend!" I exclaimed, raising my hands in mock horror. "As a matter of fact, I want to ask you a question. To put it in its briefest terms: will you marry me?"

"Yes, please," she said demurely—and was going to say something else, but I rather hindered her.

"I haven't asked you before, have I?" I asked, after an appreciable pause.

"How like a man!" Molly gurgled. "No, you haven't— not in that beautiful orthodox form, anyway, although your behaviour of the other evening was—significant!"

"Or extremely reprehensible," I murmured.

We chatted on in this light-hearted strain, gloriously happy in each other's company, until the maid brought in the tea on a trolley.

"The Master's just come in, Miss Molly," she said.

"Please tell him that tea's waiting," Molly asked her, and when the maid had gone, said to me: "Uncle's idea of tea-time is anywhere between three-thirty and six. I hope you're more punctual for meals than he is?"

"I'm *going* to be," I said.

"And at whatever time he does have his tea, it's got to be just right. It must be given to him boiling hot."

"Isn't that how tea should be?" I asked.

"But he never dreams of drinking it," laughed Molly, "until it is nearly cold. Then he passes his cup and asks for it to be really hot this time!"

"I feel that I am going to like your uncle," I said.

"I'm sure you will," said Molly. "He's got his funny little ways, of course, and is simply wrapped up in his work, but he's an old darling. If you want to keep on the right side of him, show an interest in his activities."

There was a step in the hall and the door opened.

"Hullo, Uncle!" said Molly. "Late for tea again?"

I got to my feet and turned towards the door—and looked into the smiling face of Inspector Charlton.

XI. UNCLE HARRY

Have you ever been kicked in the diaphragm by a horse? Probably not; and neither have I. But I experienced what I imagine to be parallel sensations when I saw the Inspector's tall figure standing in the doorway. I was an idiot, of course, not to have guessed it before. I expect most of my readers realized it some chapters back. My face must have been a study in stupefaction, but I managed, after swallowing hard, to answer his, "Good afternoon, Mr. Rutherford." As Molly pulled the trolley to her, he sat down, while I relapsed limply into my chair.

"You'll have to forgive our little deception," the Inspector said to me with a charming smile, "but it was rather thrust upon us."

"Not at all," I said, "but you've quite taken my breath away. You have managed to startle me several times, Inspector, during our short acquaintanceship, but this time you have excelled yourself! I thought Molly's uncle was a doctor."

"That is what they call me!" he grinned boyishly.

Molly poured out the tea and the Inspector offered me a scone, with the remark that they were some of Molly's.

"How *did* you guess that?" she asked with playful emphasis.

"I heard the to-do that attended their preparation," he laughed. "One would have thought that the Archbishop of Canterbury, at least, was coming to tea!"

"Irritating man," said Molly, blushing delightfully, as she passed his cup.

The talk passed pleasantly from one thing to another, with a great deal of banter between Molly and her uncle. They were obviously the best of friends. Then, when the

Inspector had finished his third luke-warm cup of tea and the maid had taken away the trolley, Molly rose and left us.

"I'm afraid," said the Inspector when we were alone, "that I haven't treated you too well over this business, and I hope you'll accept my apologies."

"Why, of course," I hastened to say.

"My only defence is that I wanted to get this Johnson matter cleared up without the personal element coming too much into it. You will probably appreciate my position. I persuaded Molly to abet me. But the whole thing was becoming ridiculous and that is why Molly has asked you here to-day."

"For which I am thankful," I said. "I didn't want the elusive uncle to imagine that I was carrying on a clandestine affair with his niece, and have been seeking a meeting for some time."

"I know that," he said, "and I appreciate it."

"Now that I have met you as Molly's uncle, Inspector, may I take the opportunity to ask you if you have any objection to Molly and me becoming engaged?"

"None whatever, my dear fellow," he smiled, "*when* this troublesome murder is cleared up. If you hadn't had the misfortune to find Johnson's body, things would be quite different; but you'll see that if it were publicly announced that the leading witness in the Johnson case was to marry the niece of the police official engaged upon the enquiry, there would be a certain amount of acrimonious comment."

"You prefer that I don't see Molly?" I asked. "My dear Rutherford," he laughed, "I'm no ogre. See her as much as you like—or, what's more to the point, as much as *she* likes. But an official engagement must wait until the foreman of the jury says 'guilty.' Mark you, I'm not in a position to stop Molly from doing what she likes—she's her own mistress—but you have asked me for *my* decision."

"Then let's leave it at that," I said, and he offered me his hand.

"You come of good stock, Rutherford," he smiled. "I was with your father at Mereworth."

"That's very interesting," I said. "I don't seem to remember his ever mentioning you."

"I don't expect he did," said the Inspector with a broad grin. "I was less than the weed that grew beside his door. He probably didn't realize my existence. He was Captain of the First XV when I was only a 'Sprat.' "

"Did they call the little boys that, even in your day? And you, an Old Mereworthian, prefer Soccer to Rugger?"

"Good Lord, no!" he laughed. "When I told you and Walker that at tea yesterday, that was only a gambit, working up to my little surprise. Little surprises are useful things to have by you, Rutherford. A startled man is a man at a disadvantage."

"So I have found," I said wryly.

"You and Walker went through Mereworth together, didn't you?" he asked.

"Yes," I admitted, "although it was only yesterday that I realised it. You probably know that his name wasn't Walker then?"

"Frederick Benson Langdon. He changed it in 1928. There is a pleasant little deception practised upon honest merchants by gangs of gentlemen who give each other false references, which is called a Long Firm Fraud. Jack Langdon, Walker's younger brother, got mixed up in one of these conspiracies. It wasn't innocence led astray, for Jack Langdon was always a thorough-paced young blackguard. Frederick B. went into it to get his brother out. said it was all his fault; that his brother was young and didn't rightly understand. Acted, in fact, like the Upright Elder Brother, who was the stand-by of so many Victorian novelists. But there was such an outcry—even though he was acquitted—that He had to clear out. His young brother served a term and is now living under the name of Jack Wright in Blossom Street, Whitchester."

That, then, was why Walker's cup had crashed into his saucer the day before.

"Wright seems to be living a life of strict probity, but we've been keeping our eye on him for some time. He's got some sort of a job with the *Whitchester Courier & Herald.*"

"I like Walker," I said. "An unassuming sort of chap. I thought, from his manner, that he'd been through a pretty sticky time, but I had no idea what it was. In the circumstances, it needed courage for him to come out into the open at the inquest."

"Better to come out than to be dragged out," said the Inspector, repeating, more or less, what Martin had said. "Wasn't he seen by that motorist at Deeptree Corner?"

"So there really was a motorist?" I smiled. "I thought that might have been professional inaccuracy on your part—another little gambit! But did you notice something rather strange about that, Inspector?"

"I did," he agreed, "but tell me what you think."

I hesitated for a few seconds, then said, "I don't suggest for a moment that Walker had anything to do with Johnson's death, but after we left each other yesterday, I did a bit of mental arithmetic. Walker told the coroner's jury that he passed Johnson and the other fellow at a little after twenty minutes to nine. He was then half a mile, or thereabouts, from Deeptree Corner. Assuming that he walked at about four miles an hour, it would have taken him approximately seven and a half minutes to get to the Corner from the point where he encountered the two cyclists. Just after twenty to nine—say 8.42. 42 plus 7½ equals 49½—say 50. He should have arrived at the Corner, then, at ten minutes to nine, whereas he was seen by the motorist at a couple of minutes past nine, just as he had paused, according to his own account, to refill his pipe. The question I have asked myself is: what was he doing during those eleven or twelve minutes?"

"An admirable disquisition, Rutherford," smiled the

Inspector. "It would be a great grief to me if there were lost to my family one with whom I am in such perfect accord. In plain English, Rutherford, that's what's biting me!"

"To change the subject," I said, "did it surprise you when the bicycle was found in the pond this morning?"

"I've never been more surprised in my life," he admitted.

"But wasn't it more than likely to be hidden in some such place as that?"

"Granted. But I searched that pond last Monday. I won't vouch for the other stuff—that was lying deep in the mud—but there was no bicycle when I looked. And on Monday evening the pond froze over and it has been frozen ever since!"

"There are a lot of curious things about this case," I said.

"And the most curious thing," said the Inspector, "is the other stuff that was found in the pond—I mean the constable's uniform."

"Wasn't it very likely used as a disguise?"

"How was Johnson's companion dressed—according to Walker, that is?"

"In a constable's uniform."

"He was *not*. Walker said that he was wearing a policeman's cap and a waterproof cape. It was good enough to make Walker believe that both cyclists were constables and it would have been good enough to deceive Johnson in a dark lane, with the rain pouring down. Why, then, augment the disguise with the jacket, trousers and belt?"

"Just to be on the safe side, I suppose," I said, shrugging my shoulders.

"And where is the most important part of the outfit—the cape? I am not prepared to make an unqualified statement, but, from the evidence at my disposal—and assuming that Walker was telling the truth—Johnson's murderer was wearing a constable's cap and cape a few minutes before the crime. There is no evidence to support the suggestion that he was wearing a constable's jacket, trousers and belt. I am willing to agree that a pair of regulation-pattern trousers would have proved more in keeping with the rest of the disguise than, say, a pair of flannel 'greys' and that even a blue pair with civilian turn-ups might have attracted Johnson's suspicious attention; but I cannot understand why we found in the pond a jacket that would have been a superfluous addition to the disguise and failed to find the all-important cape and the almost as essential greatcoat."

The Inspector lighted a cigarette.

"I know it sounds like one of Mr. Punch's pellucid glimpses of the obvious," he went on with a smile, "but in this case I am now faced with these alternatives: either the man who murdered Johnson was a constable or he was not. If he *was* a constable, the uniform in the pond was a red herring and Walker was telling the truth. If he was *not* a constable, I have three hypotheses to choose from:

1. The kit in the pond was what he had worn and Walker was telling the truth.

2. The kit in the pond was what he had worn and Walker was not telling the truth.

3. The kit in the pond was a red herring and Walker was not telling the truth.

"The first two of these I base on this assumption: that if the murderer disguised himself as a constable, the clothes we found in the pond this morning went to make up that disguise. Where is the sense in donning one disguise and then deliberately throwing duplicate items into a pond, where anyone can find them?"

"Molly seems to have deserted us completely, so I will run quickly through these points—that is, if you are interested?"

"Intensely, Inspector," I hastened to say. "This morning I was heartily fed up with the whole thing, but the pond episode has whetted my curiosity."

"Very well, but I hope you will bear in mind that I am regarding you as something more than one of the general public? These theories of mine are for your ear alone."

"Thank you for your confidence," I said, and couldn't help thinking of Martin's story of the Inspector laying his cards upon the table. Which was unjust, perhaps.

"My first point, then," said the Inspector. "Let me assume that the man with Johnson was a constable. To afford you yet another glimpse of the obvious, either he was Didcott or he was not. If he was Didcott, Didcott's reason for being late at Burgeston was a lie. He said, by the way, that he heard a pistol shot and stopped to investigate. If he was Didcott, he did not part with Johnson at Deeptree Corner, but cycled on with him until they passed Walker, when he murdered Johnson and then pedalled furiously along the footpath, to meet Mrs. Stevens at the other end. In this connection, one interesting point must be borne in mind: those cycle-tracks that interested me last Monday continued unbroken to the junction of the mud of the footpath with the tarred surface of the road, where they disappeared; but Mrs. Stevens said that when she met Didcott he was pushing his machine. In support of this, there are lighter tracks of a bicycle leading to a beech tree some yards along the path and more tracks going back again to the road. If, on the other hand, the second man was not Didcott, Didcott's story of the pistol shot was the truth and he did leave Johnson at Deeptree Corner. In that case, the shot was arranged by the murderer to retard Didcott's arrival at Burgeston. It is difficult to regard the shot as an entirely extraneous happening.

"Suppose that the second man was a constable other than Didcott. Of the Paulsfield Force we are left with Sergeant Martin, Harwood and Chandler. During the time the crime was committed, Martin and Chandler were on duty at the station and Harwood was at home. The whole lot of them have been having a pretty hectic time recently, as a result of this night-policing of Burgeston and Hazeloak, which has been abandoned since last Sunday night. I won't go into their whole routine. Suffice it to say that on Sunday evenings, Didcott and Johnson went off together, leaving

Martin in the station with Chandler. At quarter past nine, Harwood arrived to stand duty until next morning, while Martin and Chandler went home to bed.

"Didcott vouches for the fact that when he left the station last Sunday evening, Martin and Chandler were both there. After Didcott left with Johnson, Martin stayed in the charge-room, while Chandler went out to the shed at the back of the station, to tinker with one of the bicycles—the brakes were giving trouble or something. Harwood arrived at the station on his motor-cycle at eleven minutes past nine and found Chandler still fiddling about with the machine, while, when you presented yourself at seventeen minutes past nine or thereabouts, Martin was still in the charge-room. You were the first person to see Martin after the murder and Harwood was the first person to see Chandler after the murder. Harwood stood in the shed chatting to Chandler and had just come across the yard and through the back door when Martin called out to him. Neither Martin nor Chandler saw the other between the time Chandler went out to the shed and the time Martin saw Chandler sitting in Harwood's sidecar; but if either of them had left the station, he would have run a terrific risk from a dozen different directions.

"Now we come to Harwood. At the time the killing was done, he was off duty. I think I told you that he lives at Burgeston with his wife, who retired to the seclusion of a maternity-ward last Tuesday week. I understand,"—the Inspector smiled—"that it is a boy and both mother and child, as is happily almost always the case, are doing well. At a couple of minutes after quarter past eight, he spoke over the fence to the man next door, who was either putting the cat out or calling it in. He—Harwood's neighbour, that is—is a very talkative individual and I left him rather confused on that point! A little while after he went indoors, he heard Harwood tune in his radio to a light entertainment from the Continent and at about twenty to nine go over to the

London National. Soon after nine o'clock, he and his wife heard Harwood turn off his wireless and then start up his motor-cycle in the shed by the side of his house and ride off towards Paulsfield.

"That seems to account for Harwood, Martin and Chandler. But there's more than one police station in the country, and I have circularized stations within a radius of twenty-five miles for particulars of the movements of all constables between eight-thirty and nine-thirty. Every man could be accounted for: all those on duty were at their posts and the ones off duty have each of them reliable witnesses as to their whereabouts."

"That narrows that part of it down," I said to the Inspector.

"Now we turn," he said, lighting another cigarette, "to our other possibilities. First of all we have the hypothesis that I labelled '1' This was that the murderer was not a constable, but a man who dressed himself in a constable's uniform, allowed himself to be seen by Walker with Johnson, and, after the murder, threw certain portions of his disguise into the pond and bore off the bicycle, together with the cape, which Walker noticed, and the greatcoat, which he must surely also have worn. It is too early a stage in the proceedings to discuss this point at length. Secondly, hypothesis '2.' This was that the uniform in the pond was worn by Walker, who played the part of the man he said he saw with Johnson, in the hope that some other person would see the two men together and bring suspicion on Didcott. This seems extremely improbable.

"Thirdly and lastly, hypothesis '3.' This was that the uniform in the pond was just a blind and that Walker's story of the second constable was a lie. The first part of this is a more feasible corollary to the second part than is the first part of hypothesis '2,' for if Walker was lying—which would automatically associate him with the murder—it is more than probable that the uniform was placed by him in the pond, either before or after the crime, to add a fresh complication to the affair, should the case against Didcott fall through from lack of evidence or from any other cause.

"To my mind, hypothesis '3' is more convincing than the other two, by reason of the jacket that was found in the pond. That little extra—and to me unfelicitous—touch disposes one to believe that not only the jacket, but also the trousers, cap and belt were thrown into the pond to suggest, when they were discovered—as they almost inevitably would be—that the crime was done by some person who had masqueraded as a constable.

"To sum up, if the uniform in the pond was merely a red herring, the possible murderers are:—

Martin.

Harwood.

Didcott.

Chandler.

Walker.

A confederate of one of them.

"Unfortunately, it is not possible to exclude any member of the Paulsfield Police Force from this list, as the alibi of none of them is perfect; but, for all that, the conduct of each one of them was perfectly natural, in the circumstances. Assume that no murder took place last Sunday evening. Was it not a perfectly normal thing that Martin should be alone in the charge-room, while Chandler repaired a bicycle in the shed at the back? And was it not an equally normal thing that Harwood, in the absence of his wife, should sit alone at home listening to the radio? There are thousands of occasions in the lives of each one of us when we can produce no alibi and nothing is more difficult to explain afterwards than the thoughtless actions of complete innocence. I don't know"—he added with a chuckle—"whether that last bit is original or whether I once read it in a book."

"Whichever it was, it's perfectly true," I said. "And finally," he went on, "if the uniform in the pond was *not* a red herring, but was actually worn by the murderer, the persons I have mentioned are innocent. Conversely, if they are innocent, the uniform in the pond was actually worn by the murderer. Prove one and you have proved the other. Discover *when* the uniform was thrown into the pond and you are well on the way to finding the murderer.

"And that, Rutherford," he concluded, "Is that."

"You were good enough," I smiled, "to congratulate me on my admirable disquisition. Allow me now to return the compliment. And the attack on me last Friday, Inspector," I went on gravely, "what do you make of that?"

The Inspector looked at me with equal seriousness.

"I don't feel in a position," he said, "to say anything about that yet, but I strongly urge you to keep your weather-eye open."

"Just one more point, Inspector," I said, after a pause. "That photograph I saw in the other room on Friday last—has it any connection with your investigation? I didn't know quite what to think when I picked it up—especially as I found it so soon after your apparent business call at this house. I couldn't keep out of my mind the unpleasant idea that Molly was mixed up in the affair."

"It was careless of me to leave it lying about," he said. "I think I told you yesterday that I came by the photo in rather unusual circumstances. The postmistress at Hazeloak, who combines that position with the business of confectioner, tobacconist and what you will, brought it to me on Friday. It had been posted in Hazeloak village the evening before—or more probably during the night—and had been noticed by her because it was in a poor quality envelope which had become so much torn at one corner that it was possible to see enough of the photograph inside to identify the subject. It's quite likely that Miss Robinson, the postmistress, made the original tear worse—by accident, of course!—and the good soul was exceeding her duty by bringing it to my attention. Be that as it may, the envelope was addressed to Jack Wright, Blossom Street, Whitchester."

"Walker's brother!" I exclaimed.

"Who left his furnished room in Blossom Street last Sunday, destination unknown."

"Nothing seems to make sense in this affair!" I said.

"There is a man still at large, Rutherford," said the Inspector, "who thinks himself, as James Branch Cabell's *Jurgen* did, a monstrous clever fellow; but I have a feeling that he has been just a little bit too clever."

Molly came back into the room.

"Well, you two old gossips," she said, "have you finished?"

"A gossip, my dear," said the Inspector, "has never finished."

Then he left us and Molly and I had a little chat—but not about Johnson.

* * * *

Later on in the evening, the Inspector rejoined us for a sandwich-and-coffee supper; and afterwards got out a table for cards. We had hardly played the first hand, however, before the maid tapped on the door. Doctor Weston had called to see the Inspector. He will doubtless be remembered as the acid little medico who examined Johnson, but when he was now shown into the room, he smiled pleasantly round at us, and as we exchanged greetings, one would not have imagined that there were times when litmus turned hastily red at his approach. The Inspector supplied him with a drink.

"I see I am interrupting your game," he said.

"We've only just started," said Molly, "and it was only 'cut-throat', anyway."

"Ghastly make-shift!" said the doctor, counterfeiting a shudder. "bumble-puppy! An insult to the noble name of bridge!"

"Are you an enthusiast?" I asked.

"Who isn't after the first rubber?" he retorted.

"It certainly is a pernicious game," the Inspector agreed. "It holds you."

"It does more than I can ever hope to do to keep some of my patients alive," laughed the Doctor. "If it weren't for Auction or Contract, the venerable ladies of Paulsfield would die off around me like flies!"

"Then why not help us to play the game as it should be played?" the Inspector invited him.

"Well," said Dr. Weston, "I really came to see you on another matter, but ..." he shrugged his shoulders in surrender.

"Have I shown you my cigarette cards, John?" Molly asked.

I jumped to my feet and we left Dr. Weston and the Inspector together. As we came back into the room, after an absence of twenty minutes, the Inspector was saying:

"I'll grant you that he is the only one with an obvious motive—but what is motive, Doctor? An American woman divorced her husband the other month because he would never use the butter-knife. He might have been murdered for the same trivial reason."

The Inspector pushed a chair towards the fire for Molly, while I sat down by the Doctor on the chesterfield.

"If a murderer is not insane," said the Doctor bluntly, "he must have some reason for a crime—a motive."

"Granted," said the Inspector quickly, "but let us assume that this chap with the regrettable table-manners was not divorced, but suffered for his shortcomings the lesser indignity of death by violence. Let us also assume that just before his demise he was blackmailing one man, trifling with the affections of the wife of another, systematically swindling a third and defying a tough bunch of gangsters. Each of these had an excellent motive for killing him, but none of them did. The motive behind his murder was his irritating trick of lunging at the butter with his table-knife. There are five questions, Doctor, to which a dead body gives rise: When? Where? How? Who? and Why? The evidence of doctors and witnesses establishes the first two, the findings of the coroner's jury settle the third, the patience and pertinacity of the police (forgive my blushes!) usually fix on the fourth—and the last, Doctor, is a subject for endless debate among your casuists and arm-chair criminologists. Suppose that a man murdered an Archbishop purely and simply because he wanted to know what it felt like to murder an Archbishop. Is that what you call motive, Doctor?"

"You have been reading too much G. K. Chesterton," was Dr. Weston's smiling reply.

"I have been talking too much shop, if that's anything," laughed the Inspector. "How's the Paulsfield Amateur Dramatic Society going, Doctor?"

The Doctor snorted.

"They insist on making me president of the thing," he said, "and then they don't consult me before they choose a play. Well, when I say that, I mean they did consult me in a casual sort of way, but when I suggested 'Lady Windermere's Fan' or 'His House in Order', they turned up their twentieth-century noses and said they were in favour of something a little less neolithic. I believe they are now feverishly rehearsing some crook melodrama, in which somebody is shot before the curtain rises—and I shouldn't be at all surprised if somebody really is."

"Do you hunger for the footlights, Rutherford?" asked the Inspector, turning to me.

"Only from the comfort of a stall!" I said. "I've only performed in one show, as far as I can remember, and that was 'Twelfth Night', which we did at school. I think I had less than a dozen lines to say. 'So please my lord, I might not be admitted; but from her handmaid do return this answer'—but I'm darned if I can recall what the answer was!"

" 'The element itself, till seven years' heat, shall not behold her face at ample view; but, like a cloistress, she will veiled walk ... ' "

"That's it!" I said. " 'And water once a day her chamber round with eye-offending brine'."

Molly looked at her uncle with a wondering look.

"Do you know *everything*, Uncle?" She asked.

"Practically, my dear," he smiled.

"My thanks, good Master Modest," she retorted.

"D'you see that that little rat, Stevens, is billed for the 'Empire' this week?" said the Doctor.

"Another come-back that is doomed to failure, I'm afraid," said the Inspector.

"I'd like to see him, for all that," Molly said.

"That's your cue, Rutherford," murmured the Inspector, and skilfully dodged a box on the ear.

"The matter shall be attended to," I said.

We played bridge until half-past ten. Then Dr. Weston offered to take me back to Paulsfield in his car, which stood outside. Five minutes alone with Molly was time enough to fix on the next evening, Monday, for our visit to the 'Empire' and to settle other little matters that concerned only our two selves. At a quarter to eleven, I was sitting beside the Doctor on our way to Paulsfield. For a time he drove in silence, but after we had left Southmouth behind, he said quietly:

"You're a lucky fellow, Rutherford. She's a sweet kid. If I were twenty years younger, you'd have a rival in the field."

"She's too good for me, I'm afraid," I said.

"That's what all you bleating jackasses say!" he said with a sharp laugh. "And in almost every case, such insincere deprecation—and I'm not talking about you, my dear chap—expresses nothing less than the truth. The average man does not deserve to marry the average woman, for the average man is on a lower plane than the average woman. Bad, middling and good can be classed as A, B and C; but a woman"—he negotiated a stationary car—"is at least one step ahead, so that the classification for her are B, C and D. An A man has no right to marry at all, a B man is worthy only of a B woman and a C man only of a C woman. No man is worthy of a D woman; but it is fortunate for the human race that no D woman has ever found that out. . . . But I'm boring you. Forgive the wanderings of a crabbed old idealist."

"You're not boring me, Doctor," I protested. "You interest me immensely and I agree with everything you've said. The only thing I hope is that you haven't propounded your philosophy to Molly!"

"My dear Rutherford," he said, "do you think it would make the slightest difference to her if I did? Haven't I just said that no good woman realises that all men are unworthy of her—and never will realise it?"

He turned the window-handle by his side and threw out his cigarette-end.

"Look at this Johnson fellow," he went on. "Did he deserve anything less than he got? The man was a blackguard. A decent-spoken, obliging, courteous fellow—but a blackguard. Your modern theorist, with all his high-sounding tommy-diddle, would say that Johnson merely suffered from a complex and after a course of psycho-analysis or three months spent in a tree on a diet of green vegetables, would have become a perfect citizen. Perfect citizen, my ..."

Which of his possessions he was about to mention, I never knew, for just then he was interrupted by a dog suddenly running across our bows. After the animal had missed death by a distance that could have been measured only by a micrometer, he continued:

"Here we have this man, who was, to use the mildest word, a philanderer, done to death. What motive immediately leaps to your mind?"

"That it was a *crime passionel?*"

"Exactly so. Look for the men, I say, whose womenfolk have been victimized by Johnson—husbands, fathers, lovers, brothers—investigate thoroughly the alibi of each one of them and if you don't hit upon the murderer in the end, I'm a Dutchman. That Didcott man, he's as deep as they make 'em; and goodness knows he had enough reason for wanting Johnson nicely out of the way."

"But I thought the Maggie Wood episode was over and done with?"

"There was a later episode."

I waited expectantly. After a few moments, he said:

"Mrs. Stevens."

"But Johnson had nothing to do with Mrs. Stevens, Doctor," I suggested mildly.

"Hadn't he, by Jupiter!" laughed the Doctor.

"Even if he had," I said after a pause, "it doesn't seem to me that Didcott had any cause to kill Johnson. As far as I can see, Didcott would have been only too ready to allow anybody a monopoly of that lady's affections. The pace was getting a bit too hot for him."

"Envy, Rutherford, is one of the seven deadly sins and jealousy is a first cousin. In the case of Maggie Wood, of which I am fully informed, Didcott was jealous of Johnson. He was paying court to the Wood girl and it is possible that he intended to marry her. Whether she was of the same mind, I don't know—probably not. Then Johnson, that corn-proud popinjay, came swaggering along. Do you ever throw bread out into the garden for the birds, Rutherford? If you do, you've probably noticed that half-a-dozen sparrows are usually the first to arrive. They peck at the bread in the friendliest possible way. There is more than enough for all of them and that's all they care about. Then there drops down on to the lawn a starling—a vulgar, swashbuckling fellow, who takes no notice of the pieces of crust that have not yet attracted the sparrows, but makes a bee-line for a bit that one of the little chaps is consuming, jostling him out of the way and making himself quite unnecessarily unpleasant. No sooner has the sparrow ceded him pride of place, than the starling must leave that particular piece of bread and swagger over to browbeat another inoffensive little sparrow. In that way, I think, Rutherford, Johnson was like a starling. He always wanted what the other fellow had—only his leanings lay not towards bread, but women."

"I agree with you there," I said. "The predatory instinct was very strong in Johnson, but surely that failing was very useful to Didcott, for it allowed him to fade gracefully out of Mrs. Stevens's ken—a culmination, as Hamlet says, devoutly to be wished."

"Just a moment, Rutherford," said the Doctor. "I said a few moments ago that envy was one of the seven deadly sins; but one of the six others is pride. However tedious his association with Mrs. Stevens may have become, it must surely have hurt Didcott's pride to have Johnson playing him the same trick with Mrs. Stevens as he had done with Maggie Wood?"

"But Johnson hadn't played the same trick, Doctor," I said. "From the evidence at our disposal, Mrs. Stevens, at the time of Johnson's murder, was still infatuated with Didcott. By her own showing, she came out to meet Didcott that evening to persuade him to take her away from her husband."

"She did *what?*" said the Doctor sharply.

I could have kicked myself. That was a piece of information I should have kept under my hat.

"It probably isn't true," I said with what I fondly hoped was an easy laugh, "but that's how the story runs."

We said little more until the Doctor drew the car to a standstill outside number eighteen. I jumped out and, before I could thank him, he wished me a curt goodnight, let in his clutch and drove away.

XII. THE RETURN OF JIMMY STEVANO

There is always something rather pleasant about finding a letter propped up against the toast-rack when you come down to breakfast. As you meditatively munch your bacon and sip your tea or coffee, you think about it. From whom does it come? What will he or she have to say? Will it contain good news or bad news or, which is nearly as unpleasant as bad news—no news at all? You don't pick it up. You don't, in fact, touch it at all. You allow your curiosity to be whetted, deliberately tantalize yourself, until some arbitrarily fixed time has arrived—as soon, for instance, as you have put aside your bacon-plate and drawn the marmalade-pot towards you. You may recognize the writing on the envelope or identify the postmark, but even though you know who sent it, you defer further investigation until the appointed moment.

That Monday morning, I had an opportunity to play this innocent little game, for when I answered Lizzie's cheery summons, there was a letter lying on top of the daily paper by my plate. As I took my seat, I leant the letter against the vase of chrysanthemums that graced the centre of the table and applied myself to my bacon and egg. The news on the front page of the paper was not wildly exciting. The international situation was tense, but it is only when it isn't that the thinking man is anxious. Gradually, my attention drifted to the letter before me. I didn't recognize the writing, which was of a very ordinary characterless kind. It hardly looked like a bill. The envelope was not the usual "business-size", but of the shape used for private correspondence. There was no transparent window in it. It was post-marked Burgeston and the time was given as 6.30 p.m. the previous evening. I would open it, I decided, when the first piece of toast and marmalade had been placed in my mouth. This plan was conscientiously adhered to and, chewing that vital part of an Englishman's breakfast, I tore open the envelope. Inside was a double sheet of cream-laid notepaper and when I read what was written on it, my jaws stopped working.

> "Murder in blue
> Murder in blue
> Once there was one
> Soon there'll be two."

There was nothing more. Just that, in the same handwriting as the address on the envelope. Apart from the full-stop at the end, there was no punctuation. I read it three or four times, trying to make some sense out of it. Somebody had died. Somebody in blue. A policeman. Johnson—that was obvious. Soon there would be two. Two what? Two dead persons. Who was to be the second victim? Two in blue? Was the death of another constable contemplated? Didcott? Harwood? Martin? Young Chandler? Or somebody not in blue? Walker? Myself?

I didn't like the look of it at all. It might only be a joke at my expense, of course, but I didn't feel that it was. That Lake affair—I had been trying to persuade myself that that had been in no way connected with Johnson's death; that it was just an unprovoked attack by some hitherto uncertified lunatic. But now I began to think that the attack by the Lake had been a sequel to the previous killing. I had always laughed at those sinister letters received by intended victims in detective novels, but now that I was up against the real thing, I didn't feel too easy in my mind.

There was one clear course to take: to tell Inspector Charlton and hand over the letter to him. I was glad about one thing. By playing my little breakfast game, I had, at least, enjoyed my bacon and egg.

I called at the police station on my way to 'Voslivres' and asked Martin if the Inspector was expected there that morning. He was due in, Martin told me, at eleven o'clock. I asked Martin to tell him that I had some important news and would call in at about eleven-fifteen.

The postman had apparently also visited George's house—he lived, by the way, on the northern verge of the Common—for when I walked into the shop, he stuffed a letter hurriedly into his pocket.

"I thought it was only in the spring, George," I chaffed him, "That a young man's fancy lightly turns to thoughts of love?"

He gave me an awkward grin, but contented himself with a polite "Good morning, sir." After a decent interval, he went on, "I have an alternative theory about Johnson's murder, sir, which covers all the known facts. Would you like to hear it?"

"No, George," I said definitely, "I wouldn't. Write to me about it, care of Mrs. Hendon—if, that is, you can spare the time from your other correspondence."

George retired to the other end of the shop wearing such a hurt expression that I hurriedly apologized for my brusqueness, explaining that I was a bit worried. He was immediately all sympathy and asked if there was anything he could do for me.

"No, thank you, George," I answered. "Oh, just a moment, though. There *is* something you can do. Ring up the 'Empire' at Southmouth and book two seats for the second house this evening—stalls, if possible."

"Oh, sir!" said George, his face lighting up. "Then it is all right?"

"What's all right, George?"

"Everything, sir."

I saw what he meant.

"No, George," I said. "My aunt is coming from Chalfont

St. Vitus to stay with me and I am taking her out on the loose tonight."

His delighted smile showed that he didn't believe a word of it; and in a few moments he was having a humorously controversial conversation with the girl on the Paulsfield exchange. I left him to arrange about the seats and went out on one or two little personal errands, which occupied me until a few minutes before eleven-fifteen. The Inspector was waiting for me when I got to the police station. When I produced the letter and was explaining that it had come by that morning's post, the Inspector took it from me and waved me to a chair by his desk.

"So the fox is breaking cover, Rutherford," he said when he had read it. "Do you recognise the hand-writing?"

I shook my head and said that it looked the sort of hand they teach in elementary schools.

"It seems to me," he said, "That there is somebody mixed up in this affair who has been reading too many detective stories. Folks in real life don't send messages like this. The less attention the prospective homicide attracts to himself and his doings, the better he likes it. All this stagey On-the-stroke-of-midnight-the-Black-Hand-will-strike stuff"—he tapped the letter on the desk—"doesn't ring true. Not that we must disregard it on that account."

"Perhaps," I suggested, "it is not a threat, but a warning."

"Possibly," he agreed, and then, leaning back in his chair and staring at the ceiling, went on: "it is an interesting speculation as to whether it forms part of a plan arranged before Johnson was killed, or whether it has been rendered necessary since his death. Does somebody know something that endangers the murderer's immunity from arrest?"

He shifted his gaze from the ceiling and stared reflectively at me.

"This letter was sent to *you*, Rutherford," he said. "*Why* was it sent to you? *Why* did somebody try to drown you in the Lake last Friday? It wasn't done for financial gain, although that was the intention desired to be conveyed. Or was it? Perhaps I was intended to find those charred scraps of notes. Is the man who murdered Johnson a homicidal maniac, thirsting for a new thrill? Or has Johnson's killer a *reason* for wanting you out of the way?"

He suddenly leant forward in his chair. There was a tenseness in his pose that I had never seen before.

"Rutherford," he said, without raising his voice, "Have you told me all you know about this murder?"

"Yes."

"Have you kept back from me, however inadvertently, anything at all? Think, man, think! Your life probably depends upon it. Don't you understand that you were the one factor that wasn't taken into account? Everything else—*everything* was planned with devilish cunning. He didn't think about *you*, Rutherford, but I tell you that he's thinking about you now—and thinking hard!"

"I have told you everything I know, Inspector," I said steadily. "You have my word on that."

"But damn it, man!" he said, thumping his fist on the desk, "There must be something you saw, something you heard, that will convict him. There's no sense, rhyme or reason in this message or the trouble on Friday, if *you* don't hold a trump-card in your hand!"

I made a helpless gesture and smiled feebly.

"I'm very sorry, Inspector," I said, "but as far as I can remember, I have told you the whole of my part in the affair."

"All right," he said, "let's leave it at that, but don't forget that you are placing on me a heavy responsibility. You will understand precisely what I mean. Now, where were we?"

"The letter?" I suggested.

"Oh, yes. I think, as you yourself put forward, that this letter was sent as a warning by somebody who didn't want to see a second person go the way that Johnson went. That it was a threat, seems too ridiculous. If he wanted to indulge in such childish theatricalities, why didn't the chap send it before he launched his offensive near the Lake? Another thing occurs to me: why wasn't this warning sent before? Because, I imagine, the writer didn't know anything about that projected murder. He may not know of it even now, but has heard of a second attempt to be made upon your life. So, as I suggested to you yesterday, keep your weather-eye open. Meanwhile, I'll see what I can do with this little *billet doux*—it may give us some useful guidance."

"There's another thing I ought to tell you about before I go, Inspector," I said. "While he was driving me home last night, Dr. Weston told me that Johnson, as well as Didcott, was intimate with Mrs. Stevens."

The Inspector whistled through his teeth.

"Was he, by gad!" he said. "That's a new one on me, Rutherford! It opens up quite a new line of thought. Where did the Doctor pick up that little tit-bit, I wonder?"

He walked over and opened the door, to call down the passage for Martin. The Sergeant hastily answered his summons.

"Yes, sir?" he said, as he closed the door behind him.

"Tell me, Martin," said the Inspector, who had resumed his seat, "Was Johnson—friendly with Mrs. Stevens?"

"Johnson, sir?"

"That was the name I mentioned."

"She was running after Didcott ..."

"Sergeant, do me the courtesy of answering my question."

"No, sir, 'e wasn't—not as far as I know."

"You have never heard their names coupled?"

"No, sir, but I'll ask them outside."

His hand was on the door-knob when the Inspector said quietly, "You'll do no such thing, Sergeant, if you please."

"Very good, sir."

"Thank you, Sergeant. That is all."

When Martin had left us, the Inspector said, almost to himself:

"That would explain a very great deal.'Murder in blue, Murder in blue. Once there was one, soon there'll be two'."

He was silent for so long that I picked up my hat in readiness to leave him. This brought him out of his brown study.

"I'm sorry, my dear fellow. I had forgotten you were there," he said with a smile. "Don't let me stop you if you are anxious to get away, but there is one other point in which you may be interested."

I raised my eyebrows enquiringly.

"You remember that uniform I was slovenly enough to overlook when I carried out my first examination of the pond? Well, it had certain—provocative features."

"Such as bloodstains?" I suggested.

"Oh, no—nothing so unpleasant as that. One little oddity was that the numbers on the collar of the tunic were reversed. That is, the figures came after the Division letter, instead of before, as they should do. And the figures and letter on the tunic were entirely different from those on the cap. Oh, there were all sorts of quaint little discrepancies about the whole outfit! No policeman ever wore buttons like the buttons on that tunic!"

"You mean they came off some other uniform—a soldier's or sailor's, for example?"

"Your brain is sharper than your eyes, Rutherford," he said with a laugh. "The buttons on Army and Navy uniforms are brass, whereas those on a constable's tunic are white-metal. No, the buttons on yesterday's treasure-trove once graced the manly torso of a French *gendarme.*"

"*Quel mélange!*" I said in my best Gallic.

The Inspector smiled: then his face suddenly grew serious.

"But that is a matter of no great importance," he said. "I think that uniform played an extremely minor part. The only thing that really concerns us is where it came from and that, I think, is not a thousand miles from London, W.1.

The vital point is that you, Rutherford, have got to mind your step. I can't give you any useful advice except that. By all means go to the 'Empire' to see Stevano, but don't go home along Common Road! Stevano is an interesting little insect, falling under grade A of Dr. Weston's rather too inelastic classifications."

"Has he expounded his theories to you?" I asked.

"The little doctor," he laughed, "rides his hobbyhorse harder than ever did Tristram Shandy's Uncle Toby; but when it comes to trepanning or taking his yawl, *Placid Jenny,* round the Needles, he wants some beating."

"I didn't know he was a yachtsman," I said, as I collected my hat and rose to go.

The Inspector followed me to the door and placed his hand on my shoulder.

"Look after yourself, my dear boy," were his parting words.

George was waiting for me with a long face, when I got back to the shop. There was not a seat to be had in the house, at either performance that evening. Al Fischer and his Hotcha Club Boys were at the top of the bill, and it seemed that the cacophonous entertainment they had to offer had tickled the palates of Southmouth-by-the-Sea. I told George to let the matter slide for the moment and went upstairs to deal, rather belatedly, with the morning's post. I had been sitting at my desk some little time, when George came running up the stairs. He knocked on the door and then his face peered excitedly round it. If ever apathetic eyes like George's could pop out of his head, they were doing it then.

"What's up, George?" I asked mildly. "Is the place afire?"

"No, sir," he replied. "Her ladyship has sent along for a book and would like you yourself to pick it out."

"Right," I said, "I'll come down; but why, if it's not too personal a question, must you wear the expression of a startled prawn?"

"*Have a good look at her when you go down!*" said George in a whisper that must have echoed round the Square.

George's advice was usually worth following, so I did have a good look at her when I went down. The female in question was apparently one of the maids from the Grange: a rather florid young person of about twenty-two, in every way coarse-textured, but certainly possessed of a vulgar brand of 'IT'. She was the type of girl a sailor has one of in every port, if you understand me. In ten years, she would be completely unattractive and—what's the word?—blowzy.

"What kind of book does her ladyship want?" I asked her. "Is it for herself?"

"No, it's for 'is lordship," she answered in a voice that even now was a little harsh. "'E's just getting over a nasty quinsy and wants something to cheer 'im up, it's left 'im that low."

"What about *The Tribulations of Monty,* sir?" suggested George, who had followed me down the stairs.

"Is that comic?" she asked. "'Er ladyship said not to get 'im a comic book, but 'e likes anything of Jessica Matlock's."

Inwardly deploring his lordship's ghastly taste in literature, I took down from the romance shelves Miss Matlock's latest saccharinic splurge and handed it to her, expressing, at the same time, the hope that his lordship would enjoy it. When she had gone, I looked at George.

"Well," I said, "I had a good look at her—and now what?"

"Do you know who that was, sir?" He asked.

"One of your old flames?" I suggested.

"No, sir. That was Maggie Wood."

"What, Didcott's *inamorata?* But I understood that she'd left the Grange?"

"So she did, sir. She went to Portsmouth. I suppose her ladyship has taken her back. I don't expect Didcott will be too pleased. Portsmouth is a nice long way away from Paulsfield and Meanhurst isn't."

I went back to my office, but I had not worked for five minutes before George came upstairs again, this time with an envelope in his hand. He said that Harwood had just delivered it and was waiting for a reply. I tore it open and found inside two stall tickets for the second house at the 'Empire.' There was also a scribbled note: "Give them back to Harwood if you have already fixed up, H.C." I hurriedly wrote a few lines of thanks, which George took down to Harwood.

★ ★ ★ ★

I do not care much for the second house at a music hall. The place seems stale. The smell of cheap tobacco smoke lingers and the floor is littered with crumpled cellophane and toffee-papers. The attendants certainly make an attempt to tidy things up, but there is very little time. Even the performers seem to have a Now-we've-got-to-go-through-it-all-again air. But so intent was I that evening upon banishing dull care that I did not pay much attention to such little matters as that. The seats the Inspector had booked for us were in the middle of the fourth row of the stalls; and I murmured into Molly's ear, when we had taken up our positions in the rapidly filling auditorium:

"How was the miracle worked?"

"I got lost in a fog by Cowhanger Hill ..." she began demurely.

"I mean the other miracle," I interrupted her. "These seats. George 'phoned up early this morning and there wasn't one to be had in the whole house. Yet at midday your uncle sends along tickets for two of the best seats in the place."

"Uncle holds the Southern England Championship for string-pulling," she smiled. "He probably arranged for the people who originally booked these seats to be arrested for suspected felony against the Larceny Act, 1916!"

"You have the Law at your fingers' ends!" I laughed.

"It's in the family," said Molly.

The lights were lowered and the indicator to the side of

the stage switched from '1' to '2', a practice which always inspires in me a feeling of resentment, that the overture and the intermission should be numbered amongst the turns.

The show, like the egg of Du Maurier's curate in *Punch*, was good in parts, and most of the jokes were as old as that one—not that that prevented the man next to me, who seemed to be alone, from expressing loud and almost continuous amusement. A woman trapeze artist swung through the air, not, perhaps, with the greatest of ease, but certainly with the most fixed of smiles; while a man, probably her husband, but possibly her son, stood on the stage below making encouraging noises, but doing very little else. He might have been there in case she fell, but what he proposed to do about it if she did, I was at a loss to see.

Then a conjurer did some of those inexpressibly tedious tricks, wherein green handkerchiefs turned to red and a watch borrowed from a confederate in the audience is placed under one hat on a flimsy little table to one side of the stage, and is discovered a moment or two later, to the *utter amazement* of everybody, under another hat on an equally fragile table to the other side of the stage. The Miraculous Magician concluded his act by catching pigeons, that appeared apparently from nowhere, in a species of butterfly-net—and if those wretched birds hadn't been previously forced into the hollow shaft of the net, I'll forswear my evening tankard of Southmouth brew. It is all done, they tell us, by kindness!

At the end of the first half, Al Fischer and his Hotcha Club Boys met with a warm reception. Being, as they were, a dance-band, they followed the example of such other dance-bands as "do the halls" and concentrated on the more popular pieces of classical music, condescending to play jazz—if that word is not now demoded—only in the guise of a concert arrangement, by which "She's My Cutie on the Q.T." was made to sound like something Wagner wrote *entre deux vins*. After working himself into a quite unnecessary fever-heat over "Orpheus in the Underworld", Al came gasping to the footlights and said:

"Ladies and gentlemen *puff-puff*, you are to have the opportunity of seeing later this evening that world-famous song-writer and comedian, Jimmy Stevano *puff-puff*. I have the pleasure to announce *puff-puff* that our next number has been composed specially for us by Jimmy Stevano. Ladies and gentlemen *puff-puff*, 'Yearning For You'!"

It was a more or less commonplace little ballad, almost indistinguishable from the hundred or so songs of the same name. The refrain, as I remember it, went something like this:

> "Yearning for you,
> Yearning for you,
> Why am I so
> Terribly blue?"

That was not all, of course. There was the usual "Dreaming about you, can't do without you" formula in the middle and it finished up, with a masterpiece of virtuosity, "burning and yearning for you."

Three strapping young fellows clustered round a microphone and their emasculated voices roared the beautiful words at us through loudspeakers—a modern refinement that left me cold. The trio concluded this part of the performance by the largest of them tripping over the wire that led from the microphone to the wings—a mishap that usually accompanies the employment of a microphone on the stage.

Stevano, "in some of the songs that made him famous," was the last turn but one in the second half of the programme. After the custom originally set by B.B.C. dance-bands and later followed by individual artists, the orchestra played "Yearning For You" As Stevano's "Signature" tune; and to the accompaniment of a small amount of spiritless applause,

Jimmy Stevano walked on to the stage. For a comedian, his appearance was hardly calculated to inspire mirth in the Great British Public. He did not wear a funny hat or big boots. He didn't even have a red nose. He wore a dinner-jacket and was carrying a baby—a most extraordinary baby, as we were to find out.

"Ladies and gentlemen," he said, "I propose to sing you tonight some of the old songs I used to sing with the 'Bantams'."

The whole joke was, of course, that he didn't. It was the baby. He could not get rid of it. The back-cloth depicted a street and he tried to place the infant on the various items portrayed—a coster's barrow, the tail-board of a lorry and so on. When he attempted to hang it on a lamp-post, it dropped to the floor and bounced up again into his arms. He endeavoured to pass it over to someone in the wings, but it came sailing back through the air at him. He had a whispered conversation and the back-cloth was changed for another representing a nursery. And so it went on. It all sounds very silly, I expect, in cold print, but actually it was one of the funniest performances I have ever seen.

At last he seemed to become reconciled to the awkward encumbrance of the child and came forward. The orchestra, who had been patiently striking up various of his old tunes—"The Week That Aunt Eliza Came To Stay" and "I Like My Potatoes Cooked In Their Jackets"—only to be stopped after a few bars by Stevano's renewed attempts to dispose of the baby, now began "Yearning for You" and it wasn't until then that the full force of the song became apparent. There was something indescribably funny in this expression of an ardent desire for the company of one person, while being driven to the point of frenzy by his unsought close attachment to a second.

When he reached the "burning, yearning" point in the ballad, he flung out his arms in futile appeal to his far-away sweetheart and allowed the baby to fall to the floor, from where it sprang back, like a tennis ball, into his unwilling embrace. I thought, at this point, that the man next to me was going into hysterics, while Molly, to my other side, was helpless with laughter.

Molly hummed "Yearning for You" all the way to her home; and it was running through my head, as the train took me back to Paulsfield. The man who followed me into the compartment was crooning it gently to himself. I recognized him as the man who had been my neighbour in the 'Empire'. As I got ready for bed, I treated myself to my own vocal version of the tune and, as I am no singer, it was, perhaps, for the best that I was alone. I switched the light out over my bed and settled down between the sheets. The words were not very difficult to remember. "Yearning for you, yearning for you, why am I so soon there'll be two" ...That last line wasn't right, but it seemed to be familiar. Wasn't it from the Ten Little Nigger Boys? The big bear hugged one and then there were two. . . . Once there was one, soon there'll be two. I began it again. "Yearning for you, murder in blue . . ."

I sat up suddenly in bed.

Murder in blue! I had forgotten that confounded bit of doggerel. How well it fitted that tune. "Written specially for us by Jimmy Stevano." Jimmy Stevano. The husband of Mrs. Stevens. . . . "Running after Didcott" . . ."but Johnson had nothing to do with Mrs. Stevens, Doctor." . . . "Hadn't he, by Jupiter!" "Murder in blue, Murder in blue. Once there was one, soon there'll be two". . . . Once there was one murder in blue. . . . Soon there will be two. . . ."What about your sweetheart in blue now?"

It was cold sitting up in bed, so I lay down again, with food for thought. I had felt sleepy a few minutes before, but I was wide awake now. I'd start right at the beginning and see how it worked out.

Didcott had been intimate with Mrs. Stevens and so, according to Dr. Weston, had Johnson. If he hadn't, of course, the theory was not a very strong one. But assume that Didcott and Johnson had both been friendly with Mrs. Stevens, and Stevens had found out all about it. Mrs. Stevens had admitted to me that her husband knew of her associations with Didcott. I would assume that he also knew about her affair with Johnson. With this knowledge, he plotted revenge on the two of them. He knew of their Sunday evening ride together. He knew, too, that there had been trouble between them and that if one were killed and there were a belief that the murderer wore a constable's uniform, the other man would fall under suspicion.

Though, after the cutting of the new road, there was very little traffic along the Burgeston road, it was not nearly so safe an environment for homicide as the little lonely lane that led to Hazeloak. So Johnson was fixed upon as the victim. George had propounded a theory as we had walked back together to Paulsfield the previous morning. It seemed to fit Stevens's case very snugly. There were, of course, one or two little matters that were still not clear. There was, for instance, something a bit strange about those two bicycles. Johnson had certainly ridden the police machine and Stevens (assuming, naturally, that he was the murderer) had nearly as certainly ridden the other, which, I had every reason to believe, had originally been in the hands of Frederick Walker. But Stevens could just as easily have come by a bicycle with Walker's transfer imprinted upon it, as he could by a library-book in one of my 'Voslivres' dust-jackets. The real question was: why were the bicycles confused? It must have been a mistake on Stevens's part, as, for the proper working of his plan, no machine other than Johnson's should have been connected with the murder. If Stevens had wanted suspicion to be directed against Didcott, every trace of the presence of a third man should have been removed: the bicycle replaced in its shed or wherever it was normally kept, the constable's uniform destroyed or otherwise disposed of, together with the hitherto unidentified weapon that had been used to kill Johnson.

Yes, I thought, it could only have been Stevens's carelessness, the same carelessness as had caused him to leave the constable's kit lying in the pond, to be discovered sooner or later by accident or by the investigation of the police. He may, of course, have intended to remove such incriminating evidence when a favourable opportunity arose. But a favourable opportunity, I reminded myself, *did* arise, for had I not the Inspector's assurance that Johnson's bicycle had been thrown into the pond *after* he had examined it on the Monday morning and *before* it froze over the same night? If Stevens had been able to throw the bicycle into the pond, he had surely had an equal chance to fish out and carry off with him the constable's kit? Of course, it would have been very difficult to give a convincing explanation if he were caught with it in his possession. No, perhaps he had acted for the best, but one thing was certain: if Stevens had murdered Johnson, he had made a very grave mistake in leaving to be discovered by Johnson's body the bicycle that he himself had ridden.

There was another point, too. Was it not extremely likely that Johnson would identify Stevens when they spoke together on the Hazeloak road? But there Stevens's acting ability would have stood him in good stead. With the collar of his cape pulled up round his ears, a false moustache and an assumed voice, he might have been quite unrecognizable.

I thought about the uniform. Where had Stevens obtained that? One doesn't find one hanging on every tree. The Inspector had spoken of the unusual things about it: the *gendarme's* buttons, the numbers that did not agree. Then I suddenly saw the whole thing clearly.

That uniform was a stage "Prop". Actors in dramatic performances are not allowed by law to wear exact copies of uniforms, so the details are altered. Little inaccuracies in the way of contradictory numbers and wrong buttons are never noticed from the auditorium. That seemed to explain that. Nobody could be in a better position to lay his hands on a property constable's uniform than a man who was in the profession. Stevens might once have used it for a patter song: "Tramping On A Beat Plays Old Harry With Your Feet," or something of that kind.

I heard a clock strike one and decided that it was time I gave over this idle speculation and settled down to sleep. One thought did occur to me, as I turned over on my side. If Stevens's plot was against Didcott and Johnson, why was *I* singled out as the second victim?

XIII. THE SECOND DEATH

When I saw Mrs. Hendon the next morning, she told me that she had taken a new lodger. Only for a few weeks, she said, and she hoped it wouldn't inconvenience me. He was using one of the rooms on the top floor and seemed, she added, a respectable sort of chap. I said that I was only too pleased; and taking, as one does, a keen interest in my fellow guest, I asked her what he did for a living.

"He's something to do with newspapers," said Lizzie.

"That covers a multitude of sins!" I laughed. "Does he sell them or does he merely write for them?"

Lizzie confessed that she did not know.

"He's just finishing his breakfast downstairs in the kitchen," she added, "and you'd better be getting on with yours or you'll be late at the shop."

I obediently repaired to the other room, where my meal was waiting under a cover. I was glad to see that there was no letter for me. The previous day's mail had held enough unpleasantness for one week. I glanced at the *Daily Standard*. International relationships were still strained, so *that* was all right. Then one of the headings caught my attention—and held it. This is what it said:—

"ACTOR'S SWAN-SONG
DEATH OF WELL-KNOWN COMEDIAN"

"Mr. Jimmy Stevano, the famous comedian and seaside entertainer, was run over and killed last night by the midnight express from Southmouth-by-the-Sea to London. The tragedy occurred at the northern mouth of Burgeston tunnel and it is believed that Mr. Stevano fell from above at the moment when the express emerged from the tunnel.

"The body was almost unrecognizable, but has since been identified by the dead man's widow. On the line a brown-paper parcel was found. This contained a child's doll of unusual construction and heightens the tragicalness of his death, as it was with the assistance of this same little toy that Mr. Stevano made last night at the Southmouth 'Empire' Theatre a triumphant return to the music-hall stage that has not seen him for many years.

"It was on his way back from his first-night success that Mr. Stevano met his death. He caught a train from Southmouth to Paulsfield and set out from there to walk to the little village of Burgeston, three miles from Pauls-field, where he resided. At a distance of approximately a mile from Deeptree Corner, which is now associated in the public mind with the recent mysterious murder of Police-constable Johnson, the railway line tunnels under the Romp; and it was at this point that Mr. Stevano must have left the road, for some reason that has not, as yet, been established. The police are following up a clue that may throw some light on the tragedy.

"Jimmy Stevano, whose real name was Frank Stevens, was born at Brighton in 1891. Even in his early years, he hankered after the stage and his father, who was employed by what was then the London, Brighton and South Coast Railway, had to bring strong pressure to bear upon the boy before he would take up a position with Messrs. Willis & Thavery, the well-known firm of chartered accountants. After four months in their employment, young Frank slipped away from home and, after some difficult months, managed to get a job with a pierrot troupe, who were appearing at that time in Torquay. That was the beginning of his career. Before ten years had gone by, he was one of the most famous comedians on the South Coast. The West End never saw him, but many Londoners will remember his cheery voice calling out his celebrated catch-phrase "How are things at home?" on every pier in South England."

I put the paper down. So that was that. It looked more like suicide than an accident. If he were walking from Paulsfield, he would not be likely to leave the road on an impulse and climb to the top of the entrance to the tunnel, to enjoy the spectacle of the midnight express making its roaring exit from the hole below. There was no bridge or anything of that kind across the line. The tunnel just bored through the Downs after the line had run for a hundred yards or so through a cutting. The brickwork round the mouth of the tunnel rose to meet the grass of the Downs and the top of it was a couple of feet wide. An easily scaleable—and, to my mind inadequate—wooden fence was fixed a yard from the brink and followed the sloping wall of brickwork that flanked each side of the line. A short way away, on the other side of the Burgeston road, was the entrance to the Coppice footpath. I think I have mentioned this before.

It seemed to me that the excitement of the evening that preceded his death had proved too much for Stevens. He may have felt that he could not keep it up and that, before long, drink would again get a hold on him. Perhaps, even, he was already in its clutches when he fell under the wheels of the express.

Then there was another thing. Johnson. I remembered the case I had worked out in bed the night before. Perhaps Stevens had been prompted to kill himself either by conscience or, which is almost the same thing, the fear of being found out. But if my theory was correct, Didcott should have been the next to go—or even myself. It was only the previous morning that I had received the "Murder in blue" letter, which suggested that, at the time it was sent, it was the intention of the murderer to carry out another killing and it seemed hardly likely that the person of whose impending death he was considerate enough to send out an advance notice should be himself.

As I came downstairs after breakfast, Mrs. Hendon came

out into the hall.

"A policeman called this morning, Master John," she said, "and asked with the Inspector's compliments, who'd phoned from Southmouth, if you'd be so kind as to call in at the police station on your way to the shop."

Over her shoulder, I caught sight of a man sitting reading a paper at the kitchen table. It was the loud-laughed fellow who had sat next to me at the 'Empire.'

"Right-ho," I said, pulling myself together with an effort.

It was barely nine o'clock when I arrived at the police station, but Inspector Charlton was already there. He was calm and unruffled, and greeted me with a smile.

"Good-morning, Inspector," I said. "You must have got up early this morning."

"I haven't been to bed," he admitted with a wry grin. "I take it you have read your paper?"

"About Stevano? Yes. A nasty business. I little thought, when I watched his clowning at the 'Empire' last night, that in less than two hours he would be dead. Was it suicide?"

"Everything points that way," the Inspector answered with a nod. "He was seen walking from the station with his brown-paper parcel and was later observed, apparently sober, going at a pretty sharp pace along the Burgeston road. He must have fallen from above the tunnel a split second before the train came out. The driver and fireman saw nothing at all. What was left of the poor devil was discovered at about twelve forty-five by the guard of a goods-train."

"Was he badly smashed up?"

"Almost unrecognizable. His wallet and the property doll put us on the track. Didcott rang me up at my home and I came straight over. I was just about to get some well-earned sleep when the story broke, as the newspapermen say."

"Speaking of reporters," I said, "somebody must have put in some snappy work, for a death discovered at a quarter to one a.m. to be reported at some length in the morning papers?"

"Some free-lance picked up the story, I expect," said the Inspector indifferently, "and 'phoned it straight through."

"I wonder if it was my landlady's new lodger," I said.

"They tell me," said the Inspector, disregarding my remark, "that Stevens was in good form at the 'Empire' last night. 'A victorious come-back,' as the *Morning News* puts it."

"It was," I agreed, "In every way. Nothing at all, really, in the whole act, but extremely funny and certain to have replaced his name on the top line. It was refreshing to find a comedian who relied almost entirely on mime and not upon his patter-writer's aptitude at *double entendre*. He had the whole house laughing."

"Hardly a reason for *felo de se.*"

"I thought the same thing. Which reminds me of another idea that has occurred to me. It's only a random suggestion, Inspector, but have you explored the possibility of Stevens being mixed up in the Johnson murder?"

"You can bet your ultimate half-crown I have!" He laughed. "And I'm perfectly certain that he was. At first, I was at a loss to understand why Stevens should have murdered Johnson. I thought that, as Johnson and Didcott were much alike in build, Stevens might have killed the wrong man by mistake. That might have been feasible if Stevens had come upon Johnson suddenly and murdered him in hot blood, but, if Walker's evidence goes for anything, the slayer and his victim were together far too long for Stevens not to notice that his companion was not Didcott, but Johnson."

"But if what Dr. Weston told me was correct . . .?"

"You certainly gave me furiously to think yesterday morning," smiled the Inspector, "when you told me that, according to the Doctor, Johnson had been picking flowers in Jimmy Stevano's garden."

"I made out quite a convincing case against Stevens last night," I said, "on the assumption that Mrs. Stevens had carried on affairs with Didcott *and* Johnson. This would have been a very excellent reason for Stevano to kill them both and would give point to the 'Murder in blue' letter that was sent to me."

"That was sent to *you*" murmured the Inspector.

"Let's leave that for the moment," I suggested. "Once there was one: Johnson. Soon there'll be two: Johnson and Didcott. The case against Didcott was not sufficiently strong to convict him for Johnson's murder, so other means had to be employed. Hence the letter."

"Sent by the man you suspect of murdering Johnson and planning to murder Didcott: by a man who committed suicide before his job was done."

"I don't suggest that Stevens did write that letter."

"But he did," said the Inspector calmly. "Have a look at this."

He produced from the drawer of the desk at which he sat a sheet carelessly torn from a penny note-book, and handed it to me. I read:—

"This is the best way. Break the news gently to M. I think she will understand."

It was neither signed nor initialled. The Inspector passed me a second paper. It was the "Murder in Blue" note. I compared the two and found that the writing was identical, except that the message was a little shakier, as if written under stress of emotion.

"That was in Stevano's pocket," the Inspector explained, "when they picked him up on the line."

"They're both in the same writing," I agreed, "but is it Stevano's writing?"

"Yes. I have compared them with the odds and ends in his desk at Burgeston. I'll send them up to Scotland Yard for expert comparison, but I'll stake my oath they were written by the same hand."

In parenthesis, while putting this story together, I have included all the facts. Nothing relevant has, or will be omitted, and I assure the reader that Johnson was not killed by some ill-disposed cousin of his from Kenya, who will appear fleetingly in the last chapter but one. One of these facts, I, John Rutherford, most definitely declare, was that the "Murder in blue" letter and the note found on Stevens's body were, as the Inspector was willing to swear, both written by the same hand—and that was the hand of Frank Stevens. Let that suffice.

"How is Mrs. Stevens taking it?" I asked the Inspector. "I assume that she is the M. mentioned in the note."

"I went there in the small hours," he answered, "And she was still waiting up for her husband, who'd forbidden her to leave the house. One would imagine that he would have liked her to be at the 'Empire', but perhaps he was afraid that things would go badly. She was tearful when I broke the news to her, as the letter had enjoined, gently; but she was not as distraught as a dutiful and loving wife ought to be. In spite of the note that I had shown her, she asked me three or four times whether I thought he had committed suicide. I answered evasively that the letter would suggest that he had. Finally she said, 'do you or do you not believe that my husband killed himself?' and I had to tell her that my position as a police officer forbade me to answer that question."

"May I venture to make the same enquiry?" I asked, greatly daring. "Do you really think he was murdered?"

"Yes, Rutherford," said the Inspector simply, "I do."

"Why?"

"Because he knew too much, in the same way as you know too much. It seems to me that Stevens knew something about Johnson's murder, but that his continued silence was being bought. Then he got to know that you were also a danger to the murderer, and, suspecting that your life was in immediate jeopardy, sent you a warning to look out for yourself, for which good-natured instinct he has paid with his life. You see, Rutherford, the trouble is that, although Stevens's knowledge was a source of peril to the murderer, he was well aware of his advantage and probably made full use of it: whereas your knowledge is hidden even from yourself, until some tiny incident or casual remark gives your memory a jolt. That is why you are a greater danger to Johnson's killer than I imagine Stevens was—until his ill-advised warning to you precipitated his departure from this vale of tears."

"I was beginning to hope," I admitted, "that Johnson's murderer was no longer interested in me: that the midnight express from Southmouth had settled the matter for good."

"Don't you believe it," said the Inspector earnestly. "You were the victim No. 2 mentioned in the letter, and the attack on you has only been deferred. Before the story of this crime is finished, Rutherford, there will be fine chapter dealing almost exclusively with an attempt, perhaps successful, to exterminate you—*unless* you can remember that one little thing that would lead to the murderer's arrest."

"I have told you all I know," I said a little wearily. "Forgive my frankness, Inspector, but I think you are exaggerating the seriousness of my position."

He took this very well.

"I assure you, my dear chap," he said, "that I am not. There is not the slightest doubt in my mind that Stevens sent you that letter because he wanted to warn you of an attempt on your life; and I can see no earthly reason why the man who murdered Johnson should want you out of the way, unless you know something that may lead to his arrest for that crime. How else can one account for the lake attack?"

"I believe that Stevens was responsible," I said stoutly. "There are one or two bits that don't fit and I'll willingly concede that, for some reason or other, I was a danger to him; but I firmly contend that he gave up his murderous designs on me and abandoned whatever plans he might have had against Didcott, and took the short cut to Valhalla. How else, if I may repeat your phrase, do you account for the letter found on his body? Didn't that suggest that he committed suicide?"

"It suggests it a bit too plainly. 'Break the news gently to M.' Is that the sort of dying wish that a man in Stevens's place would normally express? He wasn't particularly fond of his wife and he must have known that he was an ache in the cervical region to her; and that the one thing that she probably wished for more than anything else was to be shot of him."

"I suppose M. *was* Mrs. Stevens?"

"Her christian name is Mary," was all the Inspector said.

He lighted a cigarette.

"I think the best thing we can do," he went on, "is to let Stevens murder Johnson and then commit suicide. I'll carry on my investigations into both matters, but I'll try to give the general impression that I feel I am wasting my time. That may lull the murderer into a false sense of safety. *You* might mention casually here and there that you have reason to believe that I think Stevens murdered Johnson and then committed suicide. It may take the murderer's mind off you."

"I'll certainly do that," I agreed, as there came a knock on the door. The Inspector walked over and opened it. Martin stood outside.

"Dr. Weston's arrived, sir," he said. "Ask him to be good enough to wait a minute or two," said the Inspector, and he returned to his chair, leaving the door still open.

"As I was saying, Rutherford," he said in a far louder tone than he had previously been using, "he had every reason for doing it. As far as we can tell, his wife was on more than friendly terms with Johnson, the uniform we found in the pond was definitely a stage property and now, to get out of what promised to be a difficult position, he has bought himself a single ticket across the Styx."

"It sounds very convincing, Inspector," I answered. "Let's hope it's true."

"I shall just carry on, of course," he continued, "and go

through the usual police procedure, but I doubt whether we shall discover much more than we know at present. I shall probably be seeing you again soon?"

"I expect so," I agreed and accepted my dismissal, which was given with a wink.

"Ask Dr. Weston to come in, Martin," the Inspector called, as I walked down the passage, and, after greeting me with an affable smile, the Doctor went along into the Inspector's room and closed the door.

Martin and Harwood were both in the charge-room. "And how's Sergeant Martin this morning?" I asked.

"Nicely, thank you, sir, except for a twinge or two of lumbago. And how's yourself?"

I told him that I, too, was nicely. "And what do you make of the Stevens affair?" I said.

"'Arwood and I were just chatting about it," Martin answered, "and we've come to the conclusion that 'e did away with 'isself."

"That's what it looks like to me," I agreed, not so much because the Inspector had asked me to continue on those lines, as because that was what I still did think. "And I've got a sneaking feeling," I went on, "that a prominent member of the Downshire County Constabulary is of the same mind."

"'Arwood's suggested ..." Martin began, but the constable cut him short. "That's all right," Martin reassured him, "Mr. Rutherford ain't the talking kind. 'E's just suggested to me, Mr. Rutherford, that Stevens wasn't at home knitting 'imself a pullover the night Johnson got bumped off."

"Frankly," I said, "I've been toying with the idea myself. The only thing that doesn't seem clear is the motive."

"The vengeance of a houtraged 'usband, Mr. Rutherford."

"I have it on good authority, Sergeant," I said, reminding him tactfully of his remarks to the Inspector the day before,"—on *extremely* good authority, that Johnson was not acquainted with a certain lady. I can't understand why this rumour persists."

"It may only be a rumour, sir," broke in Harwood, "but it would explain a lot if it was true. Stevens, so the story goes, was a funny-tempered chap and I should think 'e was quite capable of killing anybody 'oo interfered with 'is wife."

"*She* was the cause of all the rumpus," said Martin heatedly. "She raised merry Hades with poor old Did—with another chap we all know. Told 'im she was single and led him right up the garden—and then when 'e discovered that there was a fence at the bottom and not being a chap to climb fences like that, tried to . . ."

"Retire gracefully," I prompted, when he hesitated, "that's it, Mr. Rutherford—tried to gracefully retire," brutally splitting the infinitive that I had finically avoided, "She makes it damned awkward for 'im and then gets 'im all mixed up in a sticky mess like a fly in a spider's web."

The subject of our discussion came in just then and the Sergeant went on, "Still, it's not so bad for the time of the year. Well, Didcott, did you warn 'im?"

"Yes, Sergeant," smiled Didcott," 'e said he was sorry, but 'e hadn't thought about it."

"About time 'e did think about it," retorted Martin. "Leaving the blessed thing in a place like that. It only wanted another car to come round the corner and there'd 'ave been the devil to pay."

"Good-morning, Mr. Rutherford," Didcott smiled at me. He seemed to be in the sunniest of tempers, like a rather mature hen, which has laid something extra special in the way of double-yolks. In many ways, he was very much like a hen.

I met several people I knew on my way to the shop and stopped to chat with some of them. Nobody would speak of any other thing than Stevens's death; and there was obviously the widespread belief that it was he who had murdered Johnson. Previous to that day, I had heard no one connect his name in any way with the murdered constable. It must have been his own sudden end in a way that suggested suicide, that had aroused the general suspicion that he was responsible for the crime. It was the fixed opinion of all of them that Johnson had been intimate with Mrs. Stevens. Dr. Weston stopped his car by me in the High Street and leant out. His talk with the Inspector must have been short.

"It seems that I was barking up the wrong tree," he said, without any preliminary salutation. "Stevens's suicide explains it all. About the best thing he ever did, except for 'The Week That Aunt Eliza Came To Stay'."

With that, he left me.

George, naturally, was agog when I got to 'Voslivres'.

"It's proof positive, sir," he said excitedly, "and just about clinches my own theory. Who was in a better position than he to lay his hands on a constable's stage uniform and who had better reason than he did?"

"You have the satisfaction of knowing that you agree with no less exalted a person than Detective-inspector Charlton—or so I believe," I told him.

"I thought we should eventually be of the same mind," said George complacently.

★ ★ ★ ★

It was eight-thirty that evening. 'Voslivres' had been shut up at seven o'clock, George had gone home, probably to bore his family to distraction with his talk about Johnson and Stevens, and I had come back to Thorpe Street and given my attention to the chop, apple-tart and cheese that Lizzie placed before me. The fire in my sitting-room was blazing away cheerily, and a couple of hours with a book and my old briar seemed a pleasant prelude to bed. I don't often read detective-stories, but something had prompted me to take one from my shelves just before I closed the shop. I can't remember exactly what it was called, but I know it had the word "Murder" In the title, which seems to me such a good idea for a crime-book. You know, when you see the name, exactly what you are getting, whereas, if a thriller is called *Low Tide, The Eighth Heaven* or *Salmon and Shrimp,* you tend to pass it over in favour of *The Greenhouse Murder* or *Murder Hath No Tongue,* in spite of the fact that it is more likely than not a more exciting and better-written story. Mr. S. S. Van Dine, whose painstakingly scholarly detective-stories are well-known on both sides of the Atlantic, must realize this, for the title of every one of his books that I have read contains the word "Murder," not in various combinations, but always in the same form—*The Greene Murder Case, The Benson Murder Case, The Dragon Murder Case,* and so on.

I wonder whether you would be reading this book now, if I had not called it *Murder in Blue?*

But I said that it was eight-thirty and I had settled down with my pipe and a book in an easy-chair before the fire. The only thing wanting, I thought, was to have in the chair on the other side of the fire, a certain brown-haired young lady with a tip-tilted nose, who would probably refuse to go up to bed until she had finished her own book. But that, I was optimistic enough to hope, would come later. Between ourselves, it has.

My quiet evening was not to be. I had just started the third chapter and was beginning to grasp which character was which, when Mrs. Hendon tapped on the door.

"There's a man downstairs, Master John," she informed me when I had told her to come in, "who wants to see you. Something about milk, he says, and if you don't like what I give you, you ought to tell me and not be getting somebody else to bring it!"

"My dear Lizzie," I consoled her, "I have no complaints to make about the way you feed me, except that you overestimate my capacity by roughly three hundred per cent. I have never asked any man to see me about milk. Please be good enough to convey to him my compliments and say that we are already in touch with a most obliging and public-spirited cow."

Lizzie laughed and went downstairs, but was up again in a few moments.

"He doesn't want to see you about milk," she explained. "That's his name."

"Milk?" I said, with half my mind still on my book. "Milk? Oh, Milke, with an 'e'. Yes, I remember the man now. What does he want? Ask him to come up, anyway, confound the fellow!"

Milke came up, looking extremely uncomfortable and apologetic.

"Good evening, Mr. Rutherford," he said timidly. "I'm sorry to trouble you, sir, like this, but I've got something to tell you—something important."

"Sit down," I invited him, "and let's hear it. Will you have a cigarette?"

He took one from the box I held out to him.

"You probably remember me, sir," he said. "Milke's the name. I was in the 'Queen's Head' the other evening when you were there and I was out at the pond, day before yesterday, when they found the uniform."

"And were also having a few friendly words with a gentleman at the football match on Saturday?"

"That's right, sir," he said eagerly. "I showed him what was what, didn't I? Saucy sausage, that's what 'e was, sir!"

"You certainly had the last word! Now, what is it you want to tell me?"

I wanted to be rid of the quaint little fellow and get back to my book.

"Well, sir, I ain't got what you might call a regular job. I work spasmodically, as you might say. Sometimes I pick up a bit of gardening, sometimes it's minding cars, sometimes it's taking round circulars. Any old thing, I always say, as long as it'll bring in a copper or two. People are kind to me, too, sir. They help me to keep the wolf from the door, in a manner of speaking. Dr. Weston give me this 'ere overcoat."

"That was very nice of him," I said patiently.

"Well, sir," he went on, "as I was saying, people give me things, though sometimes it's only because they ain't got no use for them themselves—and what's more, I ain't got no use for them neither. I take 'em, of course, sir, not wanting to 'urt no feelings or give offence, so to speak."

"Very thoughtful of you," I smiled, still patiently.

"Well, sir"—he seemed to begin most of his remarks like that—"Well, sir, everybody's saying now that Mr Stevens knew more than he ought to about that constable what was murdered."

"It seems to be the popular belief," I agreed, "although I don't know whether there is any truth in it. Someone must have started the story this morning."

"That's what I came to tell you about, sir," said Milke, leaning eagerly forward. "I pops about 'ere and there, doing odd jobs for people and as I said, now and again they slip me something besides the money I've earned by the sweat of me brow, as the saying goes—a coat or some socks or an old pair of trahziz. Well, sir, the other day I did a bit of gardening—clearing up dead leaves and the like—for old Mrs. Gorse. You know 'er? Mrs. Gorse of 'Azeloak? You don't? She's not a bad old stick, sir, but a bit near, as you might say. Always gives me just what I'm entitled to and not a brass farthing more. But after I'd finished this job, when I told 'er that I'd better be getting along to my tea—an 'int that she's never taken since I first set eyes on 'er—she told me that she 'ad something down the cellar that I might do with. I thought it might be a bottle or two of beer and said 'What-oh' or polite words like it. I always 'ave the feeling, you know, sir, when people say they've got something I might do with, that it's going to be a bit of all right, but it never is. 'Ave you found it like that, sir?"

I thought the wretched little fellow never was going to reach the point.

"Many times, Mr. Milke," I agreed. "It is one of the most melancholy facts of life. You say that Mrs. Gorse offered you something?"

"That's right, sir. She took me down into the cellar and, 'there it is,' she says, 'over in the corner.' You'll never believe what it was, sir!"

"Well?" I asked, restraining the impulse to throw something at him.

"A pile of scrap iron, sir! Something I could do with! I thanked 'er very much when I got me breath back and, not wanting to put 'er out at all, picked up two or three bits, which was about all I could carry. 'You can probably make use of the fire-grate,' she says. 'That's what *you* say,' I says to meself, and gets out of the 'ouse with me irksing burden as soon as I could. I tramped back along the road to Paulsfield with that cargo of ironmongery, sir, until I was fit to drop. Then I says to meself, 'Milke,' I says, 'this ain't good enough. What'll you be getting out of this but back-ache?' I says. So I drops it on the grass by the side of the road and makes to go on without it. 'But supposing they finds it,' I says to meself, 'and old Mother—and Mrs. Gorse gets wind of it? What then?' So I takes it all through the gate just near where I was and pitches it into a pond—*the* pond, if you understand me, sir."

"That must have been the stuff that was found on top of the uniform," I said.

"It *was* on top, wasn't it, sir? I mean there's no doubt about it?"

"None whatever," I confirmed. "The scrap-iron was holding the uniform down in the mud."

"Well, sir, that's what I've come to see you about. Did I ought to tell Inspector Charlton?"

"Go and see him, by all means," I said, "but I really can't see how your evidence is of any great importance. The uniform was there in the pond and you came along and threw some old iron on top of it, where it was later found by the Inspector. He might like to know, of course. ..."

"Just a moment, sir," Milke timidly interrupted me, "what

I have been trying to get at is this: I threw that iron in the pond a week before Johnson was murdered!"

XIV. THE INSPECTOR GETS A NIBBLE

It took a couple of moments for it to sink in.

"Then the uniform couldn't have been worn by the murderer," I said at length.

"That's the way I look at it, sir," said Milke. "Ought I to tell the police, did you think?"

"Good Lord, yes!" I said excitedly. "It gives the whole case an entirely different aspect. If I were you . . ."

Here a doubt arose in my mind—two doubts, in fact. Firstly, the Inspector wanted it to get abroad that he believed Stevens had murdered Johnson and here was almost proof positive that he hadn't. What was it the Inspector had said on Sunday? 'Where is the sense in donning one disguise and then deliberately throwing duplicate items in a pond . . .?" Where was the sense, I now added, in Stevens masquerading as a constable, after having carefully deposited other garments in the pond a week before? Was it to the Inspector's advantage, then, for Milke to go round broadcasting what he knew? And secondly, did not the evidence that Milke could give in a court of law place his life in danger? I cut myself short, therefore, and instead of what I was about to say, I asked Milke a question that had some bearing on both these points: "Have you told anybody else what you have just told me?"

"No, sir," he answered to my relief, "I ain't breathed a word to a soul."

"That's something," I said. "I strongly recommend you not to. The only person who must know is Inspector Charlton and it is of vital importance that he should be told as soon as possible. I don't want to frighten you, Mr. Milke, but I solemnly warn you that if your information reaches the wrong ears, your own life may not be worth a tinker's malediction."

"Cripes!" said Mr. Milke.

"There is a man not very many miles from here, Milke," I went on ruthlessly, "who will go *to any lengths* to cover up his trail. He has already given proof of that."

"By killing Mr. Stevens?" Milke almost whispered.

"And more," I said. "That uniform was placed in the pond for a certain purpose—possibly to implicate Stevens, but, in any case, to help conceal the murderer's own part in the affair; and if you can go into the witness-box and prove that it was firmly embedded in the mud and *sealed* by the scrap-iron that you threw on top of it before Johnson was killed, the murderer may feel that it would be better to *prevent* you from giving that evidence."

"Blind old Riley," muttered Milke. He was badly shaken.

"Did anybody see you come here this evening?" I asked.

"I don't know, sir," he said despairingly." 'Ow was I to know that things were as bad as you say? I just came to see you like as if I was slipping into the 'Queen's 'Ead' for a pint of wallop. All open and above board as the saying is."

"Listen," I said quickly. "You came to see me to ask if I could give you some work—you understand? You thought I might have some odd jobs for you to do about the shop. And I have engaged you. Is that clear? You report to me at the shop at nine o'clock sharp tomorrow."

"But, sir . . ."

"It doesn't matter," I persisted, "If you've another job on hand in the morning. Give it a miss. Go along to the 'Queen's Head' before they close tonight and drop a hint to anybody you know there that I've taken you on to help me for a week or two—to tide me over Christmas, say that. Behave as you usually do, but for heaven's sake don't talk about this other matter."

"Yes, sir," he said, his beautiful eyes looking at me like a dog's.

"I'll 'phone Inspector Charlton tonight and ask him to come round to my shop before lunch to-morrow—and then you can tell him all about it. In that way, nobody need know that you have spoken to him ... *What was that?*"

I had heard a noise outside the room. I softly went to the door and wrenched it open. Standing at the top of the staircase, at the other end of the landing, was Mrs. Hendon's new lodger.

"Good evening," he smiled, as he turned and went down the stairs. Which, of course, he had a perfect right to do, as everybody using the stairs had to cross the landing that connected my rooms. But it was strange that when I flung open the door, he was facing me. That wasn't the way downstairs.

I murmured "good evening" and reclosed the door.

"Now, Milke," I said in a low tone, "you'd better go. And don't forget—*keep your mouth shut.* I'll come down with you. When we get into the hall, thank me for engaging you."

Even the British working-men who read out their impromptu remarks in the B.B.C.'s *In Town Tonight* programmes speak in a more natural and unforced way than Milke did when I opened the front door.

"Thank you, sir," he intoned, "for engaging me. I am extremely grateful."

I mastered a desire to tear out my hair in great handfuls.

"That's all right, Milke," I said. "I'm glad you thought to come to me for a job. I've been looking round for some extra assistance for some time. You'll be at the shop, then, at nine o'clock?"

Which sounded, from where I was, even more flat and sing-song than Milke's ghastly effort. When I had closed the door after him, I called out:

"Lizzie! Do you know Mrs. Fawson's telephone number?"

Lizzie broke off what she was saying to her new guest, who was apparently having his supper, and pulled open the door, which had been ajar.

"I can't say as I do, Master John," she said. "Isn't she in the book?"

"They've only just been connected up," I explained. "She told George to ask me to ring her."

"Won't the Exchange get her for you?" She suggested.

"O wisest of women, I'll try that," I laughed, and went upstairs, having supplied a reason (with exemplary strategy, I flattered myself) for any tell-tale tinkle that might emanate from the bell on my landing, when I lifted the receiver to ring Inspector Charlton.

The maid answered the 'phone at the other end. She was sorry, but the Inspector was engaged. Would I like to speak to Miss Molly?

Would I like to speak to Miss Molly!

"Yes, please," I said, and in a few moments, I heard Molly's voice say, "Hullo, John!"

"Darling," I said, "we mustn't talk for long. I'll tell you why when I see you. Can you get your uncle to come to the 'phone for a minute. It's about J."

"No, Mr. John Rutherford," she answered definitely, "I can't. I sent him to bed half an hour ago and there he's going to stop. The old silly was up *all last night* chasing about the countryside without his woollen scarf."

"Madame's word is law," I said, "but do please ask him to come round without fail to 'Voslivres' in the mor—" my voice suddenly fell to an urgent whisper— "*hold on and don't take any notice of what I say!*"

I had heard a creak on the landing.

"I am sorry, Mrs. Fawson," I said audibly, but not too noticeably loudly, "but I am entirely in the hands of the wholesalers. I assure you . . ."

I laid down the receiver softly and crept towards the door.

". . .that I am doing all I can to hasten delivery and as soon as the book is in my hands . . ."

For the second time that evening I wrenched open the

door, but this time the landing was empty. I ran back and lifted the receiver.

"Hullo, my dear," I said.

"Have you gone completely haywire?" was Molly's amiable enquiry.

"I'm beginning to think I have," I said. "I'll explain later."

We rang off shortly after and I went out and hung over the banisters. I could hear Lizzie still in converse with the interesting young man who now shared our roof. By the fireplace in my sitting-room was a bell-push that I do not recall ever having used before. I pressed it now and heard the bell ring downstairs. Lizzie made her heavy way up the stairs.

"Lizzie," I said, "come in and close the door."

"Is anything wrong, Master John?" she asked anxiously.

"When I said good night to Milke, Lizzie, your new lodger—what's his name, by the way?"

"Bradfield."

"Bradfield was chatting with you in the kitchen. When I rang, he was still chatting with you. Did he leave the kitchen at all during that time?"

"Yes, Master John, about ten minutes ago, but he wasn't gone long. He came upstairs."

"Do you know why?"

"A lady don't ask questions like that, Master John."

"All right, Lizzie," I laughed, "let's leave it at that. "but don't let him know why I rang for you."

When I went to bed that night, I have to confess that I locked the door and, which is a more damning admission, securely fastened the window, under which extremely unhygienic conditions, I tried to get some sleep. I don't mind admitting that I was a bit rattled. Milke's news had affected me deeply. I had been convinced, despite all the Inspector had said, that Stevens had murdered Johnson and that, with his suicide the previous evening, all danger to myself had come to an end; but now I saw that the game was still on. It would not have been so bad if I had known what to expect and from which direction the danger would come. Had I known that it was John Smith or Dick Brown who meant me mischief, I should have been ready with a nifty little upper-cut to the chin when I saw his ugly face; but when my enemy was just Mr. A, who might turn out to be the milkman, the station-master at Bumbleby Junction or the man in the moon, I felt completely at a loss. There was nothing I could get my teeth into. Bulldog Drummond or the Saint would have thrived on the suspense and gone off to sleep like a baby, with a loaded revolver in a specially made hip-pocket in his pyjamas; but I had neither their devil-may-care temperaments nor their infinitely comforting weapons.

I thought for a long time about the man, Bradfield, until finally I fell into what our novelists call a troubled sleep.

★ ★ ★ ★

I was agreeably surprised to find that I was still alive when I awoke the next morning, and by the time that I had squeezed the tooth-paste on to my brush, was beginning to feel quite Bulldog Drummondish, not to say Saintly. It's wonderful what a power of comfort there is in the jolly old sun shining through the curtains and the smell of frying bacon creeping up from below.

When I got to 'Voslivres', something in the nature of an altercation was in progress. The contestants were George and Milke, who seemed to have survived the dangers of the night as successfully as I.

"I am sure," George was saying as I pushed open the door, "that Mr. Rutherford didn't say anything of the sort."

"Yes, he did," said Milke.

"No, he didn't," returned George.

"Yes, he did," riposted Milke.

"No, he didn't," retorted George.

"Yes, he did," I threw in swiftly, beating Milke, a pastmaster at this form of debate, by the shortest of heads.

It was only then that they condescended to notice me.

"Good morning, sir. Sorry, sir," said George hurriedly.

"George," I told him, "I have asked Mr. Milke to help us in the shop. Please show him how to put our special wrappers on that lot of books that came in yesterday."

"Certainly, sir," said George obediently and proceeded to carry out my instructions with what, in the circumstances, was a surprisingly good grace.

It was only a few minutes after nine o'clock, so I hardly expected Inspector Charlton to arrive for some little time; but I felt hardly in the mood to settle down to anything and wandered aimlessly around, taking books down from the shelves and putting them back again without looking at them. George and Milke were working together at the back of the shop.

"If you put them on that way," George said patiently, "The book will be upside down when you open it. Not," he added in a vicious undertone, which he thought I would not overhear, "That that would make much difference to you."

I smiled gently to myself and idly glanced at a row of books on the shelves to the right of the door. Something caught my eye. I looked at the other two, but they were paying no attention to me. I reached up to the shelf casually and then, with my hands pushed into my jacket pockets, I strolled over to the staircase that led to my office above. When I had got upstairs and was seated at my desk, I pulled my little find from my pocket. Why I adopted these conspiratorial methods can only be explained by the atmosphere of mystery in which I have recently been existing. I had reached the point when I expected my own shadow to leap up and bite me. That probably accounts, too, for my instantly connecting a perfectly innocent little thing, that might be found anywhere, with what would be called, if this were a thrilling piece of fiction and not a pedestrian recital of facts, the Terror In Our Midst.

"George," I said about half an hour later, "You had better go and get the car out. There's a good deal of stuff to be taken round this morning. Don't forget we close at one to-day."

To tell George that he had better get the car out was like telling a small girl that she had better have a strawberry ice, and he was off down the road to the garage where we kept the van before you could have said, "George Stubbings." By the time he had drawn up the van outside, I had selected enough of the new books for distribution in various far-flung parts of the neighbourhood to keep George occupied for most of the morning; and at a few minutes before ten o'clock, I sent him off. The whole thing was nicely timed, for soon after he had gone, Inspector Charlton walked into the shop.

"Milke," I said, "if any customers call, please come up and tell me."

"Anything fresh?" the Inspector asked, as he lighted the cigarette I had given him when we were seated in my office. "Sorry I wasn't up last night when you rang, but I had been sent to bed—not, I am glad to say, without any supper."

"That man downstairs," I said, "whose name is . . ."

"Milke," said the Inspector.

"How did you know that?" I asked.

"You said it yourself thirty seconds ago," he smiled.

"I had forgotten that," I laughed. "I thought that perhaps you know something about him already."

"I must admit that I know nothing," confessed the Inspector, "apart, that is, from the fact that he visited you last evening at eight-thirty."

"When you were in bed and sound asleep," I said to cover my surprise.

"When I was in bed," he amended, "but I am interrupting you . . ."

"He came to me yesterday evening with an astonishing yarn," I said, "which I'll leave you to hear from him. But before we go downstairs, I ought to tell you what steps I have taken. You asked me to spread the rumour that you believe Stevens murdered Johnson and you have impressed upon me that my life is in danger on account of some knowledge I possess, that might bring the murderer before a jury. What Milke has told me more or less proves that Stevens did *not* murder Johnson and also suggests to me that if his evidence becomes public property, his life will also be threatened."

"Very probably," agreed the Inspector.

"I have therefore taken elaborate precautions," I went on, "to ensure that you can speak to him without arousing any suspicious interest. To explain his visit to me last night, I have engaged him to work in the shop here, for which good deed, I shall have to pay forty shillings a week, to further the ends of justice! So that it is a perfectly natural thing for him to be here this morning and an equally natural thing for you to come round and visit me."

"Very well done, Rutherford," said the Inspector, "—and I mean that. Shall I talk to Milke up here?"

"Wouldn't it be better to do it in the shop?" I suggested. "I have sent my assistant out. If you talk to Milke up here, any casual customer—and I have grown to mistrust everybody—may think it strange that Inspector Charlton, who entered this imposing establishment a few minutes ago, has apparently incarcerated himself with the man whom Mr. John Rutherford, as the whole town knows by this time, has but recently engaged."

"True," the Inspector agreed, "whereas, if we examine Milke in the shop, should anyone come in, you and I can switch over our conversation to Dalton's Atomic Theory or the opinions of Pythagoras concerning wild-fowl."

"That, if I remember rightly," I added, "the soul of our grandam might haply inhabit a bird?"

"Exactly so," said the Inspector. "As I say, we can be discovered enlarging on some such topic as that, while Milke can quickly turn his attention to some little job or other."

"Could strategy go further?" I asked as I followed him down into the shop.

"Milke," I said, "this is Inspector Charlton, who wants to hear all that you told me last night. The Inspector is a busy man, so please make it as short as possible."

Milke tried to touch the hat that he wasn't wearing.

"Please carry on with what you were doing," I continued, "and don't be surprised if the Inspector and I suddenly start talking about something else. You will understand that it is essential that nobody besides ourselves should know that the Inspector has interviewed you."

The Inspector and I sat down and Milke busied himself with the books. It is not necessary to record the whole conversation that took place, as Milke merely retold his story as I had heard it the previous evening, although this time he was not so infuriatingly circumlocutory. When he had finished, the Inspector said:

"Are you married?"

"No, sir. I live with my sister. 5, Primrose Villas, just up near the station."

"I'll remember that. Now, take my advice—tell nobody of this, not even your sister. Keep your tongue from wagging and you'll probably get through this affair with a whole sk—I think you should consider yourself very fortunate to have got such a comfortable job."

The shop door had opened, to admit P.C. Chandler.

"But I don't expect," the Inspector went on casually to me, "that the idea appeals to your other assistant, young what's-his-name—the boy with the amazing hair and the equally startling command of our tongue. Well, Chandler, what is it?"

"Whitchester 'ave been on the 'phone for you, sir," said

Chandler woodenly. "I told them you would ring them back."

"Thanks, Chandler," the Inspector replied. "I shall be along at the station in a few minutes. Tell the Sergeant that I want to speak to him before I go back to Southmouth."

"Certainly, sir," said Chandler and left the shop.

"Now that you've finished with Milke, Inspector," I said, "I have something to show you. Will you come upstairs?"

When I had closed my office door behind us, I felt in my pocket and handed him a small penny note-book. He took it from me and opened it, obviously looking, as I had looked, for signs of a page torn out. It will be recalled that the message found on Stevens's body was written on a page ripped from such a book. It did not take him long to find what I had found—that the first page had gone, leaving a ragged edge behind.

"The plot thickens, Rutherford, my boy," he murmured, and produced from an envelope in his wallet the original note taken from Stevens's pocket.

He bent back the blue cardboard cover of the note-book, laid it flat on the desk and, whistling gently through his teeth, applied the left-hand edge of Stevens's note to the rough remnant still in the book. They fitted perfectly. Still whistling softly, he folded the page, replaced it in the envelope, slid the envelope into his wallet and put back the wallet into his breast-pocket.

"An extremely interesting little experiment, Rutherford," he said when this was done.

He carefully went through the pages of the note-book, but none of them had been written on. The whole thing was fixed together by two wire staples and it measured approximately four inches by six and a half. In the middle of the back cover was the impression of a rubber-stamp. This was oval in shape and had in the centre of it "Stationers & Printers," while round the edge was printed in ⅛"-letters, "B. E. Hornbill & Co., Ltd., 64 & 65, Corn St.,

Southmouth." In the top left-hand corner of the inside of the front cover was written in pencil "1d." The pages were ruled feint and there were no cash columns. If there was anything else about the book that I have failed to mention, I do not do so intentionally!

The Inspector laid the note-book on the desk and looked at me a little oddly.

"There's something vaguely nauseating about this case, Rutherford," he said. "The man who did those two brutal murders is as fiddle-faddlesome as an elderly spinster. I can always admire attention to detail, but this fellow doesn't know when scrupulosity ends and pernicketiness begins. Phil May could sketch a face in half a dozen bold strokes, while another craftsman, without his fastidious economy of line, might apply himself for a week to the same task and produce a study which, although photographic in fidelity, would fall far short of May's hurried scrawling on the back of a menu-card. Our murderer is like that other craftsman. If he wanted to murder Johnson why the devil didn't he smash in his skull and then quietly fade away? Oh, no—that was far too primitive! Instead of that, our homicidal friend must leave a selection of clearly marked trails, which were calculated to succeed each other in leading us in a dozen wrong directions, until finally the right path through this metaphorical jungle of ours had become so obscured by undergrowth that we should never find the beginning of it. Fortunately, Rutherford, we are crafty enough not to follow a trail that has been just a bit too painstakingly blazed for us."

"You think that this note-book is another blazed trail?" I asked.

"You have examined it thoroughly, I take it, and you have seen the page found on Stevens's body and what was written on it. In spite of that, don't you see anything funny about the whole thing?"

"The only thing funny about it, as far as I can see, is that I found it on my shelves. Stevens's note was written in it and the page hastily torn out—that much is clear. But how did it get where I discovered it?"

"If I knew that," said the Inspector, "my job would be finished, but there is one little thing about this book that suggests to me that it has been deliberately planted in your shop. The whole thing's a flam. Can't you imagine the murderer saying to himself, 'That Rutherford chap, he hadn't got much of an alibi. Why not slip the note-book into his shop? The chances are that that bonehead, Charlton, won't find it there, but I'll take a chance.'? He's a foolish fellow, Rutherford, who doesn't understand the value of simplicity. He probably doesn't realize that while he is laying a false trail, he is leaving behind him an authentic one. I don't expect Hornbill's will be able to give me anything useful in the way of information about this book. They're the biggest stationers in Southmouth and they must sell dozens of them. I'll follow it up, though. A much more interesting and profitable investigation would be into the question of how the book got on your shelf downstairs. That is our authentic trail: either the murderer or an accomplice has been into your shop."

"There's one thing I will vouch for," I said. "The book wasn't there last Saturday evening, because I had all the books down from that set of shelves and I would certainly have noticed it if it had been there."

"That's something," said the Inspector in a satisfied tone. "Do you think you could let me know who has been into the shop since then?"

"That's a bit of a tall order!" I laughed. "What with one thing and another, I haven't been at my post much recently, but I expect George can remember a good many of them . . ."

I stopped suddenly and looked at him enquiringly.

"I'm afraid we'll have to keep the egregious Stubbings out of it," he said. "This little business is between you and me and, to a certain extent, the lactonomial gentleman downstairs."

"There is another way that occurs to me," I said, "although it would not be very conclusive. A large percentage of my customers, as you know, are library subscribers. People do come in here, of course, to buy books, but most of my visitors come to borrow them. So if I run through my card-index, I shall know who has been in the shop. Some people, naturally, send servants to change their books, but it is quite possible that some interesting facts may emerge."

"It's a long chance . . ." the Inspector began, when we heard footsteps on the stairs. Milke knocked on the door.

"There's a man downstairs, sir," he told me, "Who says 'e wants to change 'is library book."

From the tone he used, one would have imagined that the man downstairs wanted to hire a rocket in which to shoot himself up to the moon, or some such out-of-the-way requirement as that.

The Inspector and I went down into the shop with Milke and, while I attended to the customer, the Inspector nodded to me and left. After he had gone, I remembered that there was one more thing I had to tell him about: the strange behaviour of Mr. Bradfield.

When George came back fifteen minutes later, I slipped round to the police station. There was a crowd outside when I reached it. After a bit of pushing, I managed to see what it was that exercised their attention. It was standing against the wall inside the iron-railed forecourt: the bicycle that I had ridden when I had brought tidings of Johnson's death to Paulsfield. Stuck on the wall beside it was a large hand-printed notice, which required any person who had any knowledge of the machine to report within to the Sergeant. I went inside and found Martin at his desk. He told me that Inspector Charlton had been in, but had left after making a 'phone call to Whitchester. He believed that he had gone to Lulverton.

"It doesn't really matter," I said, and then went on with a smile, "surely, Martin, the little exhibition that is attracting so much attention outside is a little out of the usual run of police procedure?"

"One of the Inspector's ideas," said Martin. "Says he won't be happy till 'e's found out the truth about that bike and reckons that's the quickest way of getting it."

"If the crowd gets much thicker," I laughed, "you'll have the police after you for obstructing the roadway—and you wouldn't like that, *would* you?"

On my way back to 'Voslivres', I decided that a little gentle sounding of George would not do any harm. So when I saw him I said:

"We don't seem to be doing much in the sales section lately, George. How do you account for that?"

"Oh, I don't know, sir," he replied. "Sales keep pretty steady."

"Only with our old customers," I said. "We don't get much new business. Take this week. How many customers have we had in who have not previously dealt with us? Not many, I'll wager."

"We've had a fair number, sir, and the Christmas trade will be coming along soon. There was a Mrs. Beeson on Monday evening. She comes from Bank Street and hasn't been here before. She wanted a school-story for her niece's birthday. Then there was old Mr. Cartwright, who asked us to get him *The Bible in Spain;* and Mr. Dawkins, from over the chemist's, ordered a book about birds."

"But did we do business with them all?"

"Yes, sir. I've put all the orders through. Miss Howson came in and asked about a book, but she couldn't wait while we got it for her. And Mrs. Stevens wanted some black-edged notepaper and envelopes. I told her we weren't stationers."

George said "stationers" as if theirs was one of those questionable trades that are laid bare so ruthlessly by the more popular sections of our Sunday Press. He then admitted that, as far as he could remember, that was all.

"Not too bad, George," I said. "I won't sack you, after all."

At one o'clock we closed the shop and I sent George and Milke off to their homes. Behind the pulled-down blinds, I set myself to the task of examining the card-index, after first jotting down the names that George had mentioned. Each of my books had a card, which was kept inside the cover when it was on my shelves. When the book was taken out by a subscriber, the card was removed, the date and name of the borrower noted upon it and filed away in a drawer until the book was returned. I had found the note-book on the shelf so early in the day, that I felt safe in assuming that no customer could have placed it there that morning. I was only concerned, therefore, with the books borrowed on the two previous days—the Monday and Tuesday. It did not take me very long to scribble down the names and, in order that it may not be said that I am withholding evidence, here they are:

Major Hislop.	Miss Dolden.
Miss McMurtry.	Miss Bush.
Miss Riddick.	Mrs. Campbell.
Master Underhill.	Dr. Weston.
Captain Blain.	Mr. Henry Symes.
Mrs. Morrison.	Major Plunkett.
Mr. Broadfield.	Mrs. Oakman.
Master Toleman.	Mrs. Greathurst.
Mr. John Symes.	Miss Wilkins.
Miss Dilks.	Mrs. Harrison.
Mrs. Wallington.	Colonel Hawtrey.
Miss Wood.	Mrs. Fawson.
Rev. A. Brewster.	Miss Smith.
Mr. Fleming.	

I made a fair copy of this list and added the names that George had given me. Then I slipped it into an envelope with one of my business compliments cards and addressed it. to the Inspector. When I handed it over to Martin on my way home to lunch, the bicycle had been removed from the forecourt of the building.

"Have you had a nibble, Martin?" I asked.

"We have," he answered.

XV.   THE LANGDON BROTHERS TALK

After I had finished my lunch, the Inspector called. Would I care for a run with him in the car? He thought—he only *thought,* I was to understand—that I might be popping into Southmouth for some reason or another, and he was just wondering whether I might like to drive with him to Whitchester and then go back home with him to tea. He was under the impression, from certain excitement he had noticed in the kitchen, that some cakes were being made. I replied in the same spirit that some such idea had been in my mind. In fact, the information had been definitely conveyed to me on the telephone the previous afternoon that I was expected.

"And it took over twenty minutes," the Inspector chuckled, "for the invitation to be given and accepted. I know, because I was waiting to use the 'phone. The sooner you two get married, the better it will be for the smooth working of the Telephone Service."

The ban was lifted. There seemed no doubt about that. But the Inspector said no more and I confined myself to a laugh, as I took my place beside him in the car.

"Thanks very much," he said as he slipped into top-gear, "for the list of names."

"Not a bit," I said. "It wasn't as difficult as I had anticipated. I got the subscribers from the card-index and judiciously pumped George for the others—told him we didn't seem to be doing much business apart from the lending-library and he trotted out the names of everybody who'd been in the shop since Monday morning."

"I spoke to you earlier to-day, Rutherford," he said, "of

the various tempting little *culs-de-sac* down which our murderous friend had attempted to lure us. Since I left you, I have been daintily picking my way along one of them, in the hope that I may meet something interesting *en route*. This afternoon, I invite you to venture with me to the end of it, after which we will go home to tea and cakes with Molly. You probably noticed the almost unprecedented action I took this morning, when I caused that bicycle to be displayed outside Paulsfield police station? Well, it may have been eccentric, but it certainly had the desired effect; and it didn't go against what I have already hinted—that Stevens murdered Johnson—because I might very well have been anxious to trace the machine to Stevens. As I say, the exhibition did the trick, for it hadn't been out there very long before a chap went into Martin and laid certain information.

"Martin 'phoned me at Lulverton and I came over and saw the man. He said that that machine, which he readily recognized, in spite of the fact that it had been spruced up a bit, had originally belonged to himself. His name is Longfield and he lives at Hazeloak—a plumber's mate. He passed over the machine to Walker about six weeks ago in part-exchange for a new one, which he is buying on the Glad-and-Sorry system. So far so good. After I had disposed of Mr. Longfield, who, if I had let him, would have talked for the rest of the day on the finer points of plumber's-mating, I went along to see Walker.

"When I arrived at the Hazeloak Garage, Walker was taking a three-speed gear to pieces—or putting it together; I can't be sure which. I urged him not to stop for me, as I had only dropped in for a chat; and he tinkered with the cogs and so forth, while I casually mentioned that I had managed to get into touch with a Mr. Longfield, who had once owned a bicycle whose present owner I was anxious to trace. Longfield, I explained, had told me that he had exchanged it with Walker for a new machine; and I had come to him in the hope that he would remember what had happened to it after he had supplied Mr. Longfield with far swifter and more comfortable means of making his innumerable return journeys for his superior's tools—a footling little pleasantry, which got no more than a polite smile from Walker.

"He said it was a difficult question to answer, as he had sold a good number of reconditioned bicycles recently and it might be any of them. I asked him whether he kept details of the machines he bought and sold. He earnestly applied himself to the task of fitting a part of the gear's intestines into what, even to my inexperienced eye, was the wrong position; and eventually said that he did keep such a record. I suggested that he would no doubt be able to tell me from that to whom he had sold bicycles since Longfield had done business with him; and he told me that his books would show that.

" 'If you'll excuse me,' he said, 'I'll slip upstairs and wash my hands and then go through my books for you.' "

"He came back with a cash-book and turned up the entries relating to the Longfield transaction. I asked him to be good enough to jot down the names and, if possible, the addresses of all who had purchased machines from him since that date. It took him about ten minutes to make the list, which he then handed to me.

" 'Thanks very much,' I said. 'That will help me a lot. All I have to do now—unless you can call to mind to which one of these you passed over Longfield's machine?' He shook his head. 'All I have to do now is to go to all these people and check up the bicycles that you sold to them. If they still have them, all the better, but if they haven't, I'll want to know the reason why!'

"There are times, Rutherford, when I feel a complete cad. This was one of them.

" 'It won't take me long now to find out who is the current owner of that bicycle!' I gloated."

'No,' he said dully.

" 'I'll give them all a call this afternoon,' I went on, giving the screw another turn.

"Walker struck a match to light his pipe and threw it away before it reached the bowl.

" 'It'll be a tiresome job,' I said, 'but it's sure to bring out some interesting facts.'" '

" 'Oh, damn and blast it all!' Walker suddenly shouted. 'It's futile to go on like this. I did not sell that bicycle to anyone, Inspector. At six o'clock on the evening Johnson was killed, it was in my shop!'

" 'Perhaps you'd like to tell me about it, Mr. Walker?' I said.

"'I have been expecting this,' he said, 'ever since you asked me about my transfers; but you must first understand that whatever I suspected and whatever I feared, it was not until you mentioned that man Longfield that I *knew* that the bicycle I am going to tell you about was mixed up in Johnson's murder. On the night before the crime, I received a 'phone call from my brother, who is living in Whitchester. Some years ago, Inspector, there was a little bit of trouble, which made it necessary for my brother to assume a different name. It was not that he was frightened of the police. The trouble was that if he had tried to carry on under his real name, public opinion would have been against him.'

" 'I should hardly have thought it necessary,' I said. 'There's more than one Langdon in the world.'

" 'You know, then?' he asked quietly. 'I was afraid you did, when you spoke about Mereworthians last Saturday. Or has Rutherford been talking?'

"I hastened to reassure him.

" 'The County Constabulary,' I said, 'is not the figure of fun that it is made out to be by our thriller-writers. We know all there is to know about you—except what you did with that bicycle; and I feel sure, Mr. Walker, that you will not continue to trifle with me.'

" 'My brother,' said Walker, 'rang me up on Saturday evening somewhere about nine o'clock. He asked me in a whisper, which he said was necessary because he might be overheard, if I would do something for him. He wanted me to supply him with a bicycle, which I was to leave carefully hidden in the bushes near the point where the footpath through Phantom Coppice joins the Hazeloak road. I was to do this not later than seven o'clock the next evening and was afterwards to come back here and wait for him to ring me. If I did not receive a call by twenty minutes past eight, I was to leave here immediately and walk to Deeptree Corner, where he would be waiting for me. On my way there, he said, I was to see whether the bicycle was still in its place. If it was, I was to bring it back here and do no more. Should my brother not be at the Corner, I was to wait there until nine o'clock and if, by that time, he didn't arrive, I was to walk on into Paulsfield and wait for him in the 'Roebuck' until ten o'clock, which was closing-time. If, even then, he did not come, I was to go home and make no attempt whatever to get into touch with him. He explained that he was slipping away while there was still time and, if I wrote to him, my letters would be opened. When things got a bit quieter, he would write to me and tell me where he was.'

" 'And I take it,' I said to Walker, 'that you did what he asked?'

" 'I did,' he said, 'and I bitterly regret it! I hadn't the least idea what my brother's trouble was, but however much I disliked the whole affair, I felt I had to go through with it. I followed his instructions to the letter. I waited until nine o'clock at the corner, after having made sure that the bicycle had been removed from its hiding-place and then continued into Paulsfield. When the 'Roebuck' closed, I walked home again. It seems hardly necessary to add that I did not see my brother.'

" 'And since that time,' I asked, 'you have not communicated with your brother in any way?'

" 'No,' he said definitely. 'You didn't send him a photograph, for example?'

"He looked surprised and said, 'Good Lord, no!'

"I said that I was very sorry he hadn't told me all this last week and he answered:

" 'You must surely understand the position I was in then. I had no idea that my appointment with my brother had any connection at all with Johnson's death. I had left the bicycle in the hedge and, as far as I knew then, my brother had come along, pulled it out of the hedge and ridden away on it, bound for the place where he proposed to . . .to hide, if you like, until whatever storm it was that threatened had blown over. When you asked me about my transfers, certain awkward doubts rose in my mind, but I consoled myself with the thought that the neighbourhood is full of machines bearing my transfer. It wasn't, as I said just now, until you told me that Longfield had identified the machine you are interested in, that I realized that my brother and I are mixed up, in some way that I don't understand, with Johnson's murder.'

"I couldn't help seeing his point of view. '

" 'I don't know, of course,' he went on, 'but I assume that Longfield's machine was the one ridden by Johnson's companion on the night of the crime. Am I right?' "

(I was glad Walker had said that to the Inspector, because it was I who had told him that, on the Saturday before. Up to that point in the Inspector's report, I was feeling decidedly uncomfortable.)

"I agreed that that was so," the Inspector continued.

" 'Inspector Charlton,' Walker said quickly, 'do you suspect—have you any reason to suppose that my brother had anything to do with that murder? Don't you think that somebody else—the murderer—might have discovered the bicycle before my brother could take it away?'

"I avoided any definite reply to that question and left Walker soon afterwards."

I had listened in silence to the Inspector, but now that he had reached the end, I said:

"It all sounds completely incomprehensible to me. In the first place, why did Walker's brother think it advisable, to travel all the way from Whitchester to Paulsfield to obtain a bicycle? If he wanted to make a quick get-away, why didn't he buy, borrow or steal one in Whitchester and pedal madly away into the middle distance? And if it was of vital importance that the bicycle should be supplied by Walker, why didn't he ask him to bring it along to the Corner at the appointed time and not hide it behind a bush an hour or so beforehand? If he wanted the bicycle to convey him to a healthier climate, he would surely have made use of it as soon as he laid his hands on it and be miles away before Walker arrived at the Corner?"

"Those points have occurred to me," said the Inspector, "And I'll admit that, at the moment, I can't answer any of them; but I hope to be better informed after I have spoken to Mr. Jack Wright."

"Do *you* think he killed Johnson?" I asked bluntly. "There's not much doubt that Walker does."

"No," said the Inspector, "I don't. The man who killed Johnson also killed Stevens and made an attack on you—of that I am certain; and when the two later events took place Jack Wright was in London, S.W. We picked up his trail last Thursday and I've had him under observation ever since."

"When do you propose to interview him?" I enquired.

"We're on the way now," was the answer. "My man looked him up in the room he had hired under the mighty shadow of that masterpiece of modern architecture—the Battersea Power Station, and suggested that it would be as well if he caught a train to-day from Waterloo and came down to Whitchester to have a chat with me. It was not necessary to explain the alternative to Mr. Wright!"

★ ★ ★ ★

Jack Wright was shorter and more thick-set than his brother and some five years his junior: resembling him in features, but without the same care-worn look. The Front Page Sensation that had sent them both scuttling into obscurity had not left its mark, if appearance were anything, so heavily on the younger man. He greeted the Inspector at Whitchester police station with the air of one who has been ill-used, but is prepared to overlook it.

"I'm sure, Inspector," he said slightly pompously, "that you haven't brought me back to Whitchester two days before I intended to end my stay in London without a very good reason?"

"Please accept my apologies," replied the Inspector with equal dignity. "Had I known that you would so soon return, I would have waited, but I was under the mistaken impression that you proposed to be absent from your home for an indefinite period."

"Well," said Wright, "now that I am here, what can I do for you?"

"You have a brother, Mr. Langdon …"

Wright breathed in sharply.

"…who is living in Hazeloak village under the name of Walker?"

Wright opened his mouth, as if to give a swift denial, but apparently changed his mind and nodded.

"When did you last see him?"

"Some time during the summer—July or August. I can't remember exactly."

"Have you spoken to him on the telephone since then?"

"Yes, once."

"When was that?"

"Last Saturday week."

"At what time?"

"About nine o'clock in the evening."

"Had you any particular reason for ringing him?"

Wright jumped to his feet.

"I don't see why I should answer these questions!" he shouted. "If I hadn't what you police people call a criminal record, you wouldn't have dared to drag me down here virtually under arrest, to ask me questions that I have the legal right to refuse to answer! Not that I've the slightest idea what this is all about," he ended lamely.

"I assure you" (this was the Doctor's bedside manner), "That there was no suggestion of your being dragged down here. I sent a message asking if you would be kind enough to have a few words with me. You were perfectly at liberty to say that it was not convenient; and I offer you my personal thanks for discommoding yourself for me in this way."

Wright murmured something that sounded to me suspiciously like, "Oh, yeah?" I hope I was wrong.

"Your brother has told me that he was at home during the evening of last Saturday week and that you rang him up at about nine o'clock. You yourself have just confirmed this and I shall feel extremely grateful if you will tell me why you rang Mr. Walker."

"Why, why, why!" said Wright querulously. "It's always 'why,' with you police. You might just as well ask me why I clean my teeth or why I buy a packet of 'Gold Flake'. Why did I ring my brother? Because I wanted to have a chat with him: ask him how he was getting on, tell him about myself, say what nice weather we'd been hav . . ."

"Yes, yes," the Inspector interrupted him, "I quite see what you mean. Just a friendly talk on general topics. Entirely understandable, in the circumstances. Your brother says that you asked him to supply you with a bicycle."

Wright looked at him sharply.

"Yes," he said after a slight pause, "as a matter of fact I did. He's in the business and I thought he might be able to let me have one cheap. Brotherly love and all that, you know!"

"I understood your brother to say that that was your chief reason for ringing him up?"

"Well, of all the miserable fellows!" laughed Wright. "I just happened to mention it in passing: said I was thinking of buying a bike—and what about it. I ring up my own brother, after not having seen him for several months; and now he's suggesting, I suppose, that all I wanted was a bicycle at trade price!"

"Anyway," smiled the Inspector, "I'm sure he was able to supply you with a first-rate machine!"

Again Wright hesitated, but only for a moment.

"To the contrary," he said, "he didn't supply me with one at all. I had only been toying with the idea and my brother said he'd probably be able to fix me up. There things rested; and after we'd yarned about this and that, I rang off."

"You used your landlady's telephone, I suppose?"

"Not likely! If I had, a garbled report of my conversation would have been all round Downshire by now. I used an outside call-box. There's one not far from where I 'dig.' "

"Thank you very much, Mr. Wright," said the Inspector. "You have been exceedingly helpful."

"Would I be rapped on the knuckles if I asked the reason for all this?" smiled Wright. His manner was quite friendly now. "Is my brother suspected of felonious entry or some such slight transgression as that and wants me to vouch for the fact that he was at home on Saturday evening?"

"Your brother, Mr. Wright, is suspected of nothing."

"Then what's all the to-do about?"

"The interests of the police lie in another direction, Mr. Wright."

"I don't understand you, Inspector."

"I suggest to you, Mr. Wright," said the Inspector quietly, "that you have done me the discourtesy of telling me a pack of lies."

Wright began to bluster, but the Inspector's next remark silenced him.

"That 'phone call to your brother was put through from a call-box in Paulsfield."

"Of course," said Wright at length, "That was the day I went to Paulsfield. Funny how your memory plays tricks with you. Yes, I remember now. I was confusing ..."

"It will be as well," said the Inspector gently, "if you will confine yourself to the truth. And the quicker you admit that you didn't 'phone your brother that evening," he went on with sudden sharpness, "the better it will be for all of us!"

Wright sat in silence for a moment or two. Then he said: "Very well. I'll admit it."

"Why did you say that you had?"

"Because my brother asked me to."

"Can you suggest any reason for his request?"

"None whatever. The whole thing was so much Greek to me—and still is, if it comes to that. My family, Inspector, have always had the reputation for getting into hot water—and not all of us have got out of it again. My grandfather, who developed the trick of getting into debt to a fine art, met his death as the result of a carefully rehearsed accident with a rook-rifle. My father, after four extremely successful bankruptcies, died in somebody else's bed; while I, the younger of his two sons, distinguished myself in a way that you will probably remember. Poor old Freddie's always tried to restore the family escutcheon to its old spic-and-spanness; but now it looks as if the antiquated scutch has gone and got besmirched again. Otherwise you wouldn't have tracked me down to my humble apartment in darkest Battersea."

I was finding Mr. Jack Wright a rather entertaining young man. He was getting delightfully slangy.

"To which you had removed yourself," said the Inspector, "with startling precipitancy."

" 'And the night shall be filled with music'," smiled Wright.

"Would it be out of place," asked the Inspector, "to ask why *you* silently stole away?"

"Look here, Inspector," said Wright leaning forward, "let's understand each other. Are you or are you not trying to hang something on me or my brother?"

"The position is this, Mr. Wright," explained the Inspector. "A bicycle was found bearing the imprint of your brother's name. I went to him and asked him to whom he had sold it. He said that you had rung him up and urgently required him to supply you with a bicycle, which was to be hidden in a certain spot, for you to collect later. Walker said that you had told him that you wanted to slip away until the storm that you feared had blown over."

"He told you *that?*" said Wright slowly. "If he did, he was either lying or crazy. I thought from his letter that he just wanted me to establish an alibi for him. Why mix me up in some funny business about a bicycle? And why are you people so interested in this blasted bicycle?"

"We are investigating a murder, Mr. Wright."

"*Murder?*" shouted Wright. "My God!"

"You may have read in the papers," said the Inspector, unmoved by this outburst, "that last Sunday week a police-constable was done to death in a lane near Paulsfield. Near his body a bicycle was found: and it was that machine that your brother gave me to understand you borrowed a short while before the crime was committed."

"Well, I'll be damned!" said Wright. "So that's his game! Trying to fix it on this boy, is he? Inspector Charlton, I told you that I rang my brother, because my brother asked me to tell you that. I thought he'd got himself in a bit of a jam and wanted a helping hand. You'd have done the same for your brother, I'll wager. But when it's murder and Freddie tricks me into bolting for cover like a rabbit and telling a lot of dangerous lies when I'm dragged out of my funk-hole, the best thing for me to do is to desert the Brotherly Love racket and concentrate on Self-Protection."

"Sensible fellow," said the Inspector approvingly. "You say your brother sent you a letter?"

"I got it by the Saturday night's post—Saturday, the ninth. He told me to get out of Whitchester, if I valued his safety and mine: slip away quietly by the last train up to London the next day, but not to go before that, as he might have to ring me."

"Did he give you any reason why you should go?"

"No; and he asked me to tell the police, the double-crossing b—"

"Please keep to the point," interrupted the Inspector.

"He asked me to tell the police, if they asked me, that I had rung him at nine o'clock that same Saturday evening; and not to attempt to get into touch with him in any way. He would put an advertisement in the *Daily Star* when things got a bit easier."

"You still have that letter?"

"No, I destroyed it, as he particularly asked me to. It was written with his left hand—he'd injured the other."

"Which prevented you from recognizing his writing?"

"Yes."

"How was it signed?"

"As nearly as I can remember, 'Your affectionate brother, Frederick Walker'."

"Was that his usual way of finishing his letters to you?"

"No. He didn't often write to me but when he did he finished with his initials, at one time F. B. L., but recently, of course, F. B. W. and he never called himself my affectionate brother. We Langdons may have come down in the world, but we haven't sunk as low as that!"

"And after you had received a letter in a hand that you did not recognize, signed in a manner that was strange to you, urging you, for no apparent reason, to beat a hurried retreat, and, if questioned by the police, to give them false information, you did what was required of you?"

A look of amazement spread over Wright's face.

"You mean," he said, "that it was a fake: not written by my brother at all?"

"I'm not suggesting anything," said the Inspector, "except that you displayed a certain—gullibility."

"I didn't suspect a thing," said Wright. "Freddie makes his living playing about with tools and things that might easily account for an injured hand. If I'd thought at all about 'Your affectionate brother' I might have smelt a rat, but I *didn't* think about it. The only thing that struck me was: here's Freddie giving me the straight tip. It's up to me to act upon it and ask any questions later. If I suddenly shouted at you that there was a rattlesnake under your chair, you'd probably leap for safety and then go into the why and wherefore afterwards."

"We'll let the point pass," said the Inspector. "Suffice it to say that you acted on the letter. Can you tell me anything about the notepaper or the envelope?"

"It was cheap stuff—'Superlative Value, a penny the packet' kind of thing."

"Thank you, Mr. Wright," said the Inspector. "I think that is all for the moment. You are probably anxious to get back to Battersea."

Wright looked doubtful and then said:

"I suppose there's really nothing to stop me from returning to Blossom Street now."

"You should know best, Mr. Wright," said the Inspector sweetly.

★ ★ ★ ★

Before the Inspector and I left for Southmouth, the Inspector took a telephone call from Paulsfield. As we started off, he told me that Mrs. Stevens had called in at the police station and wanted to speak to him.

"We'd better see her on the way back," he said. "It'll probably make us late for tea, but she may have something important to tell me."

"That was a very successful bluff of yours," I said, "when

you told Wright that the 'phone call to Walker had been put through from Paulsfield."

"That wasn't a bluff," the Inspector answered. "I have checked up that call. It was made from that box out on the Burgeston road."

"I know the one you mean," I said. "I've often thought what a silly place it was to put a call-box. I shouldn't think anybody ever uses it."

"Very few people do now," he agreed, "but before the new arterial road was cut, all the traffic to the coast used to go along the Burgeston road—and call-boxes are always in demand on main roads. The G.P.O., I believe, have frequently considered taking the box away."

"And do you think we have reached the end of the *cul-de-sac* along which you asked me to accompany you this afternoon?" I asked.

"I'm not sure," the Inspector admitted, "but in any case, it has provided me with food for thought."

It had apparently provided him with so much food for thought that he said very little until he drew up the car outside Mrs. Stevens's house in Carnation Villas, Burgeston—a pretty name for a row of semi-detached residences exceeded in ugliness only by the railway-cutting that ran along the bottoms of the gardens. I saw the curtains in the front room pulled slightly aside and, as we went up the path, Mrs. Stevens opened the door to us. She took us into the back room, which was obviously only used when visitors came. Through the window, I could see the short, badly kept garden and, a little to the right, where the Romp rose steeply, the entrance to Burgeston tunnel—not, of course, the end where Stevens was killed.

Mrs. Stevens, who was wearing black, thanked us for coming; and I offered my sympathies to her in her loss. "Just as he was beginning to make a success of things," she said sadly. "It does seem so hard. He wouldn't let me go to see him on the stage that night at Southmouth. If I'd come home with him, it might not have happened. Everything might have been so different if he'd lived. It was only drink, Inspector, that brought out the worst in him. We might have built up our home again if he hadn't. . . . *But he didn't*" she went on with sudden passion. "I know he didn't. Frank wouldn't ever have killed himself! Some dirty tike killed him, like he killed Johnson. Somebody made him write that letter! 'I think she will understand.' Frank never wrote that willingly. The only thing I understand is that my poor husband was murdered—and what's more, I know why!"

"It must have been a great shock to you," said the Inspector gently, "but you must calm yourself. Your husband is dead and it is for you to help me to find out how he died. I think you want to tell me something? I'm sure Mr. Rutherford won't mind waiting for me outside in the car."

I rose to my feet, but Mrs. Stevens reached out and pushed me back into my chair.

"Mr. Rutherford is going to stay where he is," she said definitely. "The Tuesday after Johnson was murdered," she continued, "Mr. Protheroe, the agent, who always did what he could to help Frank, came here and told him that if he'd take it at such short notice, he'd got an engagement for him at the Southmouth 'Empire' for the next week. Somebody had been taken sick and they'd come to Mr. Protheroe to find them a fill-up. There wasn't much time to work up the act, but Frank was working hard all the rest of the week rehearsing."

There was something of an anomaly here, for, during our chat in the shop on the previous Thursday, Mrs. Stevens had said that all her husband was doing was sitting about the place with strange, ugly smiles on his face. But she had certainly added that he sometimes played with a bouncing doll.

"But," said Mrs. Stevens, "the evening before Mr. Protheroe came, Frank got back from the 'Porcupine' as tight as an owl. I managed to get him to bed somehow, but couldn't make him stop from shouting, which must have been keeping the neighbours awake—not that they weren't used to that! He eventually did stop shouting and singing bits out of those songs of his, and began to talk."

She paused and the Inspector and I waited expectantly. I felt that we were going to hear something good.

"You know how a drunk man talks?" she went on. "Round and round in circles, but never keeping to the point for long. Frank was like that then. He talked about all sorts of things: the row he'd had with a man round at the 'Porcupine', who'd accused Frank of drinking his whisky—and all sorts of other things. But through it all ran something else. About catching somebody or other at it. He went on like this:

" 'I heard what you said about me on the wireless last night. Disgraceful thing to say about a public figure like me . . .I gave Queenie a shilling . . . Distinctly remember putting it on the counter . . .So it's my drink . . .You're a miserable skunk . . . Stealing a Cabinet Minister's drink . . .If you think I didn't know who it was in the telephone-box, you're mistaken, old sportsman . . .A public figure like me. . . It's a wonder the B.B.C. allow it . . . Nothing less than slander . . . And the big bear said to the little bear, . . . 'Who the hell's been drinking my whisky?' I paid for it and I'm going to drink it. You can buy your own . . . Oh, no, old boy, this one is on me, because I heard what you said. Kept the door wedged open with your foot, didn't you, so's it wouldn't switch on the light . . . Light fantastic . . . Let's have a party and dance . . .I never did like the B.B.C. . . . Telephone people economical fellows . . . Nobody using box, no light . . . But Jimmy Stevano, finest comedian in Europe, old boy— he saw you . . . That's my drink. Keep your filthy hands off it , . . No offence meant . . . Make a note of the time, I said . . . always make a note of the time . . . Nine o'clock . . . No, not now, old boy—long time before they throw us out . . . Nine o'clock was time I saw you in . . . Funny thing, I said

. . . Haven't seen single person use that box since they cut new road . . . OOOOOOOSH . . .Cut new road . . . Just like that . . . Heard what you said about me on London Regional . . . Announcer ought to have stopped you . . . Jimmy Stevano, finest Prime Minister country's ever had . . . Thought you'd whisper, so's Jimmy Stevano wouldn't hear you . . . Ears of a tomahawk, old boy . . . Heard every word . . . said you were his brother, you wicked old storyteller . . . Wicked old storyteller, saying your whisky . . . Big Bear swallowed one . . . Then there were two . . . One for you and one for me . . . All chums together . . . Legal binder . . . One for the road . . . Two pounds a week for life . . . All I ask . . . Price of silence . . . Keep my mouth shut . . . Cheap for two pounds a week . . . Prime Minister get more than that for keeping mouth shut . . . If you don't pay, Jimmy Stevano, funniest comic in universe, goes and tells police about you . . . Scream with laughter . . . England's leading Prime Minister . . . Don't touch that—it's mine . . . How do you do? . . . Dr. Livingstone, I presume . . . Told him to put it in the bushes . . . Dr. Livingstone wasn't riding bicycle . . . Foot-slogging it through Darkest Africa . . . Kill me? . . . Wouldn't dream of it, old gooseberry . . . This is my round . . . World couldn't do without Jimmy Stevano . . . Wouldn't stand by and see old Jimmy done in . . . You can't cover up one murder with another . . . Simply isn't done, old boy . . . Alma Mater . . . Floreat Whatname and all that . . . Two pounds a week . . . Make it ten bob, sporting offer . . . Ten bob a week or I spill the beans . . . How many beans? . . . One, two, three, four, five . . ."

"Then," concluded Mrs. Stevens, "he went off to sleep."

And she burst into tears.

I went over and stood by the window, picturing that scene. The furtive figure creeping up to the telephone box, to listen to the whispering of the man inside—the man who was already preparing to murder Johnson. I saw the foot pushed back to hold open the door, the anxious plotter talking hurriedly to Walker, with his ears open for the sound of footsteps on the road, while a few inches away was another man with equally attentive ears and ready to slip into the nearby bushes when the receiver was replaced.

"Did your husband mention any names?" I heard the Inspector say when the sobbing ceased.

"No," replied Mrs. Stevens, as I turned round.

"Forgive me if I hurt you further, but to discover how your husband died, I must know the whole truth. Did your husband know of your friendship with P.C. *Johnson?*"

A look of blank surprise spread over her face.

"Johnson?" she said, as if she didn't understand, "Johnson? But I *wasn't* friendly with Johnson. I didn't even know him. I never spoke a word to him in my life!"

"That is what I wanted you to tell me, Mrs. Stevens," said the Inspector soothingly. "I hope this interview hasn't put too much of a strain on you. It is really wonderful how clearly you have managed to remember your husband's ramblings."

Five minutes later, the Inspector and I were racing through the gathering dusk, in an attempt to get back to his home in time for tea.

"Well, Inspector," I said, "to use an American idiom, that seems to let the brothers Langdon out."

"Possibly," said the Inspector, "but subtlety has no limitation of depth."

And his foot pressed down the accelerator to its fullest extent.

Wednesday, November 20th
and Thursday, November 21st.

XVI.   IN WHICH I ASK FOR TROUBLE

Just after I got home from Southmouth at about eleven o'clock that night, I heard the front door close and the sound of voices in the hall, followed by Mrs. Hendon's heavy tread on the stairs.

"While you were out, Master John," she said when she saw me, "there was a 'phone call for you. It was Inspector Charlton speaking from Burgeston and when I told him you weren't in yet—it was only about half-an-hour ago— he said I was to tell you that a certain lady had taken the same road as her husband. Them was 'is very words. He said as you'd understand and will you go to Burgeston as soon as you can, as he's waiting for you."

"Do you know Inspector Charlton's voice, Lizzie?" I asked.

"I've only heard it but twice—when he came with Sergeant Martin that evening and again this afternoon."

"Did you recognize him on the 'phone?"

"Mercy, no, Master John! I wouldn't know if it was you as was talking to me. Them plaguey things fair gives me the jumps and everybody's voice sounds the same colour."

"He didn't—whisper?"

She looked at me strangely.

"I shouldn't like to say that," she said, "but I don't think 'e did. What makes you ask that, now?"

"Oh," I said casually, "a man I know—one of my customers—sounds as if he whispers on the phone, and I was expecting a call from him."

"But this was Inspector Charlton, Master John. He said it was."

"Yes, Lizzie, that's all right," I reassured her. "You might leave the front door unbolted when you go to bed, as I may be back very late."

"You're surely not going to Burgeston tonight, Master John. Let that old Inspector wait till to-morrow."

"I don't know quite what I shall do," I said, "but don't wait up for me—and please don't say anything about this to Mr. Bradfield."

For three or four minutes after Lizzie had left me, I lay back in my chair, sucking at my pipe and looking at the ceiling. "but you're surely not going to Burgeston tonight, Master John?" That was the point. Molly and I had been sitting over the fire, when the Inspector had made an ostentatiously noisy approach along the hall.

"I'm just going out chasing wild geese," he had informed us solemnly when he had poked his head round the door, "and you'll probably be gone, Rutherford, by the time I get back. If I were you, my dear, I'd choose a diamond cluster—they've always a break-up value. Cheerio!" He had finished hastily as Molly had dashed for the door, which had been gently closed in her face.

"He suggested to me to-day," I had said when I had heard his car start up, "that the sooner we get married, the better it will be for the Telephone Service."

"He said the same thing to me last Sunday—after you'd gone," Molly had smiled, "but he didn't say anything about the Telephone Service."

"He told me on Sunday that I must wait until the Johnson investigation is filed under 'Completed Undertakings.'"

"You don't want to take any notice of that," she had laughed. "A cluster of diamonds *would* be rather nice."

So we had fixed up a shopping expedition for the next day.

The Inspector, then, I pondered, had certainly gone out, destination and approximate time of return unknown, and it was within the bounds of possibility that he was now at

Burgeston waiting for me to arrive. On the other hand, it might not be the Inspector who waited for me: it might be the gentleman who had disposed of Johnson and Stevens. Was there any way of finding out if the Inspector actually was at Burgeston? Would they know at Paulsfield police station or the 'Porcupine' at Burgeston? I reached for the telephone and then paused. Wasn't this my golden opportunity to discover the identity of the murderer? I ran a risk, of course, but it would be worth it. If I sent out an emergency call for reinforcements and we all trooped along the Burgeston road like a choir-outing, we should stand not the slightest chance of getting our man; but if I went alone and kept my wits about me, I might succeed—not, perhaps, in bringing him back bound and gagged, with a signed confession in his pocket—but at least in getting a look at him. I had a sort of feeling that one glance would be sufficient: that I knew the murderer's face as well as I knew my own. How right I was!

I pulled on my raincoat, reached for my stoutest stick and, with my electric torch in my pocket, went down the stairs. As I reached the bottom, the kitchen door opened and my fellow-lodger, Bradfield, came out. He was wearing an overcoat and carried a bowler-hat in his hand. I politely said good evening to him as I opened the front door.

"Good evening, Mr. Rutherford," he answered. "Just out for a stroll?"

I said that I was.

"So am I, as it happens," he smiled.

I did not say what was apparently expected of me.

"Do you mind if I join you?" he asked bluntly.

This was no time for conventional evasions.

"I don't want to seem discourteous," I said, "but I prefer to be by myself."

"Don't mention it," he smiled. "I know how it is sometimes."

I walked along to the corner and turned to the left into

Chesapeake Road, while Bradfield, who had followed me down the garden path bore eastward along Thorpe Street. Cruising along at a steady four miles an hour, I turned into the deserted High Street. It was turned half-past eleven and most of the town seemed asleep. As I strode along the side of the Square and gradually left the High Street behind, I got the sensation that I was not alone on that stretch of road; that I was being followed. But I told myself that the mysterious Bradfield was causing me to imagine things. When, however, the houses had thinned away and there were only hedges on each side of the road, I definitely heard footsteps behind me. I lengthened my stride, but the footsteps grew no fainter. As I drew nearer to Deeptree Corner, I decided that my follower must be given the slip; so instead of taking the right-hand fork to Burgeston, I went along the other road and, twenty yards down it, paused and struck a match, as if to light my pipe. I wanted the gentleman behind to be under no doubt as to which way I was going. When the match had burnt itself out, I started running. My rubber-soled shoes made hardly any sound on the road, and it was pitch dark. After a sprint that carried me a hundred yards down the road, I stopped, clambered over the grass bank and crouched in the ditch, to the utter ruin of my trousers.

In a couple of minutes footsteps became audible; then somebody hurried past me. When the sound of feet on the road had died away, I climbed out of the ditch and ran back to Deeptree Corner. I had left the call-box well behind me and was reaching the point where the road swung off round the Romp, when I got what I had asked for.

★ ★ ★ ★

I felt cold and my head ached damnably . . . I had been walking along the Burgeston road . . . Going to meet Inspector Charlton . . . Or somebody else . . . It looked as if I had met somebody else . . . Not that I had the faintest recollection of it . . . Perhaps a stir in the bushes, but that might have been the wind . . . Then everything had gone—they usually said black in books. But everything hadn't gone black, because it had been black already . . . Empty was the word . . . I had been walking along the Burgeston road . . . And now I was lying in bed . . . I wished my head didn't hurt so much, but they'd probably be giving me something for it . . . Aspirin or sal volatile . . . Pity the place wasn't lighted . . . Was I at home or in hospital? . . . Had the Inspector come along just in time to stop the chap from finishing the job that the pain in my head insisted on reminding me had so well begun? . . . A draughty room, anyway, where they'd put me . . . Might have the sense to shove some screens round the bed . . . I'd call out . . . No, I wouldn't call out . . . I disliked the idea of calling out . . . It would split my head like a chopper . . . Best thing to do was to wait until somebody came. . . . They had certainly tucked me in nice and snugly—so snugly that there wasn't room for my arms on each side of my body . . . I was lying on my back with my elbows pressed in above me . . . Very slowly, for every movement stirred up an assorted collection of twinges and spasms that had taken possession of my neck and head, I felt about with my hands . . . Funnily enough, there was no covering above me . . . Perhaps that was why I was so cold . . . Fine hospital that was, when patients were left with no covering above them . . . My right hand met what seemed to be an expanse of tightly stretched cloth, which gave slightly as I pressed upon it . . . I was lying in a tent . . . Yes, that must be it . . . One of those little tents that the St. John Ambulance men put up at gymkhanas and things . . . But the canvas on the other side did not yield to pressure . . . Something was behind it, some flat surface . . . The tent was erected up against something . . . The wall of a house . . . I thought I could trace the outlines of the bricks with my finger . . . Does the mortar hold the bricks together or does it keep them apart? . . . Where had I heard that foolish question and what was the answer? .

. Oh, it was devilish difficult to think and it didn't matter, anyway . . . Perhaps I wasn't in a tent . . . Perhaps I was in a hammock . . . Taken away to sea by pirates . . . Or shanghaied . . . What was the name of the book I used to gloat over? . . . Well, that would account for all the fresh air I was enjoying . . . I found that if I didn't move at all, they didn't push the red-hot pokers so savagely into my head . . . I began to feel quite comfortable . . . Cosy things, hammocks . . .

It was then that the queer rumbling began.

A distant hollow sound at first, but quickly getting louder, like an express train approaching through a tunnel . . . Perhaps I had been brought to Mrs. Stevens's house . . . Hadn't the Inspector said that she had taken the same road as her husband? . . . Did that mean that she had been murdered, because she had told the Inspector what her husband had said? . . . But Mrs. Stevens wasn't dead . . . That was only the excuse to bring me out along the Burgeston road to receive that love-tap . . . Somebody ought to shut the window . . . I was going to call out . . . I was damned if I was going to put up with the draught and noise. So I shouted out at the top of my voice, "NURSE!" Nobody came . . . That train was kicking up a row . . . But it would soon go by and then I might get some sleep . . . I certainly felt ready for it. . . .

Suddenly the whole house rocked and I rolled over on to my right side. Then for the first time for hours—or so it seemed—I heard a human voice.

"All right, I've got you!" it yelled. "Keep your 'ead! You'll be safe now! But for God's sake don't move!"

I thought it was strange that the voice came from above me and wondered to whom the encouraging cries were addressed. Then the voice cried out again, this time louder than ever:

"Hi! You in the car! Get a move on! I can't hold him much longer! Get an 'old on this, will you? Is that you, Dr. Weston? Can you give us a hand, Doctor?"

All this was bellowed above the roar of the train.

"It's the midnight express," the voice went on. "wait until it's gone before we get 'im up. It'll be out any second now!"

The roar reached its crescendo and a searing pain suddenly struck me—and as suddenly went. Then the roar changed to a rhythmic sound. "Tooting Bec, Tooting Bec," it seemed to say and then gradually began to die away.

"Now we can pull 'im up," said the man who had shouted and whose voice I now recognized as P.C. Harwood's, "but take it easy—he may be injured."

I wondered dully what the devil all this turmoil was about and hoped they'd pull up whoever it was they were going to pull up and then leave me in peace. But I was not to be left in peace, for the whole house began to sway about again. I felt hands clutching at me through the canvas; and then I was lifted and laid gently down somewhere. I looked up into Harwood's anxious face and then felt myself drifting away from everything, taking with me the memory of Dr. Weston's startled ejaculation:

"Good God, it's Rutherford!"

★ ★ ★ ★

They got me into the Doctor's car and took me to the Cottage Hospital, where I passed a reasonably comfortable night. The blow I had received had not been very serious: quite bad enough to account for my bemused condition of the night before and a foul headache that morning; but not sufficient to keep me in bed for long. The weapon by the Lake had been a sandbag, for it had left no trace; but this time it had been something a little less considerate. At eleven o'clock, with my head swathed in a becoming turban of bandages, I received my first visitor: Molly.

Her sweet expressions of concern for me will hardly interest you. I shall simply say that a tap on the head was a small price to pay for the ten minutes she sat by my bed. She hadn't known about the Lake affair, but she had taken the call from Sergeant Martin late the night before. The Inspector had rung her at eleven o'clock, to say he would not be home, as he had had an urgent call to go up to London. So she had had no car to drive to Paulsfield and the last train had gone; but the Cottage Hospital had reassuringly answered her anxious enquiry and suggested that she came to see me the next morning. And there she was.

Some little time after the nurse had taken Molly away from me, Dr. Weston came.

"Morning, Doctor," I greeted him cheerfully. "Thanks for what you did last night."

"That's all right," he said in his sharp way. "How're you feeling this morning?"

"I shall feel better when I get out of this bed and better still when I get out of the Paulsfield Cottage Hospital. The mingled scent of iodine and ether that pervades the place is beginning to terrify me!"

"Let's have a look at the head," he said, and began to dismantle my turban.

"I don't see why you shouldn't get up," he said as his deft fingers rewound the bandage round my head, "but take things gently."

"Tell me, Doctor," I said, "what happened last night? It all seems a bit murky, but somebody has apparently taken an acute dislike to me."

"You had a very narrow escape," he said gravely. "A matter of seconds."

"Where was I last night, when all that shouting and noise was going on?"

"You were hanging in a sort of cradle of canvas over the northern entrance to Burgeston tunnel, and if Harwood hadn't happened along when he did, you would have been chewed into cat's meat by the midnight express. The man who gave you the blow on the head had fixed the corners of a sheet of stout canvas to a couple of iron projections over the tunnel mouth. This made a species of hammock for you to lie in, so that just before the express emerged from the tunnel, he could release one end of the canvas and allow you to drop neatly in front of the train."

"A very pretty idea," I said grimly.

"And that, I should imagine," said the doctor, "was how Stevens 'committed suicide.' They are holding the inquest on him this morning and there's not much doubt in my mind what the verdict will be. The whole town's talking about what happened to you last night and if the nine good men and true don't snap their fingers at the evidence and return a verdict of 'Murder,' you can garotte me with my own stethoscope!"

Laughing heartily at his joke, the Doctor went his way.

I returned home that afternoon—and a comic spectacle I must have been, with my hat perched on top of the bandages. I called in at the shop and found George and Milke there. George, Sister had told me, had called early at the Cottage Hospital, to ask after me. Now his face was radiant.

"Oh, sir!" he said. "They've let you out! They told me you were all right, but I didn't believe them."

"Fortunately, George," I said, "They were telling the truth. I'm what they call a walking-casualty, with nothing much wrong with me but a scalp that feels as if it has been run through a sewing-machine."

"I'm glad to see you out and about, as you might say, sir," put in Milke.

"There are all sorts of stories going round," said George when I had thanked Milke. "Something about you being knocked unconscious by the man who murdered Johnson and Stevens, and Harwood coming along just in time to stop him throwing you under a train, and Dr. Weston bringing you back in his car. Is it true, sir?" He ended breathlessly.

"So they tell me," I said. "Personally, I remember very little. Now you be a good chap and keep things going here, while I slip home and obey Dr. Weston's instructions by taking things gently."

I nodded to them both, but paused at the shop door.

"Is the verdict on Stevens out yet?" I asked.

"Murder, sir," said George promptly, "by some person or persons unknown. And yesterday I would have wagered my hat that he committed suicide."

The first thing I did after I had got rid of Lizzie—only by telling her precisely fourteen times that there was nothing seriously wrong with me—was to telephone Molly. The only part of our conversation that really concerns this story was when she suddenly said:

"Just a moment, John. Uncle's back from London and he wants to speak to you. Hold on, will you?"

After a pause, I heard the Inspector's voice say, "thank you, Molly." What followed took me by surprise. I heard a whisper from the receiver:

"*Can you fix me up with a bicycle? You can? That's fine. No, I want you to leave it in a special place ...*"

The whispering stopped and I heard the Inspector's voice: "Did you catch all that?"

"Yes," I agreed, "I heard every word you said. What is this, if it's not a rude question—a new round-or-parlour game?"

"Yes," he chuckled, "and it's called 'Guess who it was.' That was Molly whispering to you, not me."

"What's the big idea?" was my rude enquiry.

"An experiment in sex-determination," he said blandly. "They do it with eggs." Then he went on more seriously, "Rutherford, I want to talk to you. Will you be in if I come over now? I got the fright of my life when Martin put a call through to London this morning and told me about last night's affair. How are you feeling? I rang Dr. Weston and he seems very pleased with you."

"Don't you bother about me," I laughed. "They make billiard-balls out of skulls like mine!"

"I'll come straight over," he said, and left Molly and me to abuse the hospitality of the Telephone Service.

It was tea-time when the Inspector arrived at number eighteen. I had warned Lizzie of his coming and she doubled the crumpet quota.

"Well," the Inspector said when he saw me, "aren't you proud of yourself? Did I or did I not tell you to be careful? And you fall into the first trap that is set for you."

" 'Now is the woodcock near the gin,' " I quoted flippantly. "Anyway, I walked into the trap with my eyes open. The whole thing looked a bit fishy to me, but I decided to take a chance—which wasn't very successful. I suppose it *wasn't* you who rang me last night?"

"No," he answered, "Mrs. What's-her-name—your landlady—told me about that. 'A certain lady had taken the same road as her husband.' That was a crafty one! Very nearly successful, too. Fortunately, Harwood caught him at it. He was riding his motor-cycle combination back to his home in Burgeston, after a run round to try out the engine after a 'de-coke', when he heard somebody yell out from the direction of the tunnel."

"That was my little chirrup," I said. "Somehow or other, I got the notion that I was in hospital and I vaguely remember calling out for the nurse."

"Well, you didn't get the nurse," smiled the Inspector, putting down his cup, "but the estimable Harwood was on the spot, ran his machine off the road through a gateway—the gate, like most gates in this part of the world, had been left open—followed the fence that keeps the cows from falling on the railway-line and was just in time to hear a scuffle, as our practical-joking friend made a swift getaway to the other side of the tunnel. Harwood scaled the fence, discovered you in your serious extremity, and had just started to call out encouraging remarks to the body in the bag, when another visitor arrived."

"Dr. Weston?"

"No, a fellow named Bradfield."

"Good Lord," I said rather too forcefully for the well-being of my head, "I had forgotten about him. He followed me last night all the way from my home, where he is lodging—and there are one or two other little things you may like to know about him. The other evening, when Milke came round ..."

"Don't you bother your head about Bradfield," the Inspector interrupted me. "He's one of my men. I put him on to keep an eye on you. He tells me that he had a devil of a job to pick up your trail, after you gave him the slip on the Hazeloak road."

"Why didn't you tell me this before?" I complained. "I've been imagining all sorts of things about that man!"

"I didn't tell you, because you didn't ask me," he explained. "In any case, you probably wouldn't have taken very kindly to the idea. Those tickets I sent you weren't entirely the result of a generous instinct. When young George rang on Monday morning, there were plenty of seats available—but not for Mr. John Rutherford of Paulsfield. I had seen to that!"

"You make me feel like a child of four, Inspector," I said a little bitterly. "But to change the topic, how did Dr. Weston come into it last night?"

"He was driving past and heard Harwood shouting down to you. A very lucky arrival, as they were able to get you into his car and take you to hospital."

"Can Harwood give any information about the man who disappeared when he arrived?"

"He can't even say it was a man. It might have been a woman or a boy—or a dog. He merely heard a scuffle. The assumption is that it was a human being, because somebody had to be there to release the canvas that held you, when the train came out of the tunnel."

"What happened to the canvas?"

"A pertinent question, Rutherford—and one of the first

that I asked Martin on the 'phone this morning. The answer is that we don't know. That's a black mark against Harwood and Bradfield—they forgot it. There was such a bustlement about getting you into the car, that they all overlooked that valuable piece of evidence and left it flapping in the breeze over the tunnel mouth. When Martin hurried out there after ringing off, it had gone. A great pity, as it might have told us something."

Had the Inspector held the canvas in his hands at that moment, it would have told him everything. But we weren't to know that then.

"What about the 'phone call to me?" was my next question. "Have you found out from where that was made?"

"No. The telephone people keep no record of local and toll calls. Had it been a trunk call, they could have given me full particulars."

"But wasn't it they who confirmed that call put through to Walker by the chap who whispered?"

The Inspector smiled.

"That was a case when the personal element crept in. A girl on the Paulsfield Exchange remembered putting that call through—and for the very same reason that that particular box was chosen, because it was in a lonely place and very little used. Neither she nor any of her colleagues could call to mind more than half-a-dozen occasions when that line was operated; and when, at my suggestion, the coin-box was emptied, the collector was rewarded for his trouble with the handsome sum of twopence."

"Had the girl anything to say about the voice that gave the number?"

"She said the number was whispered, followed by an explanation that the caller was suffering from a very bad cold."

"That bears out Stevens's drunken ravings," I said.

"It certainly agrees with what his wife told us," said the Inspector. He rose to his feet and walked over to the window and it was fully a minute before he returned to his chair. "I think our friend is getting a bit careless, Rutherford," he said as he sat down. "When one considers in what detail Johnson's murder was planned, this latest effort was a bit sketchy. The attempt on your life by the Lake had an element of subtlety. Had you been drowned, there wasn't much to show that it wasn't suicide or accidental death—more likely the former, because a steady-going chap like you isn't given to breaking open boathouses at dead of night, for the sole purpose of enjoying a row. If, on the other hand, our friend's homicidal intentions were not realized and you managed to avoid being drowned, the presence of the charred scraps of currency-notes on the bank would suggest that the attack had been carefully faked by you. Fortunately for your reputation, you acquired some bruises that the murderer hadn't bargained for. You got a bit too lively in the Lake.

"The Stevens's killing was put through very neatly, with all the appearances of suicide; but this latest attempt to shuffle you off this mortal coil isn't in the same class. Even if everything had gone well for the murderer and you had duly succumbed, there would have been no question of *felo de se*. Mrs. Flapdoodle ..."

"Hendon," I suggested.

"Mrs. Hendon, with her story of the 'phone call, would have convinced the most thick-headed of coroner's juries that there had been dirty work on the railroad. Stevens's death sort of rounded things off: he murdered Johnson and then committed suicide, after making an abortive attempt on your life. Everything nice and tidy. But now Mr. A makes a frantic attempt to dispose of you in the same way as he wishes the world to think that Stevens took his own life; and by so doing, completely destroys the effect that he has been at such pains to build up. It looks to me, Rutherford, as if our man is beginning to panic."

"That letter found on Stevens's body will take some explaining," I suggested. "Have the experts given the handwriting the once-over?"

"They have agreed with me that the note found on Stevens was written by himself; and I have worked out a little theory."

I tried unsuccessfully to raise my eyebrows.

"Two men were dangerous to Mr. A," he went on: "Stevens, because he knew who went into that telephone-box, and yourself, because—because what? The Lord only knows! Stevens blackmailed Mr. A, went too far and was killed. And this is where we come to my theory about the note. You remember the wording of it?"

" 'This is the best way. Break the news gently to M. I think she will understand '." I quoted.

"And M stood for?"

"Mary, I suppose. You told me that was his wife's name."

"Can you think of anything else that M might have represented?"

"Marjorie, Muriel, Minnie . . .?"

"Or Molly?" said the Inspector softly.

"You mean ..." I said slowly. "You mean that that letter was intended to be found on my body: that it was used for Stevens because the need for his death was more urgent? But my writing's nothing like Stevens's."

"Stevens didn't know that."

"I don't think I understand."

"Assume," said the Inspector leaning forward, "that Stevens was blackmailing Mr. A, and that gentleman decided that the whole thing was getting a trifle too expensive. And assume that on one of their meetings, he told Stevens that your continued existence was a danger to his safety and Stevens's income, and that he seriously considered getting rid of you . . ."

I opened my mouth to speak, but the Inspector's raised hand kept me silent.

"And assume," he continued, "that Mr. A told Stevens that his—Stevens's—writing was identical with yours, so that if he wrote a note and it was found on your body, it would be believed that you had written it. Wouldn't that explain a great deal?"

"Surely Stevens wouldn't have been idiot enough to swallow a story like that?"

"Some men will swallow any sort of story when they've had enough whisky—not sufficient to prevent them from writing legibly, but enough to make their letters the tiniest bit uncertain and wavering."

"As was the case with the letter found on Stevens."

"Precisely. Then, when Mr. A had gone away with the note-book and Stevens had had time to sober up, he was so ashamed of what he had done, that he sent you a warning."

"Which hastened his death."

"Oh, no. That had been already decided upon."

For a space, the Inspector drew at his cigarette and there was a blank, far-away look in his eyes. Then suddenly he looked at me, as if a forgotten and sought-after name had at last drifted into his mind.

"Rutherford," he said, "I need the attention of an alienist: I think I am losing my wits. That bicycle that was ridden along the footpath and whose tracks disappeared when they reached the road. I know now why they disappeared—and I think I know where I shall find that elusive sheet of canvas!"

XVII.   GEORGE'S MR. A.

It was on that Thursday evening that things came to a head; and just as it had been my doubtful privilege to raise the shout, "Gone away!" so was I also destined to be in at the death. But during the earlier stages of the last act—forgive me if my metaphors are mixed—I was in my dressing-room.

Immediately after the last remark recorded in the previous chapter, the Inspector left me and drove in his car to the station—not the police station, but the railway station. The station-master was very polite and expressed himself extremely anxious to help in any way.

"I want to go into Burgeston tunnel," the Inspector explained.

"Certainly, Inspector," said the station-master. "I'll make the necessary arrangements first thing in the morning."

"I should like to go now, if you please."

"There is a certain amount of danger, Inspector."

"That is why I didn't hop down the embankment and venture into the tunnel by myself. If I am now killed by a train, it will be your responsibility."

The outcome of it was that one of the station officials motored out with the Inspector to the tunnel mouth and the two of them clambered down on to the permanent-way. Personally I would as soon spend a jolly half-hour in a cage with a dyspeptic lion, as fiddle about in a railway tunnel, with an express train more than likely to roar through in either direction at any moment; but the Inspector was made of sterner stuff, for he stepped from sleeper to sleeper, playing his electric torch about him as he went, as if such an experience was an everyday one. The railwayman told me about it afterwards. The makers of Burgeston tunnel had had the forethought to provide periodic niches in the walls of it, so that if a train came along, it was possible to retreat into one of them until it had gone by. In the first recess they came to on the left-hand side, the ray from the Inspector's torch picked out something pushed well back against the wall. With a grunt of satisfaction, the Inspector pounced upon it.

"That's all I want," he said to his companion. "And now, as they say in talkies, let's get out of here."

After the railwayman had said that the walk back to Paulsfield would do him good and had left him, the Inspector switched on the roof-light inside his car and examined his find. It was a large rolled-up sheet of canvas, isosceles-triangular in shape, and to the two corners of the "base" short lengths of stout rope had been lashed. These had obviously been used to fasten the "hammock" to the iron projections over the tunnel mouth.

The finding of that canvas was the turning-point in the Inspector's investigation. However much in the dark he had previously been, he now saw the whole thing clearly. It was the canvas that directed him to another place, where he found three more things that relieved his mind of any doubt there may have been in it before.

The first of these things was a round black ruler, an inch in diameter and fifteen inches long. It weighed ten ounces and along five inches of it had been wound a length of sticking-plaster, to form a grip for the user's hand. The other end of it had been rounded off with glasspaper to resemble the end of a truncheon and the condition of it left little doubt as to the murderous purpose to which it had been put.

The other discoveries were two alarm-clocks, one of them a small chromium-plated affair with a square, luminous dial, and the other a big fellow, of the kind that domestic-servants are supplied with by considerate employers. Both these timepieces had certain rather unusual features.

The back of an alarm-clock is probably familiar to everyone but the idle-rich, so it is not necessary to go into any tedious details. Suffice it to say that to the alarm-spring winder of the smaller clock a ⊔⊤ shaped attachment, which mechanics, I believe, call a "dog," had been soldered. The space between the upright prongs was about an inch. It was not very clear to the Inspector at that time to what use this clock had been put, but there was no doubting the significance of the other.

The large clock was a component part of a piece of machinery. It had been mounted on a board and it, too, had a fitting soldered to the alarm-spring winder; but, in this case, it was a 2″ diametered disc of brass, with an inch-deep slot cut in the rim of it. A strip of steel, fixed in the middle, so that it swung like a seesaw, had, at one end, a small revolving projection, that rested on the edge of the brass disc. When the apparatus was set into motion by the alarm going off, the disc revolved until the projection on the steel strip was pulled down into the slot in the disc, by means of a fairly stout spring. This, of course, stopped the alarm and sent up the other end of the steel strip with a jerk sufficiently sharp to fire off the toy pistol that was secured, butt-upwards, at the other end of the board. I say "toy" pistol, but actually it was one of those little things sold by sports dealers for athletic meetings. It held one blank cartridge at a time and the barrel was solid.

I have rewritten that last paragraph four times, so I do hope the description is clear!

★ ★ ★ ★

Mrs. Hendon had cleared away the tea-things and I was sitting in my chair by the fire, thinking. When was this bothersome business going to be cleared up? Inspector

Charlton had been working hard on the case, but it didn't seem to me that he was getting anywhere. He had disappeared in great haste a quarter of an hour before, but that would probably lead to nothing. Mr. A had laid the trails to Didcott, Walker and Wright—and, possibly, Stevens—and the Inspector had followed them. With what result? Very little, as far as I could see. The only real evidence that I could call to mind was the scrap of pink paper that the Inspector had picked up when I went out with him that morning to the scene of the crime—and, for all I knew to the contrary, that had proved entirely worthless. There was the uniform, of course, and the note-book found in my shop, but the Inspector was evidently intended to discover those.

Where was the implement that had been used on Johnson? Was it the same one that had quietened Stevens and later deprived me of consciousness? Perhaps Stevens had not been knocked on the head. I didn't know what the medical evidence had been, but from what I had heard, an odd wound or two on the scalp would have probably been obliterated by the subsequent rude attentions of the train. If it hadn't been for Mrs. Stevens, it was quite likely that the body found on the line might not have been definitely identified as that of Jimmy Stevano.

And what of the canvas sheet? That would have helped the Inspector. Somebody must have bought it somewhere. Was it one of those waterproof covers one sometimes sees draped over agricultural machines—ploughs, harrows and so forth—in farmyards? Was the name and address of a farmer stamped on it?

That note-book. The Inspector had said that there was something strange about it—not about its being found in my shop, but in its relation to the page that had been ripped from it. Had he followed up his investigation into who had bought the book at Hornbill's; and had he made use of that list of customers that I had compiled for him?

I didn't want to be disloyal to the Inspector, but I was

beginning to feel that he was not making enough headway. A feeling of depression, probably the after-effects of the rough treatment I had received, began to get hold of me. I felt that we should never see the end of the Johnson-Stevens case, which for all I knew, might become the Johnson-Stevens-Rutherford case. That, I thought, with a wry smile, would make a fine title for another book by Mr. Van Dine: "The Triple Murder Case."

But that was not the way to square up to things. A dose of medicine was what I needed. When life gets a bit blue round the edges, there is always one tonic to which I instinctively turn: *Three Men in a Boat*. I got it now from the bookcase.

And while I chuckled by the fire over the difference of opinion between the kettle and Montmorency the dog, Justice, in the shape of Inspector Charlton, crouched over the wheel of his car, was on its way to Paulsfield.

★ ★ ★ ★

I have said that I was in at the death; and it was to P.C. Harwood that I was indebted for that. Soon after seven o'clock, when the shops were closing their doors, I turned the last page of my book and, with my despondency entirely banished, read: "And Montmorency, standing on his hind legs, before the window, peering out into the night, gave a short bark of decided concurrence with the toast."

With a contented sigh, I laid the book aside and refilled my pipe. Something "up to the pretty" was, I felt, called for. I levered myself out of my chair and went over to the sideboard, where the decanter that had been my father's stood beside the soda-siphon. The window rattled gently as I returned to my place by the fire, and I pulled back the curtains, to see what the weather was doing. It was a fine, bright, star-lit night and the rising wind was sending the little clouds racing over the face of the moon. There was just time for a brisk "round the houses" before dinner. I finished off my drink, got my hat and coat, called out to Lizzie in the kitchen that I should be back in twenty minutes and whistled for Spot. But Spot, apparently, was already out on a private errand, so I strode down the garden path by myself. I saw no sign of my bodyguard and wondered, as I walked down towards the High Street, whether, as a result of his shortcomings of the previous night, he had been unfrocked—or whatever it is they do to erring bodyguards.

I suppose it was just Fate that took me out along the Burgeston road that night. 'Voslivres', I noticed when I walked past it, was shut. I was nearing the last lamp-post on the left-hand side, beyond which point the Council did not consider it necessary to provide illumination, when I heard the sound of a motor-cycle engine behind me. The machine rapidly caught me up and as I had now left the pavement behind, I got well to the side of the road, but it did not pass me. The throttle was suddenly shut down and a motor-cycle combination pulled up with a jerk.

"Mr. Rutherford!" said an urgent voice.

"Yes," I said peering at the figure on the saddle. "Oh, it's you, Harwood."

"I picked you out with my light, Mr. Rutherford. Would you like to jump in? We've got the little rat on the run. He's making for the tunnel."

It didn't take me a couple of seconds to get into the sidecar and almost before I had sat down, Harwood had opened the throttle again and we were roaring through the darkness. Behind us, I heard a long imperative note from the electric horn of a car.

"That's the Inspector," Harwood shouted over the noise of the engine. "I got off the mark a few seconds before they did. My God, I hope we get there in time!"

"What's happened?" I yelled.

"The Inspector's found out who killed Johnson, but they gave 'im the slip. The car came this way."

His eyes were fixed on the road in front, and the big twin-cylindered engine swept us along at something near the fifty m.p.h. mark. The brilliant beam from the headlight picked out Deeptree Corner and from behind us came again the screech of the Inspector's horn. It seemed a little nearer now. Before us stretched the road, but there was no sign of the car in front. Harwood pulled round the lever on his handle-bar as far as it would go; and the outline of his big nose and thrust-forward, purposeful chin showed up sharply under his peaked cap.

We passed the old wooden telephone-box and quickly drew near to the entrance to the tunnel. The gate that the Inspector had spoken of was still open, and just as the road swung left, we bumped off it through the gateway into the field. As Harwood's headlight swept round, I caught a glimpse of something standing close to the hedge in the field—something that made my heart miss a beat—my little orange-coloured van.

Another beam of light shone across the field and I turned to face the full glare of it. I heard an excited shout. Harwood did not follow the line of the fence to the tunnel mouth, but swung off to the left in a wide arc, which brought us round to face the fence. The engine was roaring and we bumped across the field like a thing demented. Straight in front of us, by the fence over the tunnel mouth, a uniformed figure was standing; and the white, set face was the face of P.C. Didcott.

Suddenly Harwood screamed out:

"I can't stop the thing! The throttle's jammed! Stay where you are, for God's sake!"

The fence seemed to rush towards us and I waited tensely for Harwood to wrench round the wheel to avoid it. I saw another figure run into the beam of our head-lamp. To the right of us there was wild shouting and a mighty voice roared out:

"Jump, Rutherford, you *bloody* fool!"

There was no time to jump. I saw Didcott leap aside and then there was a frightful crash as we hit the fence. I felt something pulling at me, and the machine, with Harwood still in the saddle, slid away from me through the splintered timbers and disappeared. There was a moment's silence and then another crash, as the machine hit the permanent-way below.

I found myself sprawling in the wet grass, with somebody bending over me.

"Are you all right, sir?" said Didcott's anxious voice.

"Yes, I think so, Didcott," I said, as I scrambled to my feet. "How the hell did I get out of that sidecar?"

"You were pulled out," he said.

"And Harwood went over?"

"Yes, sir," he said sadly. "I'm afraid he's done for, poor chap."

"Didcott! Rutherford!" the Inspector's voice came across to us. "Come and help get him off the line!"

"This way, Mr. Rutherford, but go careful," said Didcott, and I followed him through the jagged gap in the fence.

As I turned to the right, to walk behind him along the top of the parapet wall, I noticed that the Inspector's car was pulled some yards into the field and that the headlamps lighted up the scene of the disaster. And I saw my little van creep quietly across the area of light, swing sharply to its right and fade away in the direction of the road.

I carefully picked my way after Didcott down the sloping flank-wall, until we were near enough to the permanent-way to jump down. The Inspector and Chandler had already got Harwood off the line, and the Inspector was kneeling by him in the narrow space between the rails and the flank-wall, while Chandler held an electric torch.

"Get that machine off the rails, you two!" snapped the Inspector without looking round, "and look sharp about it!"

The combination was completely wrecked and was lying across the rails a few yards from the mouth of the tunnel. I heard the distant whistle of a train.

"That's the up express going into the tunnel," said Didcott. "We've got about twenty seconds."

We worked frantically to get the tangled mass off the up line, but a large motor-cycle is nearly as heavy as a small car and it was not until Chandler had lent a hand, that we were able to tip it over on to the down line, just in time to avoid the express, as it roared out of the tunnel. It required the united efforts of all four of us to drag the machine along to where the flank-wall ended and allowed us to pull the wreckage well away from the line.

I straightened myself and breathing heavily, said to the Inspector:

"How is the poor chap?"

"Dead," he said shortly. "Neck's broken."

"I'm very sorry," I said.

"So am I," agreed the Inspector. "It was he who murdered Johnson and Stevens."

Ten minutes later, a voice called down from above us.

"Is that you, Dr. Weston?" the Inspector answered. "Come down here, will you?"

I heard the Doctor complaining bitterly as he made his hazardous way down to us.

"D'you take me for an Alpinist, Inspector?" he asked, as I helped him down on to the permanent-way.

Inspector Charlton did not answer, but led him to the other side of the line, where Harwood's body lay. As Didcott, Chandler and I followed them, I discovered that two more persons had joined us: the inevitable Bradfield and George.

"Why, George!" I asked him as we negotiated the rails, "What are you doing here?"

"Just lending a hand, sir," he smiled.

"He certainly lent *you* a hand, Mr. Rutherford," said Didcott, when we reached the safety of the other side. "If he 'adn't grabbed hold of your coat and pulled you out of that sidecar like a cork out of a bottle, you'd be lying there with Harwood now."

"Thanks, George," I said, and patted him on the shoulder.

"A mere nothing, sir," said George, it seemed with a little difficulty.

Dr. Weston rose to his feet and the Inspector switched off his electric torch.

"Almost instantaneous, I should think," the Doctor said.

"The ambulance will be here at any moment, sir," said George to the Inspector. "I 'phoned them from Dr. Weston's house."

"Good boy," said the Inspector.

★ ★ ★ ★

The ambulance had taken the body to the mortuary and we had all gone back to my rooms—all, that is, except Chandler, who went to report to Sergeant Martin at the police station. Three stiff ones for Dr. Weston, the Inspector and me made the decanter look a bit sorry for itself; while a quart of beer obtained from the scandalized Mrs. Hendon was sacrificed to the thirsty throats of Didcott, Bradfield and George. I passed round the cigarette box and lighted my own pipe.

"Find something to sit on," I invited them, "and make yourselves at home. It looks to me as if I owe quite a lot to all of you."

There was a chair for everyone but George, so he sat on the floor. The Inspector seemed to have regained his good humour.

"Would it be out of place to enquire, Rutherford," he asked, "why you went joy-riding with Harwood tonight?"

"I was out for a walk ..." I began.

"These walks of yours!" he said despairingly. "You should catch a tram—they're safer."

"I nearly caught a train last night," I smiled. "I was strolling along the Burgeston road, when Harwood stopped his motor-cycle just by me. He said that you'd discovered who did the murders …"

"Which was true enough," the Inspector threw in.

"And that you were all after him."

"We were all after Harwood, if that was anything."

"And would I like to hop into the sidecar and join in the fun. Which I did. I had no suspicions about the man and even when we were rushing at the fence, I stayed where I was, because I thought that, in spite of the throttle getting jammed, he would be able to avoid the fence. Actually he did shout out that the machine was out of control, but told me to sit tight until, I took it, he had had time to turn the petrol off underneath the tank or do something else that would bring us to a stop."

"He told you that," the Inspector said as he put down his glass, "because he wanted you to go with him over the top. He took the risk of our catching up with him, when he stopped to pick you up. We were only just behind."

"Why did he trouble to stop?" asked the Doctor.

"I don't know," the Inspector admitted. "by that time the danger from Rutherford didn't count for much. We can only assume that vanity was the cause. He had tried twice to kill Rutherford—and failed, the first time through Rutherford's spirited objections to being drowned, and the second time through Bradfield just catching him in the act. This evening, he saw the chance to take Rutherford with him into the Great Beyond."

"Were Mr. Bradfield and I playing 'follow-my-leader' this evening?" I asked and Bradfield smiled ruefully.

"Yes, Mr. Rutherford," he said, "and you got away from me again. I was about fifty yards behind you when Harwood picked you up—and I didn't know what to do. I hadn't any reason to suspect Harwood, so I couldn't very well stop you. Then I saw the Inspector's car coming along and shouted out to him what had happened."

"And how did you, George, and Vera, the van, get mixed up in things?" I asked.

George looked up at the Inspector.

"I'm afraid," said the Inspector, "that I was responsible for that. I picked up some pretty useful information this evening that pointed straight at Harwood as the killer of Johnson and Stevens. When I got to Paulsfield, I met Didcott on the main road and told him to pop along to the tunnel and keep watch for anyone trying to slip into it. The evidence I had discovered was actually in the tunnel and I wanted to catch Harwood in the act of trying to remove it. While I was talking to Didcott, this young feller "—he pointed to George— "Came along in that pretty little van of yours …"

"Doing a bit of delivering that I couldn't do earlier, because you weren't there to look after the shop," explained George.

"I promptly conscripted him," said the Inspector, "and told him to take Didcott to the tunnel and wait there with him, as unobtrusively as possible, until something happened. If I hadn't done that, George wouldn't have been there to save you from a sticky finish. Then I went along to the police station. Sergeant Martin was there, with Harwood and Chandler. Leaving Chandler in the charge-room, I took Harwood and the Sergeant into the back office and told them that I had received information that might enable me to fix on the guilty man. I told them about the note that was found on Stevens's body and how I had established that the book from which the page had been torn had been found in your shop, Rutherford. I told them that I knew that that book had been deliberately planted there by the murderer and *why* I knew. I told them that I had proof that the uniform had been thrown in the pond before Johnson was murdered; and that I knew how the shot had been fired that was planned to make Didcott late at Burgeston. I told them that I knew that Stevens had seen the murderer-to-be enter the telephone box and, by blackmailing him afterwards, had himself been killed. I told them that I had solved the mystery of the transposed bicycles and found out how Walker and Wright had become involved and that I knew all about the chewing-gum.

"Harwood stood up to this pretty well and maintained an air of official interest that was commendably realistic. I uncovered my big guns and fired off some heavy stuff. I told them that, if one wished to avoid attention, the best way to get from the end of the Phantom Coppice footpath to the western end of Burgeston, was to walk through the railway tunnel. Apart from the advantage of secrecy, I added, the tunnel afforded a far quicker way than the road, which was over twice the distance.

"Even that didn't seem to shake him and I admired his self-control. It had been my intention to say that I had been told where I could find the sheet of canvas and then, without mentioning precisely where I proposed to look, give Harwood the chance to slip away to the tunnel, to be caught by Didcott in the act of feverishly searching in a certain recess inside the tunnel for the evidence that I had had the forethought to remove earlier this evening. But now I changed my mind and let him have my biggest gun. The effect was instantaneous. He sagged as if somebody had really shot him and his face went white. Then he made a terrific effort and pulled himself together.

" 'That was a point, Inspector,' he said evenly, 'that I didn't think of.'

"And before Martin and I could stop him, he was out of the room, had closed the door and turned the key in the lock, and slipped through the back door into the yard, where his motor-cycle was. And the rest of that part of the story you know."

"What was the point about the chewing-gum?" I asked

"Do you remember the question I put you early last week, Rutherford? Why did Johnson take off his cap and thereby facilitate the murderer's job? And do you call to mind the small piece of pink paper that I picked up on the Hazeloak road? That was the answer to the question. Johnson was an habitual gum-chewer, wasn't he, Didcott?"

Didcott paused in dividing the remains of the beer punctiliously between Bradfield, George and himself.

"Quite right, sir," he said, "and he used to keep a reserve supply in his cap."

"A little personal eccentricity known, probably, only to a few people," said the Inspector. "That was why I took such a keen interest in your activities that evening, Didcott."

Dr. Weston had been meditatively blowing smoke through his nostrils for some time, but now he broke his silence.

"Give us your account, Charlton, of how Johnson was murdered," he suggested.

"It was a masterpiece of timing," said the Inspector, "and very nearly a complete success. A good deal of what I am going to say is, of course, theoretical, but it is all borne out by the evidence.

"Soon after a quarter past eight, Harwood spoke over the fence to his neighbour and just after nine o'clock the neighbour and his wife heard Harwood leave home on his motor-cycle. Between those times, Harwood murdered Johnson. Immediately he left his neighbour, Harwood went indoors and tuned in a Continental broadcasting station and arranged an alarm-clock, so that at a couple of minutes before 8.45, it would turn the tuning-knob to pick up the London National programme."

I interrupted the Inspector here.

"Harwood told me about that, when we were chatting together at the police station that evening. He said he had heard Lord Shawford making the Sunday-night Appeal and had been so moved by his lordship's words that he was going to send a small offering."

"That was his alibi," said the Inspector. "Actually, when that Appeal was being . . ."

"Excuse me a moment, sir," Bradfield interrupted him. "I heard that Appeal myself and it was made by a woman— Dame Mary Roxton. The B.B.C. said they were sorry that

Lord Shawford was indisposed."

The Inspector looked at me.

"Did you hear that, Rutherford?" he asked. *"That* was the little bit of evidence that you couldn't remember—and for which your life was three times in danger."

"But didn't Maggie Wood say ..." began George excitedly, but I froze him with a glance.

"When the room is less crowded, Inspector," I said humbly, "I will kick myself round it."

I recalled, as well as George, what Maggie Wood had said: that Lord Shawford was convalescing after quinsy, which meant that, when his lordship was due to broadcast, the illness was at its choking height. There was no need to tell the Inspector that, until Molly and I were safely married!

"One can imagine Harwood's feelings!" said the Inspector. "No wonder he wanted to get rid of you! Well, as I was saying, at the time this Appeal was being made, Harwood was engaged on far more momentous business than quietly listening to it. At just after twenty minutes to nine, Walker met two constables cycling along the Hazeloak road: Johnson and Harwood. One can imagine the meeting and the casual greetings of the two constables, after Harwood had run through the tunnel, hurried along the footpath, picked up the bicycle he had arranged to be hidden for him, and cycled along to wait for Johnson somewhere near Deeptree Corner:

" 'Hullo, Johnson, not much of a night for you. Thought you'd be along about now, so I waited for you.'

" 'Where're you off to?'

" 'Just popping into Hazeloak to see a chap, before I get along to the station. Bloke called Jenkins. Know him? Says he's got a fox-terrier going cheap ...'

"I don't suggest for a moment that that was what they did say, but some such conversation probably took place," the Inspector hastened to add. "So they rode together along the Hazeloak road until they had passed Walker, whose presence there Harwood had cunningly provided for. And here's where the spearmint comes in. Harwood, being intimate with Johnson, knew, as Didcott did, that Johnson kept a reserve supply inside his cap. Assume, then, that he said casually as they pedalled along:

" 'Got a bit of gum handy, Tom?'

" 'Sure thing,' said Johnson.

"So they got off their bicycles and Johnson removed his cap. Need I go further?"

"Why did Harwood ride away on the wrong bicycle?" I asked.

"For two reasons, I should imagine," the Inspector replied. "Firstly, on his way back home to Hazeloak, Walker would have discovered the body—and the bicycle. As it happened, Rutherford spoilt that little plan of Harwood's, but if things had worked out to schedule, Walker would have found the bicycle, immediately assumed that Wright had been—indiscreet and furtively returned the machine to his shop. If that had happened, I doubt if Walker would have come forward at the inquest. Secondly, I don't think Harwood's idea was to implicate Didcott. I imagine that it was his idea to give the impression that there *was* a plot to implicate Didcott. The time was certain to arrive eventually when Walker and Wright got together—and then the whole story of Johnson's mysterious companion would come out. Unfortunately for Harwood, it came out a bit too quickly. Rutherford, not Walker, found the body.

"The shot that Didcott heard was arranged by Harwood with a little piece of machinery that I found this evening in the same place as I found the clock that had been attached to Harwood's radio-set."

"And where was that, if it's not a rude question?" I asked.

"I leave it to your imagination, Rutherford. I shall merely say that it was not a hundred miles from Harwood's house in Carnation Villas, Burgeston, and that I am a qualified member of A. J. Alan's B. B. I.!"

"I take it," I said, "that Harwood rode Johnson's bicycle

along the footpath, pushed or rode it through the tunnel, emerged at the other end, carried the machine cautiously up the bank and over his garden fence, shoved it in the shed *pro tern.*, slipped indoors and turned the wireless off, and then strolled out to start up his motorcycle."

"That's about it," the Inspector agreed, "and then he quietly dumped the machine in the pond the next evening. Risky, of course, but wasn't the whole thing risky?"

"Why did you think there was something funny about that page torn from the note-book, Inspector?" I asked. "Just you try tearing a sheet carelessly from such a book," the Inspector smiled. "You may leave a few tiny fragments of it behind, but to leave a roughly serrated edge, as ragged as the coast of Cornwall, the whole length of the book, requires a certain amount of care. That was Harwood's great weakness—he was too fussy."

"How did you establish that Harwood was the man you were after?" asked Dr. Weston.

"I knew the truth immediately I had examined that piece of canvas," the Inspector replied. "It was triangular in shape— like one of the sails on your *Placid Jenny*, Doctor. A length of rope was lashed to two of its corners, but there was no rope attached to its 'apex.' "

"Well," I asked, "What of that?"

"My dear chap," the Inspector smiled, "it sticks out a mile. When Bradfield caught Harwood indulging in one of his hobbies, Harwood had that third corner gripped in his hand, waiting for the moment when he could safely let you fall."

"I am still perplexed," I admitted. "If Harwood's story of the man who disappeared when he arrived had been true, who would have been there to hold that third corner between the time the man released it and the time Harwood got his hands on it?"

"Oh," I said, "I didn't think of that."

"Neither did Harwood," said the Inspector.

XVIII.   ENVOI

It was June. Molly had been Mrs. John Rutherford for just two hours. Relatives of hers and cousins and aunts of mine that I hardly knew I had, had come to drink the Inspector's champagne and to throw confetti ....

Those seven months had gone swiftly by. The question that had not been asked on the night that Harwood died— why did he kill Johnson?—had been asked since and had been answered as fully as it ever would be. The Inspector had seen Mrs. Harwood when that sad little woman had come out of hospital with her baby and she had told him that her husband was the victim of an insane obsession: he firmly believed that he was not the father of the baby that was on the way. He had once found Mrs. Harwood and Johnson in friendly conversation and, knowing something of Johnson's reputation, must have jumped to erroneous and entirely unjust conclusions. But murder has been done with less excuse than that.

"He's a bonny little chap," the hospital sister had told the Inspector, "and he's going to have his father's nose."

If only Harwood had waited to see the perpetuation of his nose, how different things might have been!

Then there was the time when a portentously solemn George had consulted me about engagement-rings and I had offered him in return, not only the benefit of my advice, but also the managership of 'Voslivres'. I had bought back Crawhurst, I had told him, and Molly and I were going to live there. So would he take over the shop—at a salary befitting a married man, of course?

Naturally, he would want some help and perhaps he had someone in mind. . . .?

"Mr. Milke and I will get along quite nicely together,"

George had said. "I have been carefully grooming him, sir, and he is already quite invaluable."

Milke had said that he was agreeable, "In a manner of speaking," and had gone out and *bought* himself a hat, to keep up his position, "As the saying was."

But it was June. Toasts had been drunk, incoherent and much-interrupted speeches had been made and goodbyes had been said to tearfully happy aunts and noticeably gruff-voiced uncles. Rice and confetti had found its way into the innermost folds of our clothes and Molly and I had fled down the path of Holmedene into the waiting Daimler, to the back of which Dr. Weston was now feverishly tying a shoe, under the blissful impression that we didn't know what he was up to. A beaming George, impeccably attired—no plum-coloured suiting and yellow footwear for him these days!—was standing by.

The car broke into purring life and the Inspector poked his head through the window.

"Happy times, my dears!" he smiled.

We began to move forward and the assembly sent up a cheer, in which George's touch-line bellow was predominant.

"Cheerio!" I said, "and good hunting, Inspector!"

As the car gathered speed and we turned to wave to them all, the Inspector's voice came after us:

"You may call me 'Uncle'."

THE END